BOOKS BY
ALEXANDER McCALL SMITH

THE CONDITIONS OF UNCONDITIONAL LOVE

THE CONDITIONS OF UNCONDITIONAL LOVE

Alexander McCall Smith

PANTHEON BOOKS
NEW YORK

Pantheon Books and colophon are registered trademarks of
Penguin Random House LLC.

Library of Congress Cataloging-in-Publication Data
Name: McCall Smith, Alexander, [date] author.
Title: The conditions of unconditional love / Alexander McCall Smith.
Description: First American edition. | New York : Pantheon Books, 2024. |
Series: Isabel Dalhousie series ; 15.
Identifiers: LCCN 2023053549 (print) | LCCN 2023053550 (ebook) |
ISBN 9780593701720 (hardcover) | ISBN 9780593701737 (ebook)
Subjects: LCGFT: Detective and mystery fiction. | Novels.
Classification: LCC PR6063.C326 C66 2024 (print) |
LCC PR6063.C326 (ebook) | DDC 823/.914—dc23/eng/20231120
LC record available at https://lccn.loc.gov/2023053549
LC ebook record available at https://lccn.loc.gov/2023053550

www.pantheonbooks.com

Jacket illustration by Bill Sanderson;
(border) by All For You / Shutterstock

Printed in the United States of America
First American Edition
2 4 6 8 9 7 5 3 1

This book is for Sandra McGruther.

THE CONDITIONS OF UNCONDITIONAL LOVE

MODESTY," said Isabel Dalhousie, as she spread thick-cut Dundee marmalade over her slice of toast, "is not quite the same thing as humility."

This was not the sort of remark that one would hear at every kitchen table, but Isabel was, after all, a philosopher, and if there are any breakfast tables at which such statements might be made over cereal and toast, then they must be tables such as these, here in the intellectual latitudes of Edinburgh, where she lived with her husband, Jamie, a bassoonist, and their two small boys, Charlie and Magnus. And Brother Fox, of course, who lurked in the garden, although he was an itinerant, a temporary resident, having business in other gardens and nearby back streets.

Small children have an effect roughly equivalent to that of a minor tornado, leaving in their wake a detritus of abandoned toys, rearranged furniture, chocolate wrapping paper and crumbs. Isabel's kitchen table bore witness to the boys' breakfast with a half-eaten piece of bread, the teeth-marks still clearly impressed in the layer of peanut butter; an unfinished bowl of cereal, soggy with milk; and several smears of jam, honey and something that had the appearance and texture of a mixture of the two.

Isabel was fortunate. As a working mother—she was the owner and full-time editor of a philosophical journal, the *Review of Applied Ethics*—she needed help in the house. This was provided by Grace, who had been housekeeper to Isabel's father, and who had stayed on after he died and Isabel took over his house. Grace was good at her job, although she had her moments when she unexpectedly, and for obscure reasons, took umbrage. Isabel handled those situations with tact, usually by saying, "You're absolutely right, Grace." Most people like to hear that—and Grace was no exception, particularly when she was absolutely wrong, as was occasionally the case.

Grace was cheerful about her provenance. "I came with the house," she said. "I might have gone elsewhere, but somehow I didn't. So, here I am, I suppose. One of the fixtures. Part of the furniture."

Grace liked walking the boys to school in the morning, occasionally posing as their mother when she engaged in casual conversation at the school gate. Isabel had heard about this from the mother of one of Charlie's friends, and had initially been discomfited by the pretence. But then she had found out that Grace never actually claimed that the boys were hers, but would simply let people believe this, doing nothing to correct the misapprehension. That, she thought, was innocent enough, and, anyway, we all fantasised about something from time to time, and admitted it—if we were honest.

On that particular morning, Grace had arrived early to take the boys to school, leaving Isabel and Jamie to enjoy breakfast in peace. And it was against such a domestic background that this conversation about pride and associated concepts took place.

It began when Jamie, scraping the last of his boiled egg from its shell, remarked, "You know I try to like people—in general—

but there's this new violinist in the band who's just . . ." He hesitated, searching for the right metaphor. "Who just gets up my nose. Right up."

Isabel looked up in surprise. Jamie was usually moderate in his opinions and rarely expressed strong antipathy towards others.

"Pronoun?" she asked.

He looked puzzled. "Pronoun?"

"I mean, is this violinist a him or a her?"

"Him," he answered. "Very much so. Alpha male. He's called Fionn. With an *o*. Plain Finn isn't good enough for him, I imagine."

This was not a tone that Jamie struck very often. Fionn must have made quite an impression.

"He's Irish," he continued. "He played in a chamber orchestra in Dublin before he did some sort of master's programme at the Conservatoire in Glasgow. Then he got the job here in Edinburgh. That's Fionn."

Isabel listened to this. "I like the name Fionn," she said mildly. "I haven't known a Fionn before—at least not one with an *o*."

Jamie looked dubious. "I'm not sure that I like the name—at least not now that I've met this particular Fionn. He told me that he was named after a famous figure in Irish mythology—Fionn MacCool."

Isabel knew about that. "When I was a girl, I had a book on myths that was full of the exploits of Fionn. He crops up everywhere. In Scottish mythology too."

Jamie smiled. "People in the orchestra refer to him as MacCool—discreetly, of course. They think it suits him. And I must say he's pretty pleased with himself. On an ocean-going scale. He's a terrific player—extremely talented—but . . ."

Isabel interrupted him. "You're not a tiny bit envious?" she asked.

"Envious of his playing?"

Isabel nodded. "People feel envious of professional rivals. Or even of their own colleagues."

Jamie was silent.

"We don't always like those who can do things better than we can," Isabel continued.

Jamie thought about this. "There'll always be players who are better than oneself. I can name three bassoonists in Scotland alone who are more technically skilled than I am. And there are probably plenty more. But I don't feel the slightest bit envious of any of them."

"You're not an envious person," suggested Isabel. "You're lucky."

"It's not that," said Jamie. "It's just that they're modest about their playing. They don't boast. That's what counts, I think. If you're modest about your abilities, then people don't resent the fact that you're better than they are."

And it was at that point that their conversation about pride and its implications began.

"Would you call Fionn proud?" Isabel asked.

Jamie answered quickly. "Yes. Definitely."

"He's proud of his musicianship, then?"

Jamie nodded.

Isabel smiled. "Would you expect him to say that he *wasn't* proud of it?"

Jamie looked puzzled. "Of course not."

"So, there's nothing wrong with being proud?"

Jamie frowned. "There are different sorts of pride: Is that what you're getting at?"

"Yes," replied Isabel. "There's defensible pride . . ."

"Which is?"

She thought for a moment before replying, "Satisfaction in

a job well done, for instance—a sense of achievement. Nobody objects to that. You're allowed to feel it—in fact, others may encourage you to do just that. And then there's hubristic pride, where you make too much of your achievements. This is where show-offs and the smug fall down, perhaps people like Fionn—not that I can pass judgement on him, never having met him."

Jamie said that this was the sort of pride that he found so objectionable. "Proud people are arrogant. They have a false idea of their own worth. They look down on others. It's not hard to spot them."

"Pride," Isabel said, "has always been ranked well above the other vices—gluttony, lust, and so on—probably because it was seen as a challenge to the divine order of things."

"Hubris?"

"Yes, hubris amounts to saying that you are *above* the gods in some way. And Nemesis is always on the look-out for that sort of uppitiness. Her radar is sensitive to that."

"Better to be modest," said Jamie.

"Distinctly better," agreed Isabel. "I know there's a lot of debate . . ."

"In philosophical circles?" interjected Jamie.

"Yes, in philosophical circles—after all, we have to talk about *something*. There's debate about whether modesty is a virtue. If you ask me, it is, although not everyone agrees. Hume was a bit iffy about it. He talked about the *monkish virtues*—things that he really did not like at all, like celibacy, fasting, penance, self-denial, humility, silence, solitude. There were a few others."

"Not an attractive list," said Jamie.

"Humility is the interesting one there," said Isabel. "You can be too modest, I think. And then humility may become an issue."

They sat in silence for a few minutes. It was June, a few days from the longest day, and there was warmth in the morning sun. Its buttery light fell slanting on the tabletop and the walls of the kitchen, across Jamie's shoulder, onto his forearm; sunlight like this, Isabel, thought, somehow slowed down time—or gave the impression of doing so. She and Jamie could sit there at the table for the entire morning, talking about pride and modesty, about orchestral politics, about all the small things that made up everyday life. And there was nothing wrong in sitting about and talking—so many people were afraid of inaction because they were addicted to doing things. And she, she decided, was one of them. She felt guilty if she passed a day without achieving at least something: That came from her protestant work-ethic genes, bequeathed her by cautious ancestors on both sides—the forebears of her *sainted American mother*, as she called her, and of her Scottish father were all believers in the virtues of hard work and prudence. Had they come from a Mediterranean culture of olive trees and siestas it might have been different, and she might have taken a more relaxed view of life.

Then Jamie said, "Some of the players would like to get rid of Fionn. It's an open secret."

Isabel was interested. "How can they get rid of him? That's for management, isn't it?"

"Of course," said Jamie. "But there's a lot of ill feeling. And one or two of them have good cause, I think."

Isabel pointed out that people muttered all sorts of things, and meant very few of them. What did he mean by good cause?

Jamie sighed. "Fionn thinks he's God's gift to women. Handsome Irishman. Pretty good musician. Good singing voice too. They like him—a lot."

"And?" Isabel encouraged.

"There's a flautist called Andrew. He had a girlfriend called Dawn. They'd been together for three years or so, but when Dawn saw Fionn, she couldn't contain herself. She flirted with him at some party and he was only too willing to go off with her—for a few months, at least. After that, he moved on to some other woman. Dawn was left homeless—she had been living with Andrew, but that ended when she went off with Fionn."

Isabel rolled her eyes. Life was precarious enough—even for people of cautious habits. Those who allowed their heads to be turned by appealing Irishmen were at even greater risk of disaster. Sex was a dark, anarchic force in some respects, and was often at odds with reason and good sense. But she understood, as anybody who had ever fallen in love must understand. These things just *happened* to you—you did not choose to be struck by lightning.

Jamie continued the tale. "Fionn asked her to leave his flat when he started his next affair—and she had nowhere to go. She ended up living in the box room at a friend's place down in Maxwell Street—a tiny cupboard, really, with just enough room for a bed—and nothing else."

"Poor woman," said Isabel.

Jamie looked thoughtful. "Yes. But she made the choice to go off with Fionn. You could say she brought this upon herself." He paused. "She made the bed in which she chose to lie." He paused, adding slightly reluctantly, "It really was her fault, I suppose."

Isabel shrugged: yes, but no. "Of course, anyone may find herself in a mess because of what she's chosen to do. But that doesn't necessarily mean they don't deserve our sympathy." She paused. "People who smoke may end up with—what do they call it? Chronic obstructive pulmonary disease? Like that poor man we see going into the bakery sometimes with his oxygen cylinders. They're left gasping for air. We still help them, even though smokers may have brought the whole thing on themselves."

"Of course," said Jamie.

"So, I don't think we should spend too much time thinking

about *why* Dawn has ended up in her cupboard. The fact is—she's there. That's what counts."

She lowered her eyes. She had sounded—even to herself—a bit censorious, as if she were giving Jamie a lecture. Now she said, "I'm sorry. I'm not suggesting you're being harsh. I was thinking aloud."

Jamie reassured her that he had not taken offence. "It was just a thought," he said. "But of course, you're right."

Isabel asked him whether he knew Dawn. "I've met her quite a few times," Jamie replied. "I still see her now and then—she was always friendly with Robert, who's another flautist—and who was a good friend of Andrew—and still is. She's nice enough. She's a nurse. She works in an infectious diseases ward down at the Western General Hospital. That's why I think the accommodation issue is a problem. She has to work night shifts from time to time, and the flat's noisy during the day. Her box room has a small window on the common stair. She gets a lot of noise while she's trying to sleep."

Isabel frowned. "Can't she get something else?" she asked.

Jamie shook his head. "It's really hard to find a flat in this city," he said. "And then rents are pretty high. It's not easy." He paused. "We're lucky."

Isabel did not need to be reminded of her good fortune. She was comfortably off, and they lived in a large house. She was well aware of that—and took none of it for granted. And now that Jamie reminded her, it triggered something that was always just below the surface with her: the thought that she could do something to make things better. And not only *could* do something, but *should* do it. What counted was whether a person needing help had come within what she called her circle of moral recognition; once that happened, help needed to be given.

Isabel had become aware of Dawn's plight. She did not know her, but Jamie did, and that meant she was not a moral stranger: She was somebody who was now morally proximate—another term she used to set out the boundaries of moral obligation.

"I should meet her," Isabel said quietly.

Jamie did not conceal his surprise. "Dawn? You want to meet Dawn?"

"Yes. I think I might be able to do something—you never know."

Jamie struggled. He had always discouraged Isabel from taking on the troubles of the world, and she had always found a reason why, in any particular case, she felt that she had to do something. Now he realised that in telling Isabel the story of Dawn and Fionn, he had evoked exactly such a response. He sighed. He wished she would not burden herself in this way, and yet this was what Isabel did. He could not change her—and he did not particularly want to change her. All that he might like to do, he decided, was to moderate her sense of moral obligation—that was all. But he rarely succeeded. Isabel became involved irrespective of what he said, and then he was largely powerless to do anything but watch events unfold.

He was not surprised by what came next.

"I've been thinking of that room next to the attic," Isabel said. "It's comfortable enough, and it has that kitchenette. That needs to be cleaned up a bit . . ."

"I can do that," said Jamie.

She smiled. "You don't mind?"

He shook his head. "It would be a good thing to do."

"Will you speak to her?" asked Isabel.

"I will," said Jamie.

He got up out of his chair and went round to her side of the table. He kissed her. He kissed her for her kindness. She kissed him back.

"You've left some marmalade on me," he said, reaching up to rub it off his cheek. "But I don't mind."

ISABEL FINISHED HER COFFEE and made her way into her study at the front of the house. This was her inner sanctum—not only the private domain in which she could sit undisturbed and think, but also the editorial office of the *Review of Applied Ethics*. It was a large room, at the end of which was a fireplace with a carved wooden mantelpiece. Jamie had rescued the mantelpiece from a scrapyard, suspecting—correctly—that underneath several thick coats of green paint was a delicate relief. He was right: Paint stripper and gentle sandpapering had revealed a late Victorian tableau in which the figures of Faith, Hope and Charity dispensed advice to a number of attentive small children, their hoops and hobby horses laid to one side. The message of enlightened education was a clear one, and Jamie arranged for it to be given further cleaning and then installed. Isabel was delighted with the gift, and often stole a glance at it across her desk while she was struggling with some demanding editorial task. How different an image it was from that which, as a student, twenty years ago, she had pinned to the wall of her study-bedroom: the tight-trousered rock star, almost shirtless, caressing an electric guitar. Tastes change, she thought, and smiled, although she understood what she had seen in the rock star. There would be countless student bedrooms in any university city where images of rebellion adorned the walls. At least she had not had a smiling Mao, as some of her acquaintances had.

It was here that the pages of the journal were put together, telephone calls made to the printer, proofs corrected, and books received for discussion and review. A number of these books—currently more than twenty—stood in piles at the end of the table near the window. Those were the titles that would be sent out to reviewers, but they were not the only ones in the office. On another table, tucked behind the door that led into the hallway outside, was a further stack of books, less fortunate than those in the other pile. These were the books that would not be reviewed but would, at least, be mentioned in the "Briefly Noted" column towards the end of the *Review*, after the "Forthcoming Conferences" section. A mention was better than nothing, Isabel thought, although she felt considerable sympathy for the authors of these less-favoured works. They would be the result of long hours of research and writing, of months, if not years, of work, and now, in publication, there was every chance that they would be read by virtually nobody. There were some books, in fact, that Isabel was convinced were read only by the author's close family: The mothers of authors are often a much put-upon group, having to struggle with the unreadable works of their offspring when there was so much more for them to do.

That was the case, Isabel was sure, with Christopher Dove's latest book, *Event Individuation in the Philosophy of Action: Critical Issues*. The oleaginous Christopher Dove was how she thought of him, although she was not sure whether the word *oleaginous* suited Dove. She had gone to the dictionary to check, and had discovered that there were two principal meanings: covered in oil, and obsequious. Dove was definitely not obsequious—in fact, he was anything but. Dove was pleased with himself, and his approach to others was to imagine that they shared that high opinion, particularly if the others were women. So if she was to continue thinking of Dove as oleaginous, it must be in the oily sense, and there she was not certain that the word was quite right.

There were oily people in the strictly physical sense—people whose sebaceous glands secreted too much oil and made their skin glisten. That was unfortunate, and was of course not a subject of moral comment. One could not criticise oily people of that sort, and Isabel would not do that. And yet there was that man behind the counter in the local post office who was terribly oily, poor fellow, and who could have been helped, she thought, by one of those lotions that reduced skin oil. But that was not something one could take up with a complete stranger, even if he might have benefitted from the suggestion.

Dove was not oleaginous in that sense. Dove had a good complexion, which somehow seemed to go with his self-satisfied manner. He was certainly good-looking, although, as Isabel had pointed out to a friend, he was also "rather creepy." He was oleaginous, then, in the way in which he slipped his way into things, usually with a patently obvious intention of benefitting himself in some way. Now he had written this book of event individuation, on the jacket of which there was a large picture of the author—too large to fit on the rear flap and therefore plastered all over the back cover. She had extracted the book with some distaste from the padded envelope in which it arrived, and had held it away from her as if it were infected with some noxious chemical. And then she had seen the picture on its back, and her eyes had widened with surprise. There was Christopher Dove, in full colour, sitting back in an armchair in what could only be described as a deliberately seductive pose, the top three buttons of his shirt undone. Isabel had stared at this for a few seconds, and then burst out laughing.

Professionalism had triumphed, though, and she had turned to the description of the book's contents printed on the front flap. Event individuation was a recondite branch of philosophy in which events were dissected into their component parts. In this way the larger act of getting up in the morning could be described as a series of minor acts—putting one's foot out of bed and onto the floor; turning on the light; standing up; reaching for some item of clothing—and so on. It was all very tedious, Isabel thought, and she did not read beyond page three before the book was consigned to the *Books Received* pile.

But then her conscience had troubled her. Isabel's conscience was always asking awkward questions. Jamie was well aware of the problem, and had tried to persuade her to ignore at least some of its promptings. Isabel, though, had found that difficult, with the result that she often went back over a decision she had taken, subjecting it to scrutiny that it did not always survive. Now she wondered whether she had been too quick to dismiss Dove's book, swayed by her dislike for its author. *Never judge a book by its author* . . . The variation on the old saying about books and their covers seemed apt here—and persuasive enough to make her move the book to the review pile. More than that, she would ask Professor Robert Lettuce whether he would review it—an outcome that would delight Dove, who had long been in Lettuce's camp and who could not hope for a more favourably biased reviewer. Her conscience would probably trouble her about this decision too; if Dove's book was to get a full review, then what about the other books in the unfortunate pile: Did they not deserve to be given equal consideration? She sighed. She would ignore that possibility for the time being because . . . well, because she simply did not have the time to be as punctilious as she ought to be. *We are all imperfect*, she thought, *all of us, and the occasions of imperfection are too numerous to list* . . .

Now she sat at her desk and looked at the stack of letters in the old shoebox of her mother's that she used as one of her in-trays. The box had seen years of service and would not last much longer, but Isabel was attached for sentimental reasons. Her mother had used it for storing desk items that were not easily stored elsewhere—rubber bands, drawing pins, paper clips and so on—and Isabel had taken it over, jettisoning the detritus of the past and using it for letters. The box had originally housed a pair of Salvatore Ferragamo shoes—her mother's only significant weakness, although she also liked expensive bottles of cologne, which she ordered from a perfumier in Munich.

Grace had collected the mail from the front hall, where Graham, the postman, had pushed it through the letter box. There were seven or eight items—three letters, a couple of journals and a handful of bills. Isabel extracted the journals from their wrapping: There was the latest issue of *Ethics* from the University of Chicago Press and an issue of *Mind*. These were moved to the other side of the desk, to be dipped into at her leisure. She particularly enjoyed *Ethics*, in which she always found articles that caught her attention. *Neuroscience and Responsibility*—she saw that this issue was a special one, and she could not resist the temptation of running her eye down the list of contributors. She knew one or two of them and had heard of some of the others. She would keep it as a treat, to be savoured later, perhaps in the precious half-hour of reading that she allowed herself before bed.

She picked up the first of the letters. It was from a reader of the *Review* who objected to the tone of her editorial in a previous issue. Isabel had written a defence of the free exchange of ideas which had not gone down well with this particular reader. "There is absolutely no moral equivalence between those who would deny others their right to live as they wish and those who would stop the deniers from being heard," the letter began. "Freedom of speech does not include the right to make others uncomfortable."

It does, actually, thought Isabel. *That's one of the things, surely,* that freedom of speech is all about. We *need* to feel uncomfortable from time to time.

She would reply politely—she always did—although she was wary about entering into correspondence with some of the *Review*'s readers, who seemed adept at perpetrating long arguments. She sighed: There were so many people now who seemed to be prepared to close down debate on the grounds that somebody, somewhere might take offence at what others might say. She was in that firing line, she supposed, and she would have to defend freedom of speech, although she did not enjoy the atmosphere of intolerance in which any exchanges on the subject tended to take place.

She picked up the next letter. The envelope gave no clue as to the sender: It was addressed to Isabel personally, but her name and address had been typed rather than handwritten. Inside was a single sheet of folded writing paper that, when unfolded, identified the sender immediately. *Professor Robert Lettuce*, said the heading, and after the name came a string of letters, some obvious, others obscure. Isabel looked at them with amusement: *FRSE* (Fellow of the Royal Society of Edinburgh). That was genuine enough—the Royal Society of Edinburgh was the national scholarly academy, and it was reasonable enough that Lettuce should be a member now that he was based in Edinburgh. Then came *D.Phil (Oxon)*, which, once again, she supposed Lettuce had earned at Balliol, his old college at Oxford. He was entitled to that, but then came *D.Litt. (Hon, Univ. Mult.)* That, of course, was a reference to the conferment of honorary doctorates from multiple universities. Once again, Lettuce might well have received these plaudits, but to mention them in this way was a breach of academic, not to say personal, etiquette. It would be different if Lettuce were German, which of course he was not: German professors were expected to list their honorary doctorates and to use *mult* if they had more than one. German *Professor Dr. Drs* were a standing joke in academia, even if the joke was savoured fondly. British professors, along with their American, Canadian and Australian counterparts, never did this. In some cases, they even eschewed the title professor, and used nothing other than the honorifics available to the ordinary citizen—the Ms., the Mr., and so on.

But it got worse, decidedly so, and quickly. The next post-nominals were the icing on an already over-decorated cake: *Kt of the Order of St. Lazarus* and *Chevalier d'Honneur (Palme d'Or)*. Isabel knew about the first of these, a twelfth-century crusader order that had been sporadically revived by enthusiasts in Malta and elsewhere, and now had a branch in Edinburgh. Members paraded harmlessly from time to time in robes and feathered bonnets, conferring on each other various medals, honours and distinctions. Lettuce was clearly fond of ceremony, and would have enjoyed being a knight of such an order: She could imagine the heraldic devices he would use—a shield on which four lettuces would be painted in the green that heraldic artists called *vert*. And Dove, were he to be conscripted by Lettuce into the order, would bear an equally predictable device—a dove, in flight, painted in *argent*, which did for both white and silver in heraldic terms. She smiled as she imagined the two of them in some fanciful procession, in long *vert* cloaks, with Dove carrying some of Lettuce's doctorates for him as there were so many.

But what was this Golden Palm under which Lettuce claimed to shelter? She wondered whether she should ask him outright. "What's all this about golden palms?" she might say, trying not to laugh. And he would engage in bluster as he always did, and go on about some obscure French academic order.

She stopped herself. It was easy to laugh at Lettuce and his pretentions, but she reminded herself that mockery was almost always cruel. Puffed-up people were puffed-up for a reason: They felt that they needed the boost. And Lettuce was the same as any of us: We wanted to be valued, to be loved, if possible, and sometimes the world did not provide them with what they needed. It had once been brought home to her that there had been sadness in Lettuce's life, and she had resolved to remember that. Now she reminded herself, and she put aside these delicious imaginings of Lettuce and Dove in full flood.

But then she read the letter, and her charitable feelings were quickly strained.

"Dear Miss Dalhousie," he began—a bad start because even if she had never had any *palmes d'or* conferred on her, she was still Dr. Dalhousie. She would never insist on that—and indeed rarely used her doctoral title—but Lettuce *knew* she had a PhD and must have omitted it deliberately.

"You may recall," Lettuce continued, "that at a previous meeting we discussed the possibility of our holding a joint conference at some point, the idea being to bring out the conference proceedings as a special issue of the *Review of Applied Ethics.* You may further recollect that a possible topic for this conference was the role of the virtues in the modern world. I thought—and I may have suggested to you at the time—that a possible title for the conference would be *Virtues in a World of Vice.*"

Isabel remembered this—but only vaguely. She was guarded in her reception of any ideas from Lettuce, as he was, in her view, an inveterate plotter—of schemes that were always somehow to his advantage. Neither of them had taken the idea any further, but now Lettuce was bringing it up again. Why?

The answer was not long in coming. "Since we spoke, I have been giving the matter more thought and now, I am happy to say, it seems that the auspices for such a project are looking increasingly favourable, and indeed I am tempted to say that, barring disaster, funding for such a conference will be readily available.

"You may know," he continued, "of a trust established by a late and much regretted Scottish industrialist. He was a great believer in education—as these men of little learning often are . . ." This stopped Isabel in her tracks. Academic snobbery appalled her, and the condescension in Lettuce's reference was breathtaking. She thought she knew who the industrialist was—a self-made man, and self-educated, too, for which she thought he deserved every credit rather than this high-handed dismissal. He may have been a man of little formal education, but he knew more about the world than Lettuce and Dove put together, and, moreover, was modest about his money and his success.

"I happen to know the person who runs this trust," Lettuce went on. "We are both members of a bridge club that meets fairly regularly. He has indicated to me that there is an underspend this year—one or two projects that they were supporting never got off the ground and another, a medical research programme, failed to get the approval of the relevant research ethics committee. Tut-tut, not that it's any of our business! Anyway. This has left them with surplus funds that they are keen to put to good use.

"I sent them a draft proposal that I am happy to say they accepted without quibble. I have suggested that they fund the conference in full, and that they also provide for the publication of the papers presented at it. I hope you don't mind that I told them that you could provide a suitable publication platform through the *Review*. They accepted all this and indicated that once they had a detailed budget, we could expect their approval. They very helpfully suggested a figure for the support they can give. It is a very generous one, as you will see in the budget I have attached.

"I think it would be simplest if I were to chair this conference, perhaps using, for administrative purposes, the title of Conference Director. I hope that you will serve on the conference committee, along with Christopher Dove and one or two others, including my assistant, Gloria MacFarlane. Gloria has very kindly offered to be Chief Rapporteur—I know that you will find her very easy to work with when it comes to preparing the papers for publication."

Isabel took a deep breath. *She* was the editor of the *Review of Applied Ethics*. Anybody called Gloria MacFarlane would have no say in what appeared in the *Review*'s columns, and nor for that matter would anybody called Lettuce or Dove.

That was the end of the main body of the letter; now she ran her eye over the budget that Lettuce had attached, and if she had been shocked by what Lettuce had said in the main body of the letter, then her reaction to his budget proposals was even more marked. The overall budget of the conference was to be one hundred thousand pounds. The cost of hiring the venue, the provision of a conference dinner, and the travel and hotel expenses of the speakers came to fifty thousand pounds. That was what these things cost, thought Isabel, but then . . . But her eyes widened at what followed. "Conference Director (Professor Robert Lettuce) honorarium and administrative fee: twenty thousand pounds. Administrative assistant fee (Ms. G. MacFarlane): eight thousand pounds. Honorarium and administrative fee for Deputy Director (Dr. Christopher Dove): five thousand pounds. Office and printing costs: three thousand pounds. Laptop computer purchase for Director and administrative staff: six thousand pounds." And so it went on until the grand total of one hundred thousand was reached. An item for five hundred pounds caught Isabel's eye: This was to be a publication grant to the *Review of Applied Ethics* to support the printing and publication of a special issue devoted to the conference papers. She thought: *Five hundred pounds—one fortieth of what Lettuce was proposing to pay himself.*

She slipped the letter and its accompanying budget into a desk drawer. She would have to consider her response to Professor Lettuce, but that would take time. One thing was clear to her, though, and that was that she could never, under any circumstances, be part of what in her mind amounted to a criminal misuse of a supporting trust's money. She thought of Lettuce's share of the dripping roast: *twenty thousand pounds.* Did he seriously imagine that the trust would not question that ridiculously inflated fee—or the fee being proposed for Ms. MacFarlane, with whom Lettuce must be having an affair? *Eight thousand pounds* was going her way—and for what? For dancing attendance on Lettuce who, anyway, was being handsomely paid for such administrative work as the conference would entail—not that it would be overburdensome. This was fraud—even daylight robbery. It was brazen; it was unashamed.

The whole project was outrageous, thought Isabel. She would tell Lettuce as much—tactfully, she hoped, but in unambiguous terms. The conference, she imagined, could be put together for fifteen thousand pounds *at the most.* But that would not allow for a fee for Lettuce, and he would certainly not approve of that. She sighed.

She wondered how she might reply to Lettuce's letter. "Dear Professor Lettuce," she might write. "How dare you? Yours sincerely, Isabel Dalhousie." But the question mark worried her: Was *how dare you* a question or an exclamation? She was not sure, and if you were going to write a letter quite as direct and unambiguous as that, one would want to get the punctuation correct.

She closed her eyes. Writing to Lettuce in those terms would constitute a declaration of war—and she wondered whether she wanted to make an implacable enemy of him. There was so much conflict and confrontation in the world: Did she want to add to it, in her own small circle? Lettuce was selfish and self-serving—she was in no doubt about that—but would going head-to-head with him in a no-holds-barred exchange do anything to change him? She doubted it. Would it not be better to point out, in a courteous way if possible, the grounds of her concern? If she told him that his budget was perhaps just a little bit overgenerous when it came to payments to him and the undoubtedly very competent Ms. MacFarlane, he might be more inclined to examine the issue and even to do something to correct the flaw. That was possible, she supposed, and it would leave her feeling less uncomfortable. Conflict made her feel raw—it dirtied things, she thought. She did not want to add to the already immense burden of conflict under which society laboured. It was all very well saying that this was a minor issue, but it was on these tiny local battlefields that the greater moral battle drama was enacted. Small, apparently inconsequential acts defined the greater moral climate; local discord, as every concertgoer knew, made a difference to the sound of the larger orchestra.

She got up from her desk and crossed the room to stand before the window. The day had started sunny, and the sun was still there, on the shrubs and on the hedge that shielded the front garden from the street. She now made a conscious effort to think positively of Lettuce. She would not retreat into the security of animosity, of hatred. Lettuce only wanted to be loved, to be given the recognition that he felt he was due. She should not laugh at that; she should not mock his parading of his qualifications and honours.

It was hard, but she did it. She returned to her desk and began a note, in longhand, on a piece of headed notepaper. There were no accolades listed on this paper—just Isabel's address. She wrote: "Dear Robert, I was pleased to hear about your proposed conference. This is a wonderful idea and of course the *Review* will be pleased to provide a home for the papers. I have looked at your draft budget and it seems to me that you have covered all the foreseeable expenses. I am slightly concerned, though, about balance. I'm sure that you would wish to achieve that balance, and I wonder whether we should perhaps allocate less to administrative fees and a bit more to looking after those who attend? Just a thought, but I am sure that it's one that you yourself will be only too willing to address."

She re-read what she had written—more than once. Words were such powerful things: A few words could end a world, or equally might heal one. Now she inserted, after the final sentence, "I know how sensitive you are in the way you deal with such matters, and I am sure that you'll come up with something that deals with my concerns."

She signed the letter, folded it, and inserted it in the envelope. Then she placed it in the other old shoebox that she used for outgoing mail. On the side of the box she could just make out an ancient, faded label: *Salvatore Ferragamo*, and she thought of her mother, as she often did. Then she thought of Jamie, and of the boys, and of Grace, who even now was making a cup of tea for her and would be bringing it to her study, the cup rattling on its saucer as she carried it. It was the sound that tea made, Isabel had decided. Everything had a sound, even those things that looked silent.

She gave the letter a final glance as it lay in the box. She sighed—she so longed for a few weeks somewhere warm, perhaps a small villa on an Italian hillside dotted with ancient olive trees. And with the smell of thyme and the sound of cicadas in the noonday heat . . . Scotland, she thought, had become far too cautious a place, riddled with self-reproach—to the extent that it was impossible to do anything without worrying about it. Italy was different; it would be a place of tolerance and freedom, and yet . . .

She heard the rattle of the teacup. Then there was the knock at the door—which occasioned further rattling. But Grace never spilled the tea. Isabel had a private horror of saucers into which the contents of a cup had spilled. It was a small and ridiculous thing, but of such preferences and dislikes was life made up. *Get the small things right,* her sainted American mother had told her. *Get those right, and the rest follows.*

Grace came in. "Tea," she said.

It was what she always said. Just "tea"—but what else, Isabel asked herself, was there to say?

CHAPTER TWO

DAWN ARRIVED FOUR DAYS LATER, climbing out of a taxi with two battered suitcases which the taxi driver cheerfully helped wheel to the front door. Jamie was there to meet her, and led her into the hall.

"That's everything?" he asked, eyeing the luggage.

Dawn smiled. "My worldly possessions," she said. "Or the ones I currently use. I've got stuff at my parents' house. They live out at West Linton." She paused. "You know how you never really move out of home?"

"No, you don't, do you? And parents keep your bedroom as it was when you left. They make a shrine of it."

Dawn said that this was exactly what her mother had done. She gestured towards the suitcases. "This is mostly clothes. I've left books in the flat—the one I was sharing. They had empty bookshelves and I put mine in. They don't mind keeping them for me."

"It's good to travel light," said Jamie.

"Except that these cases seem to weigh a ton," said Dawn. She looked at the staircase that led off the hall. "I gather I'm up at the top."

Jamie laughed. "A garret—I hope you don't mind a garret."

"You're being so kind," said Dawn. "You and your . . ."

"Isabel."

"And she hasn't even met me," Dawn went on.

"You'll like her," said Jamie. He glanced towards the closed door to Isabel's study. "She's on the phone right now. She edits a journal—that's her office through there."

He moved to pick up the suitcases.

"Let me take one," said Dawn.

"I'd be balanced. One in each hand."

"No. I must."

They made their way up the two flights of stairs leading to the attic bedroom that Jamie and Isabel had prepared the previous day. Dawn liked it. "Look at this view," she enthused. "Trees. Look at that oak tree. And the garden. This is beautiful, Jamie. I love it."

"There's a bathroom of sorts right next door," said Jamie. "There's a shower. The washbasin tap needs a new washer—it drips a bit. And there's a kitchenette, although you're more than welcome to use the kitchen downstairs. Both Isabel and I would be happy if you did. The kids make a mess of it, but there's everything there."

"I'll keep out of your hair," said Dawn. "You won't notice me—I promise."

He told her there was no need to do that. She could join them for meals in the kitchen. There was plenty of room. But she demurred. "You don't need me cluttering up the place," she said. And then, lowering her voice, she continued, "I've been stupid. You know about everything, I suppose. You know about what happened?"

Jamie was tactful. "I heard a bit . . ."

Dawn looked pained. "I didn't realise at first that everybody

would hear about it. But they did. The whole orchestra knew—
and their partners. I take it that you heard that I . . ."

Jamie interrupted her. "I heard that you and Andrew had
split up."

"Split up is putting it politely. I left Andrew because I fell for
Fionn. Did you hear that bit?"

Jamie had to admit that he had. "Yes," he said. "I think that
everybody knew you had . . . gone off with Fionn."

Dawn gave him a piercing look. "And they disapproved?"

Jamie took some time to answer. "I don't think it was necessarily disapproval. Surprise, yes. And also, I suppose people thought
that you were making a mistake."

Rather unexpectedly, Dawn laughed. "And they were right—
as it turned out."

"We all make mistakes," said Jamie quickly.

Dawn looked rueful. "But some mistakes are worse than
others."

"I suppose so," Jamie agreed. "Marching on Moscow in the
winter—bad mistake. Selling Alaska if you're the Czar of Russia.
Bringing in a large wooden horse left outside your gates by a group
of Greeks. There'll be other examples."

"I'm paying for it now," said Dawn.

Jamie looked away. He was embarrassed. Then he said, "We
hope you'll be happy here."

Dawn said that she felt she would. "My old room was so noisy.
It was driving me mad. This is so peaceful."

Jamie began to leave. At the door he remembered something.
"You'll bump into somebody called Grace," he said. "She's the
housekeeper. She used to work for Isabel's father. She's . . ." He
stopped. He was not sure what he was going to say. It was difficult to say much about Grace to somebody who had never met

her. No description he could think of would do her justice, he thought.

Dawn was waiting.

"She has fixed views on some matters," Jamie continued. "Most matters, in fact."

Dawn looked at him with interest. "You're warning me about something?"

"Not really," said Jamie, but then said, "Well, I suppose I am—in a way. Grace is a spiritualist. She's interested in what she calls 'the world of spirit.' She goes to séances."

Dawn looked interested. "I had an aunt who was like that," she said. "She was a Highlander. People up there are often said to be a bit . . . what's the word? Fey? They claim to see things other people don't see."

"I'm not sure if I believe any of that stuff," said Jamie. "Not that I'm being dismissive. Some things, I suppose, are difficult to explain."

"Like telepathy?" suggested Dawn.

Jamie said that he had never had a telepathic message. "But there might be something in it," he conceded. "People say that dogs know when their owners are coming back well before they appear."

Dawn nodded. "Sometimes, when my phone goes, I know who it is before anybody says anything."

Jamie grinned. "That's because it displays the caller's name and number."

She gave him a playful glance. "I'm not making it up," she said. "I really do know—sometimes."

"That could be because you're guessing," said Jamie.

"Think of a number between one and ten," Dawn said suddenly. "Go on. Just think of it."

Jamie closed his eyes briefly. "All right."

"Send it to me."

"Sending."

Dawn's brows were knitted in concentration. "Three," she said.

Jamie's eyes widened. "As a matter of fact . . ."

She cut him short. "It works best if you do it spontaneously," she said. "If we tried again, I probably wouldn't get it right."

He looked at her. He was not sure that he was entirely comfortable with her having telepathic abilities—if she did, indeed, have them. Would such a person know what another was thinking even before anything was said? That was a disturbing thought, as we all thought things that we would not want others to know we were thinking. Jamie remembered that he and Isabel had once discussed what she had called the "intrusive thoughts" that elbowed their way into one's mind from time to time. These were thoughts that we would not normally entertain because they were out of character or because we were ashamed of them. Isabel had said that it was quite normal to think such things because it was the mind's way of reminding us of what we would not do.

For a few moments they stared at one another. Jamie was sure that Dawn knew that he was thinking about the possibility that she could tell what was going on in his mind, and he now made a conscious effort to think about something quite different. And that resulted in his asking, quite out of the blue, whether she liked the music of Peter Maxwell Davies.

She looked puzzled. "I've never heard of him," she replied.

"He was a composer who lived up in Orkney," said Jamie. "He wrote a wonderful piece called *An Orkney Wedding, with Sunrise*. A piper joins the orchestra at the end of that. It's electrifying."

She looked slightly embarrassed. "There's so much I don't

know," she said. "Every day I discover that I seem to know less and less."

He was quick to say that he was in the same position. "I'm playing in a performance of one of his pieces," he said. "That's why I was thinking of him."

"Oh, yes?"

"I was just interested to know if you knew his music. He's not as well known as he should be, I think." He paused. "But I don't know what your taste in music is."

"Everything," she said. "I like everything except heavy metal and rap. Too noisy. Too aggressive. I like folk music. I sometimes go to the folk clubs. Sandy Bell's, for instance."

"Of course."

"And Icelandic," she continued. "Sigur Rós. Amiina. I'd like to go to Iceland."

"You could," he said. "It's not far away. Our neighbour, in fact."

She asked him whether he had been. He shook his head.

"I can't seem to get away," he said. "Two small children. The gigs I play in." He looked about him. "All this. Life."

He reminded himself that she had arrived with no more than two suitcases; he, by contrast, had so many things. She was free, but he was burdened by the weight of what he had acquired over the years: his collection of musical scores, his vinyl records, his stereo equipment, the old harmonium that Isabel had given him as a birthday present and that was still awaiting restoration, his bicycle with its expensive titanium frame . . . These were things that kept him from going off to Iceland on the spur of the moment, and he remembered the title of a piece he had fallen in love with when he had first discovered early music: "In Nets of Golden Wires." It was often not chains that bound us or weighed us down: It could equally well be nets of golden wires.

He looked at his watch and said that he would have to get on with things but that if she liked to come downstairs in fifteen minutes, she would meet Isabel and they would all have a cup of tea.

She gave him a look that he found hard to interpret. It seemed to him that she was pleading with him.

He hesitated before the door. "Is there something?"

She lowered her gaze. "I'm sorry . . . There was something I was wondering about."

He waited, and then she said, "What will Isabel think of me?"

He shrugged. "I'm sure she'll like you."

"But she knows?"

He was not sure what to make of this. "About?"

"About what happened? About how I went off?"

He held her gaze. "Yes, she knows."

"And she disapproves?"

He felt a sudden surge of sympathy. "Isabel is not one of those people who goes round disapproving of other people. She's very . . ." He searched for the right word, and decided upon "understanding."

"And anyway," he continued, "we can all fall for other people without thinking about consequences. Who hasn't done just that at some point in their lives?"

"All of us?"

"Yes," he said, emphatically. "Everyone—if they're honest with themselves."

Dawn looked away. "If I could turn the clock back," she said. "I would."

Jamie made a gesture of acceptance. "Once again, who hasn't wanted to do that?"

She gave him a look of gratitude.

"I have to get on," he said.

He closed the door behind him and made his way downstairs.

THEY INVITED DAWN to join them for an early dinner that evening, but she declined. "It's very kind of you," she said, "but I really don't want to be in your hair."

"You wouldn't be," said Isabel.

"No," agreed Jamie. "We'd like you to come. We mean it."

But Dawn was not to be persuaded. "I'd rather not," she said. "Sorry. It's really kind of you, but I'd feel much more comfortable if you treated me as a lodger."

Isabel caught Jamie's eye. "I understand," she said. "You need your independence. That's fine by us."

"Yes," said Jamie. "But if you ever want a chat or anything, don't sit up there all by yourself."

"You're both so kind," said Dawn.

Over dinner, Isabel said to Jamie, "I like her, you know. But I think that she's . . . well, I think there's an air of sadness about her."

"Regret," said Jamie. "She feels regret over what she did."

"Going off with that man? Leaving a nice man for a known Lothario."

"Yes." He paused. "She said something about wanting to turn the clock back if she could."

Isabel sighed. "Poor woman."

Jamie thought that she would probably find somebody else, and that would deal with her regret. Isabel considered this, and then told him that she did not agree. That would be too simple of a sort that never really worked—a flawed folk wisdom. "I don't think that a new lover is a cure for an old one. I don't think it works that way."

"Possibly not," said Jamie, and then added, "Except sometimes."

"You could say that of any rule," said Isabel. "Every rule will have its exceptions."

"That proves the rule," said Jamie.

Isabel had studied logic. "That's just not true," she said. "An exception is more likely to disprove a rule. Or at least restrict its application." She toyed with the food on her plate. "Unless there's something else troubling her—not just simple regret over a love affair gone wrong."

Jamie was surprised. "You mean . . . guilt over something else she's done?"

"Perhaps."

Jamie looked doubtful. "So, we might have taken in somebody who's done something . . . something worse than simply leaving one man for another?"

"I didn't say that," said Isabel. "But that sort of thing has happened, I believe."

Jamie said that he doubted whether Dawn was anything other than what she appeared to be. "She was very frank with me," he said. "She didn't seem to be hiding anything."

Isabel was silent for a few moments. "I hope we haven't done the wrong thing."

"I don't think we have," Jamie reassured her. "We've simply taken in somebody who needed somewhere to live for a while. That's the right thing, I think."

"What was it that T. S. Eliot said?" asked Isabel. "Something about how bad it was to do the right thing for the wrong reason."

"Why?" asked Jamie.

"It must be because you get credit that you don't deserve," Isabel suggested.

Jamie said that he did not see what was wrong with that, but then added that if you were wrongfully credited with something, then you should correct the misapprehension.

"That's simply an aspect of the duty to tell the truth," Isabel said. "You can lie to people in more ways than one. Letting some-body believe something untrue is another form of lying to them."

But had they acted for the wrong reason? Isabel sighed. "I suppose that sometimes one does something because it makes one feel better, rather than because it is the right thing in itself." She glanced at Jamie, as if apologising for the question she was about to ask. "Is that what we've done here? Have we given Dawn that room because it makes us feel that we're doing some-thing that needs to be done, rather than because that's what *she* needs?"

He reached out to take her hand. "You make everything so dif-ficult," he said. "So what if you feel good when you give a hungry person the money to buy a meal. So what? The point is that you're helping somebody. That's not acting for the wrong reason . . ."

"It's a side effect," suggested Isabel. "Is that it?"

Jamie nodded. "Yes, it is. It's exactly that. And I don't think you need to worry too much about side effects."

Isabel pushed her plate away. She had had enough. She sighed. "Going through life is much easier if you aren't a philoso-pher. There must be far fewer problems in the unexamined life."

He laughed. "We are what we are," he said. "You can't help being a philosopher and I can't help being a musician. We both have to do what we have to do."

She looked thoughtful. "We could go away," she said. "I could give up the *Review*. You could resign from the ensemble. You could tell the Academy that you're no longer going to teach. We could pack it all in."

"Go where?" he asked.

She waved a hand. "To live on a Hebridean island. Mull. South Uist. Harris. Or even Canna. Remember how we loved Canna when we went over there from Arisaig. We walked along that road past the farm. There were wildflowers. I remember the wildflowers. And the sheep on the hillside, and the sound of the birds. People actually live there—not many, but they do. There's a tiny, tiny school—a handful of children. The boys could go there."

"And what would we do?" he asked.

"Grow a few vegetables. Keep sheep. You could have a fishing boat. You could put down creels and catch mackerel."

"And if somebody needs to go to the dentist? Or needs to buy new clothes?"

Isabel had an answer. "There's the ferry to Mallaig. There are shops there. The mainland isn't all that far away."

"And when the boys get bigger and need to go to secondary school?"

"Mallaig again. The school there takes weekly boarders. They go back home at weekends."

Jamie said that she made it sound so straightforward. And it was, Isabel said. "We're the ones who complicate our lives," she said. "It doesn't have to be like that. We want all these comforts that we have. We want to travel. We want more and more material possessions. You don't need most of those things."

He looked at her intently. "Are you serious?" he asked.

She did not reply immediately, and when she did, there was a note of sadness in her voice. "It's not an entirely fanciful suggestion. There are a lot of people who do it. They tend to be happy with their choice. They thrive."

"I'd have to stop playing music with other people," Jamie said.

"You could start an island orchestra—just a small one. People would be keen, I imagine. We could even build a tiny opera house—one with thirty seats and get Scottish Opera to come and perform for us. They love taking things to remote places—it's part of their outreach programme."

Jamie laughed. "Possibly. The *Ring* cycle on Coll—or Tiree perhaps. I can see it. Island people would be so proud of it."

He smiled. He loved Scotland. He loved it so much.

"And I would have to stop doing philosophy with other people."

"I think I could get bored with fishing," he added.

"Who wouldn't?" agreed Isabel. "But you could read, of course. You've often said you wish you had more time to read."

"I suppose so," he said. "I definitely need to read more."

"Well, you'd be able to do that on the island."

"There are so few escapes still available in this life," Jamie said. "Although we're lucky, aren't we? Scotland is one of the few places where you can really get away from all the things that there are to dislike in the world today."

"We like to think that," Isabel warned. "But I'm not sure that it's the case."

"Oh well," said Jamie. "Illusions. We all need illusions about ourselves."

"Even in front of the mirror?" asked Isabel.

"Especially then," Jamie answered.

Jamie would never have had cause to fear mirrors. She was sure of that. In her eyes he was perfect, a figure from a Renaissance painting, somehow delivered to her, to be gazed upon, to be cherished, which she did, of course. She loved him so much that it hurt. That was the real test of love, she had always believed: Did it hurt? Of course it hurt. Love *always* hurts. That's the discovery you made when you were in your teens and it stayed with you for ever. It was something you just knew.

Then a disturbing thought occurred to her. Would she love Jamie any less if he were not so beautiful, if he were not the double of the young man in Botticelli's *Portrait of a Young Man Holding a Roundel*? The beautiful had love lavished upon them—unmerited love, because they had done nothing to earn it. That was so unfair, even if it was an inescapable concomitant of the way things were.

A thought came to her out of the blue. "Do you think life is inherently unfair?" she asked.

Jamie was surprised by this unexpected question—although Isabel occasionally came up with observations or questions that seemed to have little bearing on what they had been talking about. That, he thought, was a philosopher's prerogative.

He looked at his watch. He needed to do some practice.

"Later," he said. "Let's talk about that later." He rose from the table. "Next month? Shall we discuss that sometime next month?"

She laughed. "Or next year?"

He bent down to kiss her. "There's so much to talk about. So many questions . . ."

"And so few answers," said Isabel.

CHAPTER THREE

THE FOLLOWING MORNING, Grace gave Isabel a list of things that the household needed: garlic, washing-up liquid, bananas and goat's cheese. To this list, Jamie had added potatoes, as he had offered to make potato dauphinoise for dinner that evening. He would also make a salmon mousse if she would get some smoked salmon from the fish shop at Holy Corner. The potato dauphinoise would be served to accompany lamb chops, which she would need to get as well if she happened to be walking past the butcher's. "Other than that," he said, "I think we have everything we need."

It was a ten-minute walk to Bruntsfield Place, where most of these items—with the exception of bananas—might be bought. That was where the delicatessen was—the one formerly run by her niece, Cat, and now managed by Hannah, with Eddie as her assistant. Isabel was fond of Eddie, who had worked with Cat for some time. Eddie's confidence had increased recently, and his nervous, rather diffident manner had become less noticeable. Isabel had always known that Eddie was a damaged young man who bore the scars of a traumatic childhood; she encouraged him as best she could, and he responded well to the interest she showed in his career. She had paid for him to go on an advanced food hygiene course, and he had come back from a week in Glasgow with a raft of proposals as to how refrigerated displays should be cleaned, how boards should be colour-coded to prevent meat being dealt with on surfaces reserved for fish, and just how long one should wash one's hands for even before donning blue food-handling gloves. He also had temperature charts, lurid blown-up pictures of various hostile organisms, and a discouraging book on the way in which infections could be transmitted by skin-to-skin contact or by droplets emitted by sneezing or even breathing.

"Breathing's very dangerous," Eddie had said to her after he returned from the course. "You may not realise it, Isabel, but just by breathing you're spreading all sorts of toxic organisms."

"That may be true, Eddie," Isabel admitted. "But I hardly have much alternative, do I?"

He had looked at her reproachfully. "You can keep away from food," he said.

"But again, one can't do that indefinitely," she pointed out. "We have to eat, just as we have to breathe. We're basically pretty unhygienic."

"Don't make fun of toxic organisms," warned Eddie. "A lot of people don't know how dangerous they are. E-coli, for example, have you heard of them? Everybody should read up on e-coli. They're everywhere." He paused. "I'm serious. They're in your nose, for example."

Isabel raised an eyebrow. "Mine, in particular?"

"Everybody's. Not just yours. Some people, though, have large colonies of e-coli in their nose." He gave her a look that made her imagine that he was assessing her nose. She did not think it was a particularly tempting refuge for e-coli, but she could be wrong . . .

"There's a guy in Glasgow," Eddie went on. "He was a butcher, see, and he made some pies from meat that had e-coli crawling all over it. He hadn't kept it in the fridge and he thought it would be all right. But it wasn't, and he made these Scotch pies and this man came in and bought one. He almost died—he didn't quite, but they said it was a close thing. He was seriously ill in hospital in Glasgow and they thought he was a goner. A priest came and did . . . what do priests do when they're told you've got e-coli and are not going to make it? Put olive oil on your forehead? Something like that?"

"It doesn't have to be olive oil," said Isabel. "It can be any sort of oil."

"Even engine oil? That thick stuff you put in engines?"

Isabel was not sure. She thought not, but said that it probably didn't matter too much.

"Well, he had that," said Eddie. "And then the next morning he felt much better."

"That's a good ending," said Isabel. "I was worried that the story would not end well."

Eddie looked thoughtful. "I heard about it from a cousin of mine," he said. "He lives over in Glasgow. His father knew the guy who ate the pie. He said that he was really cross with the butcher. He went round to his shop and punched him in the face. That was once he was out of hospital and was strong enough to do it, of course. But the butcher still knew why he punched him."

Isabel sighed. "That's not very edifying," she said. "The butcher did not mean to harm him. He didn't knowingly sell a pie that was full of e-coli, did he?"

"He should have kept the meat in the fridge," said Eddie. "Butchers know that. They go to courses like the one I've been on. There were two butchers there when I did it. One was called Sammy and he came from Northern Ireland originally. He had a tattoo on his arm that said *No Pope Here*. He showed it to me."

Isabel sighed once more. "That's rather sad," she said. "People should try to get on with one another, and it doesn't help if some of them have unfriendly remarks about the Pope tattooed on their arms. Mind you, I suppose as a statement it was clear enough: It indicated that the Pope would not be welcome if he were to try to take the young man's arm—he would be rebuffed. Strictly speaking, it was a statement that made sense."

"Are you serious?" asked Eddie. "Sometimes it's hard to tell, you know."

"I was digressing," said Isabel. "We were talking about e-coli and somehow we got on to talking about the Pope and Northern Ireland. There's no obvious connection, of course, but sometimes conversations drift."

"Well, you have to be really careful about e-coli," Eddie concluded. "That's all I'm saying."

"And that's very good advice," said Isabel, and smiled at Eddie, who returned the smile appreciatively, and was even more pleased when Isabel admired the certificate he had been awarded for the successful completion of the food hygiene course. It was probably the first certificate he'd ever had, and she could see how much it meant to him.

"I'm going to get that properly framed for you," she said. "Would you like that, Eddie? If you give me the certificate, I'll take it to the framers down the road and get them to put a good big frame on it."

Eddie handed over the certificate. "You're really kind, Isabel," he said, and then added, "You're the kindest person I know. No, I mean it. That's true—you are."

Embarrassed by his praise, she made a dismissive gesture. "I'm not," she said simply. "You mustn't say things like that, Eddie. You mustn't exaggerate."

He might have demurred, and left it at that, but Eddie had the intensity of youth. "No, I really mean it. You do all these things for people—all the time. I've seen it all along. Nobody else I know does that."

Isabel turned away, keen to change the subject. She saw a large jar of salted almonds on the counter, and said, "Those are so more-ish, aren't they. Eat one, and you end up eating twenty."

Eddie's attention was successfully diverted, and the conversation moved on.

NOW, AS SHE REACHED Bruntsfield and saw the deli on the other side of the road, she checked her list. There was a small supermarket a few blocks towards town—she would get the potatoes and garlic there, and see if there were any bananas to be had. They stocked very little fruit there, though, and she would probably have to go out of her way to get those. She could leave them off the list altogether, though, without their being missed. Grace sometimes made a banana loaf for the boys, and she suspected that was why they were needed. If the banana loaf had to wait until the next trip to the larger supermarket in Morningside, then so be it. One's life should not be regulated by bananas, she thought.

She bought the potatoes and washing-up liquid before going to the deli. She still thought of it as *the* deli, and mentally called it that, although Cat now ran another deli on Morningside Road, and there was the possibility of confusion, but the habit was entrenched and Jamie and Grace usually knew which one she was talking about. Jamie referred to Cat's new shop as "Cat's place" and Grace called it "that cheesy place," which could be taken as a reference to its principal product, or, alternatively, to its smell, which she found too strong. "Cheese doesn't *have* to smell," Grace said. "Look at cheddar. Does it smell? It does not."

Isabel could have bought the goat's cheese at *the* deli but decided to walk further down the road to get it from Cat herself. She had not seen her niece for some time and she wanted to know how the comparatively new shop was faring. She had no real fears on that score—Cat may not have had a talent for spotting reliable men, but she lacked nothing in her ability to run a business. In the past, Isabel had nursed a secret hope that Cat would one day consult a relationship counsellor of some sort and be told where she was going wrong in her choice of boyfriends, but she knew that she would never be able to suggest this. You could not tell people they needed to see a psychiatrist or a therapist—you simply couldn't. It was far easier to tell them they needed to use a more effective deodorant, although that was hardly thought to be a simple thing to do. Fortunately, thought Isabel, I have never been in a position where I felt I had to impart that particular piece of sensitive advice to a friend. None of my friends, Isabel reflected, has personal freshness issues . . . The thought amused her. There were many grounds on which one might congratulate oneself, but that, surely, must be one of the most obscure ones. This made her smile. Isabel often smiled to herself, which amused Jamie, who would say "Descartes!" when he noticed it—a reference to an occasion on which he had, rather wittily, thought Isabel, said, *I think, therefore I smile.*

Cat was not in when Isabel arrived at her deli. Her boyfriend— and business partner—Gordon was behind the counter, though, and he gave Isabel a broad smile as she came through the front door. There were a couple of customers who had just made a purchase, and they left a few moments after Isabel came in. Gordon watched them go, and made a face as they left.

"Those two are a pain," he said. "They like to sample everything before they buy it. They end up having a complete two-course meal on the house."

"I haven't come to eat anything," said Isabel. She looked about her. "Is Cat around?"

"She's taking the day off," said Gordon. "She's gone to see a friend in St. Andrews. I could call her, if you like."

Isabel said that she would see Cat on another occasion. "I'm very happy just to see you," she said to Gordon. "We haven't spoken for a while."

"No, we haven't," he said. "Cat and I were thinking about that the other day. I don't know where the time goes."

Isabel examined a bottle of wine on one of the wine shelves that took up a whole wall of the shop. "You have some rather nice wines," she said. "Western Australia, I see."

"It's very nice," said Gordon. "Margaret River, not far from Perth. Their whites are lovely—very floral."

Isabel peered at the label. "Is that a eucalyptus flower?" she asked.

"I believe so," said Gordon. "I love anything to do with eucalyptus. I gave Cat some eucalyptus soap the other day. I've been using it myself."

"And this one," said Isabel, moving along the shelf.

"That's English. People forget that the south of England is now good territory for white wine. It's still a bit pricey, but people love wines from that part of the world. Even the French, who can be very sniffy about wine from anywhere outside France, have come up with grudging praise for that particular vineyard."

Gordon gestured to a chair. "We could sit down, I think. There's hardly anybody around at the moment—I don't think we'll be disturbed."

Isabel accepted his invitation. She liked Gordon and his easy manner. He was friendly without being too gushing, and he seemed to weigh carefully what was said to him before he responded.

"Is everything all right in the shop?" Isabel asked.

Gordon did not hesitate to reply. "Perfect," he said. "May was our best month since we started. This one's a bit quieter, but I think that's because of the weather. It's been a bit wet, and you know how people think twice about going out if it's pouring with rain."

Gordon gestured for her to sit down on one of the chairs behind the counter. "I've been meaning to get in touch, but . . ." He looked about him. "But this place takes up so much time."

Isabel said that she could well believe it. "I've heard that having a business is like having another child. It requires much the same commitment."

Gordon agreed. "You have a business yourself, of course. You must know what it's like."

"The *Review*? I suppose it's a business, but it's different."

"You have to deal with awkward customers too, I imagine."

Isabel thought of Professor Lettuce—he was an awkward customer by any standards. And Christopher Dove, of course. Now she said, "Are you getting help here?" There had been talk of taking on a counter assistant, but Cat had complained about the difficulty of finding somebody reliable. She had tried one or two young people, but they had been bad timekeepers and she had given up on them.

"We're managing by ourselves," said Gordon. "And I always take the view that somebody will turn up. That happened on the yacht. We'd be a crew member short and then somebody comes strolling along the dock, looking for a job."

Gordon had worked on a large yacht in the Caribbean until an issue with a homicidal chef prompted him to look for something else. Isabel had heard the story of the chef and now she wondered whether he had been recruited in this way. If he had, it was an object lesson, perhaps, in being a bit more careful in choosing whom to employ.

Gordon sat back in his chair. "You know something, Isabel?" he said. "I'm really happy—probably happier than I've been for years."

She glanced at him. He *looked* happy—he had that air about him. Happiness—like misery—could make an unmistakeable impression on a person's features. Now she found herself wondering why he should be so happy. Was it because he had found his niche—running a small deli in Edinburgh? Had that been his ambition all along? Or was it just sheer pleasure in being on dry land after a demanding job at sea? Sailing, she had always thought, was uncomfortable—in some respects the most uncomfortable state of all: You were wet; your clothing, damp from seawater, would never get dry; your bunk was too small; and if conditions became too rough, seasickness could wrap its nauseating tentacles about you.

But it was not this at all. Gordon was happy, as he now explained to Isabel, because he was in love with Cat.

"I wouldn't normally talk about this sort of thing," he confided. "But I'm really smitten. Cat is . . . well, she's everything I've dreamed of—and never found, until now."

He blushed.

"I don't want to go on about it," he continued, "but I think this is the first time I've been in love. In the past I may have thought I was in love, but what I felt was nothing like what I feel now—nothing like it at all."

Isabel looked down at the floor. She was embarrassed by this sudden opening up; it was not as if she knew Gordon at all well, and hearing about his emotional state was not something she was prepared for. But she did not wish to sound discouraging, so she said, "It's a wonderful state, isn't it?"

He was staring at her. "Are you in love yourself?"

Isabel felt distinctly uncomfortable under his gaze. She did not think that this was a question one should ask somebody out of the blue. It was not the business of anybody else whether one was in love or not. And even if she gave a frank answer, she was not sure what it would be. She loved Jamie—of course she did—but was that the same thing as being *in* love? Certainly, there was none of the head-spinning intoxication of a newly minted love affair. The love that you felt for your spouse was a more comfortable love—like the feeling one gets from wearing a familiar pair of old slippers, as it had once been described to her.

"I hope my question doesn't embarrass you," said Gordon.

"No, it doesn't," Isabel said. Of course, it did, but if one confessed embarrassment on being asked whether one was in love with one's spouse, then what conclusions would others reach? *When asked whether she was in love with her husband, she declined to answer . . .* She would have to say something.

"Of course, I'm in love," she replied. "But I'm not head over heels in a . . . walking-on-air sense. That's a different sort of being in love."

Gordon agreed. "I know it changes. I know that after you've been with somebody for a couple of years, it's different. A bit less overwhelming. But when you're actually experiencing it, it's pretty intense."

She said that she knew exactly what he meant. "And I'm happy for you and Cat—assuming that she feels the same about you." She paused. "Sorry, that sounds a bit grudging. I'm sure she does."

"I think she does," said Gordon. "At least that's what she's led me to believe. And why shouldn't she be fond of me? We get on pretty well." He scratched the back of his neck. Body language experts might read that as a sign of puzzlement, thought Isabel, but there seemed to be nothing puzzled about Gordon. Quite the opposite, in fact.

Gordon continued, "I'm really pleased that she's waited for me—I mean, that she hasn't really committed herself to anybody else before."

There were occasions when such was Isabel's astonishment that her usual calm deserted her. That did not happen now, although it almost did. She felt that she might splutter and choke, although all she eventually did was say, rather mildly, "Really?" Then she blinked and added, "Well . . ."

A comment unfinished may be more eloquent than one considered, refined, fully punctuated and delivered. Gordon, though, was unaware of the reaction his remark had provoked. "Yes," he said. "This is her first serious relationship."

He spoke with a reticence tinged with pride. Isabel's eyes widened. Had she heard correctly? "Her first?" she asked.

"Yes. I'm not saying Cat hasn't ever been involved with anybody else—I'm not saying that. She's probably had a boyfriend or two in the past—who hasn't?"

Isabel swallowed. A boyfriend or two? She wanted to say, "I've stopped counting" but did not; she simply swallowed again and said nothing.

"Of course," Gordon continued, "I don't think you should ask anybody about their love lives—before you, that is. You assume that people have been involved, but you don't ask directly." He paused as he gave Isabel an enquiring look. "You don't, do you? I know that this is the sort of question you like to think about when you're doing your . . . your philosophy, I suppose you'd say. Do you say *doing philosophy*? Is that what you say you do?"

Isabel hesitated. She would answer that question first—that, at least, was uncontroversial. She confirmed that *doing philosophy* was exactly what one might say. Or one might say *practising philosophy*, although that sounded a bit like practising the piano. Mind you, the analogy of piano practice was a useful one, she thought. It involved developing neural pathways for a specific activity, and that was something one needed to do in all sorts of contexts.

"I suppose what you do is like playing chess," Gordon remarked. "You have to sit there and think of your moves, one by one. You have to make sure that you think of what the other side is going to do. I suppose in your case that means thinking of the arguments that other people are going to make."

"Yes," said Isabel. She was still thinking of what Cat had said—if she had said it. People often misunderstood what others said, and it was entirely possible that Cat had not actually said what Gordon thought she had said. People in love—and it was obvious now that he was deeply in love—misinterpreted things. Gordon might want to be the first great love of Cat's life, and might have convinced himself that this was so without having been misled in any way by Cat. That was quite possible.

But now he pressed her on the other question he had raised. "Do you agree with me? Do you think that you shouldn't ask people about these things?"

"About their previous love lives?"

"Yes. Should you ask them directly? I don't think you should." He answered his own question—quite emphatically, Isabel thought.

"It depends," she said. "As a general rule, I'd probably agree with you. Perhaps you should leave it up to the other person to raise the subject. If he or she wants to say something . . ."

"To go there," Gordon suggested.

"Yes, if he or she wants to go there, then he or she should be allowed to." She hesitated. "Although that raises the issue of whether it's right for somebody to bring up a subject that they're not sure the other person wants to hear about." She paused.

"There are proper limits to any conversation we have with another person."

He waited. Then he said, "You mean you shouldn't go there if you think the other person might not want to go there? Is that what you mean?"

"Yes. And that, I think, is why we have certain assumed no-go areas in what we say to others. You don't make negative comments about their appearance, for instance. Or you don't ask them about whether they ever suffer from constipation. Not as an opening gambit in a conversation, that is."

The irony seemed to escape Gordon, who burst out laughing. "Who cares about constipation?" he asked.

"The constipated," replied Isabel.

He frowned. "What about them?"

"They care about constipation. And they probably can't talk to their friends about it."

Gordon did not see why not. "I wouldn't care," he said. "It's nothing to be ashamed about."

"But it's not something that people like to talk about," Isabel responded. "And anyway, we're talking about love lives, and on balance, I'd agree with you. You shouldn't ask because it's an area of life that *may* be—not necessarily *is*, but may be private. We have to keep some sense of privacy in our lives."

As she said this, she realised how out of date she must sound to those who lived their lives on social media, who disclosed to the world every detail of what they did and what happened to them. It was a curious attitude, she thought, because it amounted to liv-ing in a glass box, a show to any passer-by. Such people led their lives in front of an open window, she imagined, and those who looked in were voyeurs. Or was that too extreme? she asked her-self. It was. It was not unnatural to want to share your experiences with others.

Gordon now said, "Anyway, these are big issues, aren't they? And you're the philosopher—I just run a deli. I should leave these questions to you, I think."

Isabel shook her head. "These are questions for everybody," she said. "Philosophy isn't just for philosophers—it's for everybody. Every single day we're faced with questions about what we should do. You can't go out of the house without tripping over a philosophical question."

He looked thoughtful. "Yes, I suppose you're right. Do you give money to the character sitting on the ground next to the cash machine? Do you bother to reply to a text message from somebody you don't want to hear from? That sort of thing."

"Yes," she said. "That sort of thing."

Gordon suddenly got up from his chair and rearranged some packets of pasta on a shelf. "People move these things," he said. "It really gets on my nerves when they take something off the shelf, look at it, and then put it back in the wrong place." He turned to Isabel. "I'm going to ask her to marry me, you know."

Isabel tried to smile. "Oh," she said.

"Do you think I should?"

She looked away. They had been discussing things you should not ask others. This was exactly such a question. You should *never* ask that, she thought, because if the marriage proves to be a mistake, then you have burdened another with some degree of responsibility for it.

"I don't think I can answer that," she said. "It's up to you. Do you want to marry her? I suppose you must—otherwise you wouldn't be asking."

Gordon smiled. "Actually, what I'm asking is this: Would you marry Cat—if you were me, that is. You know her well. Better than I do, I suppose, since you've been her aunt . . . well, for all her life."

Isabel reminded him that she and Cat, although aunt and niece, were not all that far apart in age. Twelve years. That came from an age difference in their parents. "It means that I don't really look upon myself as her aunt—not in the *real* aunt-like sense. Aunts are usually much older than their nieces."

"I know that," said Gordon. "But I'm still asking: Do you think I should marry her?"

Isabel responded with a question of her own. "Have you thought about it long enough? You shouldn't rush these things."

He was quick to tell her that he had thought about it for weeks. "Three weeks—non-stop. I've thought and I've thought."

Isabel looked at her watch. She did not want to answer him, at least not yet. Now it would be her turn to give the question careful thought. But just as she was thinking this, a customer came into the shop, and Gordon was diverted. Isabel rose from her chair. "Must go," she whispered. "You look after your customer. We can talk some other time."

Gordon nodded. "Some other time," he said.

The customer, a thin man wearing a corduroy jacket, glanced briefly at Isabel, then pointed at a bottle of wine on a shelf. "Is that stuff any good?" he asked.

Gordon nodded. "Wonderful," he said. "All our wines are wonderful."

If you are in love, thought Isabel as she left the deli, you think that sort of thing. Everything seems wonderful, and perhaps it was always going to be left to others to tell you, as gently as they could, that this was not necessarily the case.

CHAPTER FOUR

ON HER WAY BACK to the house, Isabel was burdened both physically and mentally: with her purchases, which had been more numerous than she had anticipated, and with the thought of Gordon's declaration—for that is what it had been: a declaration of love for Cat. In itself that was not particularly concerning—Isabel thought it rather touching that he should have opened up to her about his feelings—but what worried her was the possibility that he fundamentally misunderstood what Cat was like. Gordon was clearly a good man—Isabel had formed that impression when she first met him, and further acquaintance with him had confirmed it. Cat, however, was far from straightforward. Isabel was fond of her, and was prepared to make allowances, but there were limits, and she had always been aware of her niece's tendency to chop and change her affections. Cat, Isabel had reluctantly concluded, was inconstant, a fact of which Gordon was quite unaware. And so, not for the first time by any means, Isabel found herself faced with the unsettling question of whether she should become involved in another's private affairs. She knew the answer that Jamie would give if she asked his advice: He had raised with her time and time again the question of limiting the extent to which she took it upon herself to interfere—and that was the precise word he used: He did not say *help* or *assist*, he said *interfere*.

She walked slowly up the path leading to her front door, still thinking of Gordon and his boyish confession. She thought she would have to speak to him—she really had no alternative. She would have to tell him about Cat . . . But then she stopped: What exactly should she say to him? That far from being a novice, Cat was an emotional veteran? The list of her boyfriends was a long one, even to the point of invoking the lyrics of a Jacobite song, "The Highland Muster Roll," with its intoning of the names of those appearing for the uprising of 1745: MacIntosh, MacRabie, Macdonald, Mackenzie, Macpherson, the wild Maccraws . . . Cat had been catholic in her taste for men: Isabel now remembered Bruno, who had been a tightrope walker; and Eamonn, an apprentice stonemason; and Mick, who had not lasted very long, and who had preceded Toby, with his crushed strawberry corduroy trousers and his perfect *annoyingness*—he being what Germans would call a *Nervensäge*, a "nerve saw." And then, of course, most recently there had been Leo, with his mane of light brown hair and his calculating manner—not unlike that of a hunting lion. Had she missed out anybody? She realised that she had, because there had even been another Gordon—Gordon Leafers, who had been a mathematics teacher, and who had eventually married a botanical artist. That Gordon, Isabel heard, was now the father of twin girls and, according to somebody who had seen him recently, blissfully happy. And had there not been a muscular Canadian who was reputed to hold an unverified world record for free diving and who, although apparently able to speak, never uttered a single word in Isabel's hearing? "He must be saving his breath for his descents," Isabel remarked to Jamie, who simply shook his head and observed that he had never seen the point in free diving. "There are far less stressful ways of risking one's life," he pronounced.

She thought again of the mathematics teacher, of his blameless life, and his happiness. Cat would have been wrong for him, she told herself—Cat would be wrong for just about anybody—until she learned about emotional loyalty and acceptance. That was her problem, Isabel felt: acceptance. We have to accept our situation in life, which means that we accept people for what they are and do not spend our time looking for perfection in them. Cat was looking for the perfect man, and needed to learn that he did not exist. She obviously became bored with men and thought the next one would be better. But he would be the same—and that was the lesson that we should all learn about our appetites for anything.

She thought it likely that this new Gordon was unaware of his earlier namesake and all the others. Of course, it might make no difference to how he felt about Cat, and there was a sense in which that was just how it should be. It was long past the time when women were expected not to be experienced—that had always been an outrageous, lopsided expectation by men who felt themselves entitled to freedom they denied women. That was all over now, at least in the society in which she and Cat lived, even if there were vast swathes of the world where it remained an expectation. If men could have the personal freedom, then so too could women. Both should be judged—if judgement were to come into it—by the same standards.

Isabel felt uncomfortable. Cat was her close relative, and she loved her—in a complicated sort of way; she wanted her to be settled and happy. She also wanted happiness for Gordon, although, as she took her keys out of her pocket and prepared to open her front door, she mentally conceded that his happiness should be of less concern to her than Cat's. And that worried her. Immanuel Kant would have made no distinction between them, she thought—and she was not sure that she should either.

She put the key in the door just as it was opened from within.

"I saw you coming up the path," Grace said, reaching out to relieve Isabel of one of her shopping bags. "Things get heavier the longer you carry them, don't they?"

Isabel nodded her agreement. "That's true." She paused. It was true in a broader, metaphorical sense too, she thought. She smiled at Grace. "Like the secrets of the past. I suppose they increase in weight the longer you carry them."

Grace shook her head in disapproval. "Best to have none," she said.

Isabel went inside and Grace closed the front door behind her.

"I'm not sure there are many people who have *no* secrets," Isabel remarked as she deposited her remaining shopping bag on the hall table. "We all have some, surely."

Grace looked unconvinced. "I don't think I do," she said firmly.

"Then you're very fortunate," said Isabel. And she asked herself: Would a life without any secrets at all—even small and insignificant ones—not prove to be rather dull? Secrets added spice to life—within reason, of course. That thought, though, led to another, which was to ask herself what her own secrets were. She frowned. She could think of nothing in particular, unless . . . No, that was not a secret. She had talked to Jamie about that—he knew. And as for . . . She stopped herself. John Liamor—her first husband. She had nurtured an affection for him well after they had parted, and the secret was that she had telephoned him on several occasions after they had separated, simply to hear his voice, and had felt ashamed of herself afterwards. That was a secret, and even now she would not want to reveal it to Jamie.

Grace had been cleaning the kitchen floor, and Isabel followed her as she went to switch off the steam cleaner.

"There was strawberry jam on the floor," Grace said, adding, "It was raspberry yesterday."

Isabel sighed. "It's the boys," she said. "If you keep small boys in the house, you get strawberry jam on the kitchen floor as sure as night follows day."

Grace laughed. "Little imps."

"But nice little imps."

"Of course." Grace paused. "Except when they bite."

"Nearly all small children do," said Isabel. "It's early orality. They grow out of it. Freud . . ."

Grace had no time for Freud, but she loved the boys. "Of course. You know, I sometimes wonder which one has the most mischief in him. And you know what I've concluded?"

Isabel waited.

Grace spoke with the air of one announcing the results of a contest. "I've decided that there's no difference between them. They both have the same amount of mischief brewing inside them."

"I think you're probably right," said Isabel. "They share a lot of genes—including the ones that produce mischief."

As she said this, she thought of a paper she had just approved for publication in the *Review*. It had been submitted by a Dutch medical ethicist who had recently published a book on genetics and responsibility. If personality disorders had a genetic basis, he suggested, then psychopaths could not be held responsible for their actions. Nobody *asked* for their genetic inheritance—it was handed out on conception—and if your genes made you do things, that was not your fault. But, of course, that led to genetic determinism, and determinism was incompatible with life in society: People *had* to answer for their actions, or, quite simply, human society would not work. That meant that even if our lack of freedom were theoretically true, we had no alternative but to behave as if it were false. The nineteen-year-old Isabel might have decried free will, but the mature Isabel, wife, mother and editor, knew better.

Grace addressed a remark to her, but Isabel missed it. She had been thinking of psychopaths and their genes.

"I'm sorry," Isabel said. "I was miles away."

"It's your job," said Grace. "People expect you to be miles away, don't they?"

"I suppose they do." Isabel paused. "Sometimes I feel life would be much simpler if I didn't have to think very much. But then I ask myself whether simplifying your life doesn't involve as much thought as leading a complicated life. It's quite an effort to clear your mind, I believe."

"Buddhists," said Grace.

"What about them?"

Grace began to unpack the shopping bags. "Buddhists try to clear their minds of distractions. We had a talk about it last week. There was a speaker at the centre I go to. A big crowd came—the speaker had been on television, and if you're on television lots of people want to hear you."

The items removed from the bag were now on the kitchen table: the potatoes, the garlic, an iceberg lettuce, the washing-up liquid in its bulky green bottle, the lamb, the goat's cheese that Gordon had recommended, the salmon she had bought at the Holy Corner fish shop, and one or two other purchases she had added to the list Jamie had given her.

As Isabel put away the shopping bags, she became aware of Grace's eyes upon her. She turned and smiled encouragingly. "Is there anything . . ."

She did not have time to complete the question.

"Yes," said Grace. "There is."

Isabel sensed what it was. "Our guest?" she asked.

Grace nodded silently.

Isabel sat down at the kitchen table. Grace remained standing in spite of Isabel's invitation.

"She's gone off to work," Grace began.

"Yes," said Isabel. "She's a nurse—at the Western General. She works in the infectious diseases ward down there—or one of them. I think they have more than one."

Suddenly it occurred to her what the issue might be. If you worked with infectious diseases, others might feel endangered in some way—it was an understandable concern. Grace was anxious—that was it. "You don't need to worry, you know," she said reassuringly. "They're not dealing with Ebola or anything like that. Lots of ordinary illnesses are caused by infection. It's nothing special."

Grace shook her head. "No, it's not that."

Isabel waited. She wondered whether Grace and Dawn had had some sort of altercation. Grace had pronounced views, and there might have been a disagreement. "Did you speak to her before she went off to work?" asked Isabel.

"Yes," said Grace. "We chatted."

"And?"

Grace was tight-lipped.

"She seems nice enough," Isabel volunteered. "I don't really know her. Jamie met her through one of his orchestra people. She needed somewhere to stay . . . She wasn't quite homeless, but she was cooped up in a box room in a small flat and we had that room up at the top."

Isabel trailed off. Grace seemed unconvinced by her explanation. She decided to try again.

"She's often on night duty," she said. "It was difficult for her to get sleep where she was. People made a din on the stair—that can be a problem, as I imagine you know. You're drifting off to sleep and somebody starts clattering about."

She glanced at Grace. Her expression—one of unambiguous disapproval—had not softened. And then it occurred to Isabel: Grace had heard of the reason for Dawn's homelessness and had taken exception to it. Of course, that was it. In a liberal society it was easy to forget that there were those who took an unbending view of these things. Perhaps Jamie had explained to her how Dawn had been turned out of her previous flat. Perhaps Grace thought that she deserved everything that she got. That was something that the homeless often had to contend with, she believed. People assumed they had done something to trigger their exclusion—an argument with parents; a row over something comparatively minor that might precipitate an expulsion from the family home; economic incompetence or the loss of a job that led to rent not being paid—but there were manifold routes out onto the street, and many of them had nothing to do with fault at all.

Now she asked Grace directly whether Jamie had said anything about how Dawn had found herself in her predicament. The answer was that he had not.

"He didn't say much about her," Grace said. "He introduced us. And I thought that it was a kind thing to do—to offer her a roof over her head."

So it was not that. And Isabel had decided that now was not the time to tell Grace about the reason for Dawn's misfortune.

"Well," said Isabel. "She's here now and I hope it helps."

"I'm not saying it won't," Grace said quickly. "It's just that I went into her room—after she had gone off to the hospital. I went in to give it a quick vacuum. I took the portable Dyson. The blue one."

Isabel looked nervous. Drugs? Cannabis had a distinctive smell that everybody would recognise. Nothing had drifted down from above, as far as Isabel could tell. So perhaps it was a man: Perhaps Dawn, unbeknown to them, had smuggled a man into her room. That would raise legitimate issues: It was not the fact that he, if he existed, was a man, but the fact of his being another person. There was one bed up there—not two. Guests should not seek to extend the invitation they received—that much was obvious.

"I'm not one to snoop," Grace announced. "You know that, don't you?"

"Of course, you aren't," Isabel said hurriedly. And Grace was not; she was tactful and discreet, which was not always the case with those who did the job that Grace did. Her friend Janet had a cleaner who was anything but, and had once been found bent double, listening at a door. She had fallen over when the door was opened. Grace was not like that.

"Well, I went into the room," Grace continued. "It was tidy enough. Everything neatly put away."

"Nurses are trained to do that," said Isabel.

"But I saw something that surprised me."

Isabel sighed. She had not anticipated that this sort of thing would arise—whatever this sort of thing turned out to be. "What did you see?" she asked.

Grace hesitated. Then she said faintly, "I don't want to say anything."

Isabel stared at her with astonishment. "But you can't leave it at that. You can't say that you saw something, and then not tell me what it was."

Grace became adamant. "No, I don't want to discuss it."

"But you can't leave me up in the air like this," Isabel protested. "What am I to think? Do we need to do anything? You have to tell me, Grace."

Suddenly she wanted to burst out laughing. This was pure *Cold Comfort Farm*. Aunt Ada sees "something nasty" in the woodshed and is never the same again. It is left unexplained what it was that she saw.

"I'm not easily shocked," Isabel said. "*Nihil humanum mihi alienum est.*"

She immediately regretted what she had said. One should not quote Latin to others without explanation—or even *with* explanation: It sounded too much like flaunting. "I'm sorry," she went on. "It's something my father used to say. You remember how he used to like Latin expressions? His favourite was *mirabile dictu*— marvellous to relate. *Nihil humanum* might be roughly translated as 'nothing surprises me'—more or less."

Grace was defensive. "I shouldn't have raised it. *Mea culpa.*"

"Just tell me. Go on, I'm not going to create a fuss. We may have to do something, but it's best to know."

Grace now appeared to retreat. "It wasn't anything serious. I'd tell you if it was. I'd tell you if it was a firearm, or something like that."

"Well, I'm relieved it isn't that. Not that one expects infectious diseases nurses to be armed."

"It's just that I wasn't prepared."

Isabel sighed. "Prepared for what?"

"I think we should leave it," said Grace. "It was nothing, really."

Isabel felt increasingly irritated. "You really should tell me, you know. You owe it to me to tell me."

You owe it to me to tell me. The phrase hung in the air. It was completely pertinent to her own position vis-à-vis Gordon, and now she was struck by that. Isabel owed it to Gordon to tell him.

Grace became business-like. "I'm sure I'll get on fine with Dawn," she said. "I really shouldn't have worried you. It was nothing at all. She'll be fine." She paused. "It's her aura, though."

Isabel felt a surge of relief. This was it: Grace had taken exception to Dawn's aura. She often talked about people's auras. She had always had her reservations about Cat's aura, which she described as excessively red. Was this what it was all about?

"Her aura's weak, you see."

Isabel was puzzled. "So that's what you saw. Do people leave traces of their aura when they leave the room? Is that the problem?"

"No, it wasn't that. I just said that her aura is a bit weak. That can sometimes happen if you're run down."

Isabel's relief at discovering what was troubling Grace was short-lived. She realised she would not be able to find out—just yet—what she had seen in Dawn's room. It was ridiculous, but Grace was stubborn.

Grace had been looking down at the floor. Now she looked up, and for a brief moment met Isabel's eye. There was a moment of hesitation—as if she were trying to make a decision. Then it came out. "There was one of those magazines—that one I particularly object to. You know the one."

Isabel breathed a sigh of relief. This was hardly serious. "The one that . . ."

Grace cut her off. "Yes. That one."

Isabel looked away. This was almost risible, but she knew that if she laughed, or even smiled, Grace would be offended. The magazine in question was one of the best-known magazines aimed at younger women. It was glossy, smart, and explicit. Grace was known to disapprove of it.

"I see," said Isabel. "Well, a lot of people read that sort of thing now, Grace. It's harmless enough." She paused. Grace was looking at her defiantly, and Isabel added quickly, "I know you don't think some of these matters should be paraded in public. I understand that. But these days . . ."

Isabel was not sure where to start. Women's magazines had long since changed their focus. They were no longer full of homely articles. They had an edge now, because that was what their readers wanted. The days of reticence were over, but Grace had not caught up with that.

"And I noticed that there was one of those steamy novels," Grace went on. "You know the sort?"

Isabel did. "But I don't think you should take against somebody just because she may read things like that."

She looked at Grace and realised that further discussion would be unlikely to resolve the issue. The path ahead, though, was rocky. If Grace took against somebody, it was difficult to shift her; Dawn's presence in the house would be a source of tension, however much Isabel tried to pour oil on the waters dividing them.

Isabel became brisk. "Let's not worry about what people read," she said. "That's really up to them, I think."

"There are children in this house," Grace muttered. "What if children read that sort of thing?"

Isabel could not help but smile. "The boys aren't great readers yet."

Grace sniffed. "I'd better get on with my work," she said. "The boys' room is a mess."

"Thanks," said Isabel. She had not intended to be dismissive of Grace, whose position, if somewhat prudish, nonetheless revealed moral concern about how people treated one another. In a society in which the notion of the private disappeared, a blunting of the moral sense could occur without being noticed. Slowly, perhaps imperceptibly, might tolerance become a lack of concern for human dignity. And that was the issue here, Isabel realised: human dignity. Grace had a point.

She looked at the other woman and then, with real fondness, said, "I'd be lost without you, Grace. You do know that, don't you? I really appreciate everything that you do."

"It's my job," said Grace.

"But not everybody does their job as well as you do yours."

Grace was silent. Then she said, "That's very good of you to say that."

"I mean it," said Isabel.

CHAPTER FIVE

JAMIE HAD BEEN GIVEN tickets to a concert that night at the Queen's Hall.

"A recital," he said. "I've been given comps. I think we should go."

Isabel had been unsure. Her reading pile had grown, and she had thought of suggesting that Jamie delay his potato dauphinoise and salmon mousse until the following day. She could make them scrambled eggs on toast for an early supper, or they might even eat fish fingers and peas with the boys.

Jamie, though, was keen to go to the concert. "It's a recital," he said. "Jamie MacDougall. He's a tenor. You've heard him before. You'll enjoy it."

"Babysitting?"

He had already spoken to Grace, and she was free.

"Was she all right?" Isabel asked.

Jamie frowned. "Of course. Why do you ask?"

Isabel hesitated. She had been the one to suggest Dawn be offered the room, but that had been as a result of Jamie's first mention of her plight. If there was going to be a problem with Grace's objections to their guest, then Isabel would not want Jamie to be embarrassed by it. So she decided not to mention it—at least not for the moment. There was a good chance that the issue would go away, and that Grace would discover that she could get on perfectly well with Dawn. That sort of thing had happened before, when Grace had taken umbrage and then suddenly appeared to forget, or forgive perhaps, the initial cause of offence.

Isabel shrugged. "You know how she is."

Jamie gave her an enquiring look. He could tell when Isabel was keeping something from him. "Come on," he cajoled, "there's something, isn't there?"

She hesitated, but then replied, "She's taken a scunner against Dawn."

Isabel used the Scots word, *scunner*, which, like many Scots words, was particularly expressive—although in this case it was a bit extreme. A scunner was usually a loathing: Grace had expressed disapproval, but not that strongly.

Jamie looked dismayed. "But why would she do that? Did Dawn say something?"

Isabel explained that it was nothing that Dawn had said. "She went to clean her room," she explained. "She found a copy of a mag open at some article or other that she took exception to. You know the sort of thing they publish when they've got nothing else to fill their columns with. Salacious stuff that's usually rather dull and predictable. It's not easy to say anything new about sex. It's been around for rather a long time."

Jamie laughed. "And yet we all read that stuff."

"I know," said Isabel. "Grace, though, has a tendency to be strait-laced. She doesn't approve. And she also objected to a book that Dawn brought with her. One of those steamy novels that can hardly be taken seriously."

Jamie rolled his eyes. "These days, nobody cares about what other people read. Nobody." He looked to Isabel for support. "Don't you think this is a storm in a teacup?"

Isabel agreed. "Yes, and like all those teacup storms it'll probably blow over in a day or two. They might even become friends—who knows?"

"I hope so," said Jamie. "I feel bad about this. I didn't think about how Grace might react to having somebody else in the house. Perhaps I should have discussed it with her before we invited Dawn. What do you think?"

Isabel was robust. "We don't have to consult Grace over everything we do."

"Not everything," said Jamie. "But this is different."

"Dawn won't be with us indefinitely," Isabel pointed out. "The idea was to tide her over."

Jamie raised an eyebrow. "I hope she understands that." He added quickly, "Not that I'm in any hurry to get her to go."

"No, of course not."

He gave her an anxious glance. "It can be awkward if guests have nowhere else to go. How do you get rid of them? Drop hints?"

Isabel thought that there were tactful ways of moving guests on. "You can say that you need the room," she suggested. "That's clear enough."

Jamie considered this. "Except that we don't. And she may have noticed that there are four spare rooms in this house." He smiled. "I suppose we could say we need them all."

"I would hope that she'd take the hint," said Isabel. "You said that she was very tactful about not infringing our space."

"She was," Jamie confirmed. "She turned down an invitation to join us for a meal. I think she'd be quick to pick up any suggestion that we wanted her to leave."

"Then let's stop worrying about it. And Grace could come round—as I said."

"She could."

They left it at that, but Isabel could tell that Jamie was still concerned. For her own part, she did not regret inviting Dawn to stay—if you had more room than you could use, offering it to others was clearly the right thing to do. There might be no moral obligation to do so—not in any strong sense—but if you could do something to meet the needs of others, then ideally you should do it. Of course, if you had a great deal of space—say three or four houses—then the duty to help became much stronger. Those who had could not simply shrug their shoulders and walk away from those who had not—they were obliged to help, because we were all mutually dependent.

Nothing more was said about Dawn, who had not returned from work by the time that Grace arrived that evening.

"Dawn has her own key," Isabel said. "I don't know when she'll be back."

Grace nodded—grimly, Isabel thought. There was an atmosphere—she was sure of it—but she simply breezed her way through it, as did Jamie. Once outside the house and on their way, by foot, to the Queen's Hall, Isabel said, "She still a bit sniffy. Did you notice it?"

Jamie shrugged. "We'll see."

They walked off towards Bruntsfield and the Meadows. The evening sun was on the rooftops, painting them with a gentle, warm gold. Jamie took her hand and squeezed it conspiratorially. I shall never be happier than I am now, thought Isabel.

He looked at her and grinned. "Are you glad we're going out?" he asked.

She was. "We should do it more often."

"Even go out to dinner? On a date?"

Isabel smiled. "If you ask me."

"Or you ask me," he said.

"Either or."

A man walked past on the other side of the road. He had a

black Scotch terrier on a leash, and he raised his hand in a salute that Jamie returned.

"That dog is lucky to be alive," Jamie remarked. "He ate a poisonous mushroom."

"Like the old King of the Elephants in the Babar books?"

They both knew Babar off by heart, through reading the books to the boys, although they both carefully avoided the account of Babar's mother being shot by a hunter. "We can tell the boys about that when they turn eighteen," said Isabel.

Jamie laughed. "I suppose there are people who put the truth off until then. *We spent your education fund on that car—remember it?* That sort of thing."

Isabel looked thoughtful. "You may joke about it, but it happens, you know."

"People spend their kids' money?"

Isabel shrugged. "Possibly. But I was thinking of someone I knew whose grandparents were in a Japanese prison camp during the war. They didn't tell her about it until she was eighteen, and then it all came out. She had no idea about what had happened. Her grandmother sat her down and said that there was something she should know—and told the whole harrowing story."

Jamie was silent.

"The grandmother was a young woman then, of course," Isabel continued. "She started off quite fit. Older people did not do so well. They died all the time. She just made it, although she said that had the war lasted a week or two longer, she would have died of starvation. She said that when they heard about Nagasaki they danced in the camp. Isn't that a terrible thought? That people should dance when something like that happens. And yet for them that dreadful event spelled liberation from all that cruelty."

Jamie asked why they had not spoken about it before. "Why

did they feel their granddaughter shouldn't know about it? It wasn't their fault that they were prisoners."

"No, of course it wasn't. But victims feel shame for things that happen to them. Look at Eddie. He felt that, you know."

Jamie understood. "He's much better now."

"Yes," said Isabel. "We all feel much better, I think."

He gave her a quizzical look. "What do you mean by that?"

She looked about her. "Enlightenment? People are just so much more honest than they used to be. There's less darkness. We're less frightened of the things that have been used to frighten us for an awfully long time. Auden puts it rather well."

Jamie smiled. "You would say that, wouldn't you?"

Isabel saw no reason to apologise. "Well, if he does, then why shouldn't I? The thing about great thoughts is that they are almost always thought by other people." She paused. They had to cross the road that ran through the Meadows, and one should not quote poets while dealing with traffic.

On the other side, Jamie said, "Auden?"

"He wrote a tribute to Freud. He talked about the liberating effect of psychoanalytical theory. He said that after Freud it was harder for tyrants to frighten people."

Jamie liked that. "That's great. I hate bullies—especially if they're conductors."

"Who doesn't?" said Isabel. Then she continued, "Auden said in that poem that 'the proud can still be proud, but find it a little harder.' I love that line so much."

"Why?"

Isabel thought for a moment. "Because it's true. And it expresses a profound truth so succinctly—which is what poetry is all about. Proud people find it much more difficult now because in the light of Freud we can see their pride for what it is—nothing but the strivings of an insecure ego." *Professor Lettuce?* she asked herself. "That's something that Freud did—he helped us to understand what the ego was."

"And Buddhism too," said Jamie.

"Yes. Freudianism and Buddhism. They both help. They are both about freedom, in a way."

They were nearing the Queen's Hall. Isabel thought of the concert ahead. "What will he sing?" she asked.

"It's a programme of Scottish songs," said Jamie.

"Burns? 'Ae fond kiss'?"

He leaned over and kissed her lightly on the cheek. For the second time that evening, Isabel thought, I shall never be happier than I am now.

ISABEL WAS NOT SURPRISED that Jamie seemed to know everybody, or just about everybody, at the concert. As they went into the Queen's Hall, a converted church that still retained the features of Scottish ecclesiastical buildings of its time—box-like pews under a projecting upper gallery, and an almost Scandinavian simplicity—various members of the audience already there looked in their direction and waved. Jamie acknowledged the smiles and the greetings while Isabel looked for seats. She was used to being in Jamie's shadow at these musical events: This was his world, rather than hers, and although she had met a number of his musical friends, there were many she did not know.

They were early, and decided to have a drink before the concert. They left the hall for the bar, where Jamie was immediately recognised by a percussionist friend who was alone at one of the tables. They moved through the crowd to greet him, and Jamie offered him a drink.

Isabel said that she would go up to the bar. "You stay here and chat," she said. "I'll bring the drinks over."

It was busy, and Isabel found herself standing behind two young women. They had spotted Jamie, and were talking about him. In their conversation she heard her own existence being doubted. This was a particularly striking moment, she told herself—it was not every day that one might hear somebody denying the only fact of which we may each be completely certain—that we exist.

"Apparently he's married," said one of them. "Or so I've heard. Somebody said that she's actually a philosopher."

Isabel realised this could only be her. Instinctively, in her embarrassment, she had looked over her shoulder to where Jamie was sitting. He was deep in conversation with the percussionist, but he smiled encouragingly at her.

"I don't think he is," said the other young woman. "I think that's somebody else."

"No, it's Jamie. It's him."

"I don't think she exists. People invent partners if they don't want to have to fend people off. People like him must be chased after all the time—twenty-four-seven."

Isabel almost intervened. "I do exist," she was tempted to say, but realised that this would cause mortification, and would be unkind. She could leave the queue, but it was now almost her chance to be served and Jamie and his friend were waiting expectantly.

"He's so dishy."

"Yes, he is. But the dishy ones are usually snapped up. Do you know a single dishy man who's available, so to speak?"

This brought a sigh, and the sigh was followed by a change of subject. Isabel smiled. Being married to Jamie would not be easy if one resented the fact that he turned heads wherever he went. She had overheard such conversations before, but never one in which her very existence was doubted. At least it had not been *disproved*. That would have been a more unsettling experience.

To be a non-existent person was, of course, an impossibility, in the strict sense that x cannot be x and not-x at the same time— something that had been explained to her in the first weeks as a student of philosophy, and yet, in a broader sense, when x was a moral quality . . . she thought of the many examples of people who had become "non-people" at the whim of various oppressors. In the era of slavery, there had been all those people snatched and transported from their homes, treated as cargo and not as human beings. Africans had borne the brunt of that egregious crime, but there had been numerous Europeans, too, taken by Barbary Corsairs and sold into slavery in North Africa. Then there had been Koreans taken by the Japanese and those captured by Germans and Russians in the Second World War and forced to perform slave labour. The burden of guilt, acknowledged or unacknowledged, flowing from this was so widespread as to be almost universal. Human history, it seemed, was a great well of sorrow and suffering.

She gave her order and took the drinks back to the table where Jamie and his percussionist friend were sitting.

"Former people," she muttered to herself.

But she had been audible to Jamie. "Former what?" he asked.

"Sorry. I was thinking about something else altogether."

Jamie turned to his friend and smiled. "Isabel has a tendency to think about things," he said.

The friend laughed. "Well, you're a philosopher, aren't you."

"You remember Andy?" said Jamie.

Isabel nodded. "We met, didn't we? After that concert in Glasgow. A party in the West End somewhere—somebody's flat."

"My girlfriend's," said Andy. "I remember it."

"Former what?" repeated Jamie.

"Former people," said Isabel. "I was thinking about the people that the Bolsheviks described as 'former people.' They were anybody whom they regarded as enemies of their revolution. It's such a chilling term. They had no rights to anything, really—no right to work, no property, no freedom. The only right they had was the right to be shot."

"They actually used the term *former people?*" asked Andy.

"Yes," said Isabel. "It's chilling, isn't it? And that sort of attitude has had many followers: Nazis, Pol Pot, Jean Kambanda in Rwanda—it's quite a big club. Deny somebody else's humanity and human worth and you're on a very well-worn and familiar road."

"Not a very cheerful subject," said Jamie.

"No," agreed Andy.

"I'm sorry," said Isabel. "My fault. It's just that I find that once I start thinking along a certain line, I go after it . . ."

"Like a terrier," interjected Jamie. "But enough of that. Andy was telling me that his partner's having a baby."

Isabel gave her congratulations.

"She's the one who deserves the congratulations," said Andy breezily. "My part in it was quite brief . . ." He blushed.

"But a necessary one," said Jamie.

"Congratulations all the same," said Isabel. "It's very good news. We need a few more babies—for demographic reasons, that is. There are too many . . ."

"Former babies?" Jamie suggested.

Andy laughed. "We like a joke in the percussion section. Percussion and brass players are pretty uncomplicated types. Lots of noise—no refinement."

They discussed the programme they were to hear that evening. "I know Jamie," said Andy, adding, "Not you, Jamie—Jamie MacDougall—the tenor who's on tonight. He has a wonderful voice."

"All tenors have wonderful voices," said Isabel. "It's the nicest sound of all. I find sopranos a bit too shrill, and basses a bit too gravelly."

"Like the porridge in the story of the Three Bears," suggested Andy. "I know what you mean. Goldilocks was looking for something in the middle, wasn't she?"

Isabel said that she assumed that she was. "Although she shouldn't have been there, should she? Goldilocks was definitely in the wrong—going into the bears' house like that."

Jamie looked thoughtful. "Now, I read about that," he said. "Somewhere . . ." It took him a few moments to remember, but then, "Yes, it was a Freudian explanation of that story. Somebody said that Goldilocks was self-centred and difficult because she must have had an excessively liberal toilet-training. She felt that she could treat other people's property as her own because she had always had her own way."

Andy laughed. "And the bears?"

"Daddy Bear was the stern father-figure," said Jamie. "No surprise there. Baby Bear was obedient and well-behaved—as a result of a stricter toilet-training. And Mummy Bear—well, she was mother, in Freudian terms. Mother is always there, isn't she? She represents comfort and refuge. But her bed can be a bit too soft—as it was in the story."

Andy looked at his watch. "They're going to ring the bell any moment. We should get to our seats."

They finished their drinks quickly and made their way into the hall. Several people waved to Jamie. Isabel looked for people she might know, but did not find anybody. She noticed that a woman seated in the front row looked up sharply when they came in. This woman held her gaze for a moment or two, and then looked away briefly before returning with an intense stare. Isabel was sure that she had been recognised, but could not work out who the other woman was. There was a certain anxiety in her manner, and Isabel wondered whether this was somebody who might have written to her and not received a reply. She was careful about that sort of thing, but inevitably, with the volume of mail that she received for the *Review*, there were private letters that fell through the cracks. Perhaps she is angry with me, thought Isabel. Perhaps she is angry with me because she thinks I have ignored her letter and now I am setting out to ignore her. I try not to ignore *anybody*, she thought: It was one thing that she really tried *not* to do, in spite of the fact that Jamie says that we have to do a certain amount of ignoring if we are to survive. "You can't respond to absolutely everybody," he had said. "I don't."

He was probably right, she thought. But now, as she took her seat, she glanced in the direction of the woman who had been looking at her. She still was.

THE CONCERT BEGAN. Isabel stopped thinking about the woman who had been staring at her, and immersed herself in the programme. The tenor was accompanied by a Romanian pianist who had set up a piano school in Glasgow and who had an easy, fluent style, well-suited to the singer's approach. Isabel had hoped for Robert Burns songs, and was pleased to see that there were six of these on the programme. "Ca' the Yowes," "Ae Fond Kiss" and "A Red, Red Rose" were rarely missed from any Burns recital, and they were there that evening, but there were others that were less well known too.

She closed her eyes when "Ae Fond Kiss" was sung because she knew that if she listened to it with them open she would have to wipe away the tears. How could one not cry, she thought, when one heard the words:

Had we never lov'd sae kindly,
Had we never lov'd sae blindly,
Never met—or never parted—
We had ne'er been broken-hearted.

It was impossible not to be moved by Burns, because he said, so simply, what we all felt about things like love and friendship and, yes, sympathy. That was it. There was a sympathy there that struck a chord because it was so honest, so direct. There were those who thought Burns could stray into the sentimental, but sentiment was the whole point, Isabel thought. We felt sentiment because that was how we were *designed*. Sentiment was natural— we needed it to live peaceably with others. We *needed* to well up inside when we thought about love and affection—it showed that our sympathetic responses were doing what they should be doing. It was precisely those responses that made us treat one another with consideration. And if we did not have that basic concern for each other, then there could be no civilisation—no concerts at the Queen's Hall, no hospitals, no schools, no certainty about anything.

The interval was a short one, and she and Jamie did not leave their seats. Andy, who had been sitting a few rows away, came over to continue his conversation with Jamie, but the two of them had become immersed in some issue of orchestral politics, and Isabel quickly lost interest. She had picked up a leaflet setting out the Queen's Hall's future programme, and she busied herself with that. There was to be a performance of *Carmina Burana*, which she might come to by herself, she thought, as Jamie would be playing at a concert in Glasgow on that night. Perhaps she would invite Grace to come with her, as she knew that Grace had enjoyed a performance of the piece a few months ago, transmitted live from a concert hall in Berlin. "Poor swan," she had said, of the heart-rending plaint from the bird on the spit. "It sounds so sad, the song it sings. I could never eat a swan after hearing that."

"You couldn't anyway," Isabel had observed. "Wild, unmarked swans have special protection in this country. They're not on the menu."

"I know that," said Grace defensively. "They belong to the King, don't they? Although where he finds the time to bother about things like that, I have no idea. Do you think he eats them himself?"

"I doubt it," said Isabel. "He doesn't have that look about him." She was not sure how one might look if one was in the habit of eating swans—did Professor Lettuce have that look about him? He was a bit overweight and puffy about the face, and she could just see him sitting down at the table with a great roast bird in front of him. And Christopher Dove would wield the carving knife, gleefully, she thought, because he had that calculating, determined look about him, and he always seemed willing to do Lettuce's bidding. "You carve, Dove," Lettuce would order.

She came back to Grace. "You can eat swan in Orkney or Shetland, though, I'm told—not that anybody does, of course. Something to do with special laws they have up there. They're as Norwegian as they are Scottish, I think. And I believe that some of them would like to attach themselves to Norway once again."

Grace shook her head in disavowal. "I don't feel at all Norwegian, although my mother used to say that we had Viking blood in us—way back. My grandfather had red hair, you know, and he was tall—just like the Vikings were."

"Well," said Isabel, "there you are. Perhaps we all have a bit of inner Viking."

Grace shuddered. "I have no desire to eat a swan."

"Nor I," agreed Isabel. "Lovely creatures." She paused. "This is a very odd country. There are some very strange rules when you look closely."

Now she thought of the babysitting issue. If she invited Grace to *Carmina Burana*, then she would have to find another babysitter, and although there were several teenage girls in the area who were willing to earn a bit of pin-money, she was out of touch with them and thought they might have gone off to university by now. Of course, there was Dawn. She was not sure, though, whether she should ask her: It might be hard for her to refuse because she felt beholden for the room. And Isabel would not want her to feel that the offer of the room had come with strings attached. There were plenty of people, she had read in *The Scotsman* recently, who were taking advantage of students desperate for accommodation, requiring them to work as unpaid cleaners in exchange for a roof over their head, or worse. And Dawn, she felt, was not the babysitting type. She was not sure why she thought this, because virtually anybody could babysit, especially for children who were sound sleepers, as theirs were—you just had to sit there and watch television or read and eat the cake that thoughtful parents left out for you. And there were parents who were happy enough for you to bring your boyfriend or girlfriend with you, which, if you were a teenager, was an attractive proposition.

When the interval came to an end, the singer and accompanist reappeared. There was no more Burns, but a selection of Hebridean songs. Isabel had always liked "The Eriskay Love Lilt," and Jamie knew this. His arms were folded, but he touched her elbow with a finger as the love song reached its yearning climax, and for a moment or two she rested her head gently against his shoulder. Then the song died away, and the appreciative audience burst into applause.

"That one never fails to hit the spot," whispered Jamie.

Isabel dwelled on the line they had just heard, *Sad am I without you*, and thought of the island of Eriskay, which she had visited years ago, on her twentieth birthday. She had wondered then, as the boat left the rocky shore to return to South Uist, whether she would ever fall in love—completely in love, that is, and not just in love in a shallow or passing way. Now she knew the answer to that. Love could creep up on you slowly, until suddenly you were aware of it and realised that it had you in its nets. "In Nets of Golden Wires." Jamie often mentioned that song, because he had a particular affection for it. She knew why he should love it. It was because it was so true—*In nets of golden wires/With pearl and ruby spangled/My heart entangled* . . . My heart *is* entangled, she thought—and I would not want it otherwise.

JAMIE MacDOUGALL PERFORMED an encore, and then the concert was over. On the way out, Isabel stopped briefly to have a word with a friend whom she had not seen for a few months, and was briefly detached from Jamie, who had wandered ahead towards the front door. Her conversation over, she went to catch up with him, and it was at this point that she became aware of the presence at her side of the woman who had been staring at her earlier on.

"You're Isabel Dalhousie, aren't you?"

Isabel turned to face the woman who was addressing her. She was about Isabel's age, and attractive. There was a hint of olive in her colouring—a Mediterranean look, thought Isabel. "I am, yes. And . . . I'm sorry, have we met? I'm sure we have."

The woman shook her head. "No, we haven't actually met. I live quite close to you, though. I'm in Tipperlinn Road." She gave Isabel an embarrassed glance. "I feel as if I know you."

Isabel smiled. "I think I may have seen you. I sometimes go that way to get to the supermarket."

"I've seen you too," said the woman. "And I think you know my neighbour Jean Morrison."

"Of course." Isabel and Jean Morrison had been at school together for a few years. Jean's parents had gone to live in Brussels when their daughter was fifteen, and so she and Isabel had lost touch for a while. Now they met only occasionally—like Isabel, Jean had a young family that kept her busy, as well as a part-time job as an actuary. They got on well together, though, and found that they could easily pick up where they left off, as old friends so often can.

"She's in my book group," the woman went on. "Or was—she left a few months ago. We have a book group you see, in Tipperlinn Road—and for the area round about. There are people from other streets too."

Isabel said that she thought that Jean had mentioned this to her. It made her keep up with her reading, she said.

"That's the great thing about book groups," said the woman. "My name is Roz, by the way. Roz Mack. Rosalind, actually, but nobody calls me that."

Isabel glanced towards the throng of people at the door. She could not see Jamie.

"I'm sorry," said Roz. "I shouldn't hold you up. You're with your husband—I saw him." Her eyes conveyed a message as she said this. Isabel was not sure what it was. A conspiratorial look? *Yes, he's very good-looking, isn't he?* Was that it?

"He'll be all right," Isabel reassured her. "We're in no hurry. He knows quite a few people here tonight and he'll be chatting to them outside, no doubt. He's a musician, you see, and there are people here he plays with."

She waited. She got the impression that Roz wanted to talk to her about something, but she was not sure what it was.

She did not have to wait long. "I was hoping to have a word with you," Roz said. "But I've been a bit . . . well, I'm not very good about approaching people."

Isabel picked up the note of apology. "That goes for me too," she said.

Roz seemed relieved. "Actually, I wanted to ask you to help us out with our book group. We need to keep numbers up."

Isabel showed her surprise, and Roz became flustered. "I know it's a bit of a cheek on my part," she said quickly. "Asking you out of the blue like this." She gave Isabel a searching look. "Are you in a book group already? You probably are."

Isabel shook her head. "Actually, I'm not. Just about everybody I know happens to be in one. I've never got round to it."

This seemed to give Roz hope. "Do you think . . . I mean, would you consider it?"

Isabel frowned. "I haven't really thought about it." She looked at Roz. This woman was *pleading* with her—she could see it in her eyes. And, in a moment of impulse, Isabel said, "I don't see why not. It's just round the corner, after all."

Roz showed her delight. But then her expression became serious. "It's not just numbers. There are other issues, I'm afraid. In fact, the reason why I was particularly keen to ask you to join is that somebody said . . ." She trailed off.

Isabel suppressed a sigh. She was not sure what was coming, but she already wondered whether she had been too hasty. Of course she had been—and Jamie would tell her that later on, no doubt.

"Somebody said that you helped people sort things out," said Roz. "They said you had a great talent for that."

"I'm not so sure," said Isabel. "People get undeserved reputations, you know."

Roz laughed. "I suspect you deserve yours." She gave Isabel another imploring look. "Could we meet for coffee? Would you like to drop in at my place? I could tell you about it."

Isabel knew that she would not be able to say no, and so she said yes, which was what she almost always said. I'm weak, she said to herself. I need to become much, much firmer.

"You're very kind," said Roz.

I need to become much unkinder, Isabel thought. But that, of course, is much harder than . . . than not being unkind. She looked towards the door. Jamie had come back into the hall and was waving to her to attract her attention and hurry her up.

She made a quick arrangement with Roz. She would call round the following morning at eleven, but would not be able to stay too long, as she had journal proofs to read. Then she went over to join Jamie.

"What was all that about?" he asked.

She did not answer immediately. He looked at her. "Isabel?" he said, a note of reproach in his voice. "Have you just said yes to something?"

"I'm not sure," she replied. "Maybe." And then she added, "Just an invitation to join a book group. That's all."

"Oh, that's all right," said Jamie. "I thought that you might have agreed to sort something out—you know, your normal thing."

"Well, it might be a book group with issues," Isabel said.

Jamie gave her a disapproving look. "I should have guessed that," he said. Then he added, "From what I've heard, *all* book groups have issues."

Isabel thought about this. He was right, she decided. Most of the people she knew who were in book groups complained about something or other; no book group, it seemed, was perfect. It might be a know-all member who paraded superior knowledge; it might be somebody who overdid the entertaining side of things and made others feel their own hospitality was inadequate when it was their turn to host a meeting; it might be somebody who deliberately and consistently chose obscure and unreadable titles; there were many reefs on which book groups could founder, many respects in which comity might falter.

Jamie was silent as they crossed the road near the old veterinary college. Isabel looked at him anxiously.

"I know what you're thinking," she said.

It took a few moments for him to respond. "Yes," he said at last. "That's what I'm thinking."

"You feel this is going to lead to trouble?"

He nodded, then added, "That's exactly what was going through my mind. And yet . . . and yet . . ."

"I don't blame you for taking that view," said Isabel. "You give me good advice, and then I seem to ignore it—every time. I'm sorry about that—it must really try your patience. All I can say is that I don't set out to do the opposite of what you tell me I should do."

Jamie reached out to touch her forearm. He did not want her to think he was controlling—he would never want that. That was not the nature of their relationship at all—he would never be overbearing and she would never accept that sort of thing anyway. "No, you don't try my patience—not really. And I don't want you to be any different from what you are. I've said that before; I think you're you—I'm me. That has to be the basis of any marriage. You can't *be* the other person—no matter how much you love her— and she can't be you. That's not the way it works."

She listened.

"You can't resist the urge to help people," Jamie continued.

"That makes you special. And it's a good quality. Far better than being selfish, which is what I suppose I must seem to you. I'm just plain, ordinary selfish."

She laughed. "You're not. You're just not. You're kind. You're generous. You're nice. Look what you did for Dawn."

He stopped, and Isabel stopped too. "I hope we've done the right thing, there," he said. "I'm beginning to get the feeling we may have made a mistake."

She sought to reassure him. "Of course we haven't. And give her a chance—it's only been a couple of days."

He remained uneasy. "You know something," he said. "I have the distinct feeling that she's . . . she's watching us—spying on us, in a way."

Isabel looked incredulous. "You're letting your imagination run away with you. Spying on us?" This was quite unlike Jamie, who was the least paranoid person she knew. She gave him a searching look.

"I feel it," said Jamie, a note of apology in his voice. "I don't know why, but I feel it. I think she's watching us."

Isabel shook her head. She could not believe this. "In a voyeuristic sense?" she asked.

Jamie was uncomfortable. "I wasn't going to say that, but yes."

They started off again. Isabel tried to make light of what had been said. "You're as bad as Grace," she said. "That business with the magazine."

"I'm not. It's just that I feel a bit uneasy."

"I feel uneasy about a lot of things at the moment," Isabel said.

He seemed surprised. "Do you? I thought your life was relatively straightforward. The *Review*. The children. Philosophy."

"You could add yourself to that list," Isabel said playfully. He would be at the top of her list of priorities—joint first, along with the two children. Immediately below them, she thought, would be the *Review*, which was almost childlike in its dependence on her.

"Me? Yes, well I didn't want to presume."

She laughed. "My life may seem uncomplicated on the surface. Underneath, there's a long list of things I need to worry about. What to do about Cat, for instance."

"Ah," said Jamie. Cat was always there, he had to admit. Cat was definitely an issue.

"And Robert Lettuce."

Jamie made a sympathetic noise. "What's he up to?"

"Fraud, or something not too far off fraud."

Jamie raised an eyebrow. "Ah. And the other one? Lettuce's second-in-command?"

"Christopher Dove?"

"Yes, the elegant one. Christopher Dove. I don't really know him, but on the few occasions I've seen him, I've got the creeps. Badly."

Isabel had to agree. She had never liked Christopher Dove. He had no excuse, she felt, no possible justification. There had been times when she had felt sorry for Professor Lettuce—after all, it could not be easy being him. He was all wrong—that was the only way she could think of it, and if somebody is all wrong then pity, rather than dislike, might be invoked. And yet it was difficult to see beyond Lettuce's monstrous sense of self-importance. She remembered his notepaper . . . Could you judge somebody by his or her notepaper? Was notepaper that eloquent?

"Christopher Dove," she said, "tests our capacity for tolerance. Charity requires of us that we see in people a glimmer of something of which we can approve. With Dove, it's not easy. And yet, I suppose I should try. *Caritas*. It's better in Latin, I think.

Caritas says: Look for some redeeming quality in those you judge unredeemable."

Jamie smiled. "I remember when I was at college there was a professor who taught music history. He was called Stave, would you believe it? Talk about nominative determinism. Professor Alfred Stave. Nobody liked him. He wasn't interested in us—he was one of those professors who regard students as a nuisance. He wanted to be left alone to write his whacking big five-volume history of Western music—something like that. Anyway, one of my class-mates, Harry, said of him, 'At least I like his car.' It was so funny. He couldn't think of anything else that was remotely positive. He had a beautiful old car, you see—a Jaguar. It was deep blue and had gorgeous lines. Harry also said, 'I'd like to take that car on a date.' He had a deadpan way of saying things like that. It's strange how you remember these little things after quite a few years. They stay in the mind."

Isabel laughed. She liked it when Jamie talked about his stu-dent days, as he occasionally did. She had met one or two of his friends from those times, and she could imagine the life they had led together at that stage. She had never met Harry, but this was not the first time Jamie had mentioned him. She was sure she would like him, and now, unbidden, a story was unfolding in her mind. A student called Harry admires his professor's blue Jaguar. He summons up the courage to steal it—no, borrow it unofficially. He drives off in the purloined car. The professor is bereft. He comes across Harry—on his date with the car. And he forgives them—Harry and the car. He says, "I'm happy for you to carry on seeing my car . . ."

Jamie was looking at her. "What were you smiling at?"

Isabel shook her head. "Thinking of something ridiculous. About yearning—and blue Jaguars."

Jamie wanted to get back to the issues she had mentioned. "So," he began, "you have these problems . . ."

She interrupted him. "They're not massive quandaries—I'm not saying that. Just little ones, I suppose. Most of them seem to raise the same questions: what to say, if anything."

"Sometimes the answer to that must be nothing," Jamie offered. "In fact, isn't that the answer most of the time? Speak when you're spoken to. Don't say anything about anything that isn't your business. Least said, soonest mended—and so on."

"I wish it were that simple," said Isabel.

They had reached the point where a path that came over from George Square joined another, diagonal crossing. A young man and a young woman were standing there, under a tree, in the last light of the long summer evening, locked in a passionate embrace, largely oblivious to the world. The headlights of a passing car, illuminated prematurely, as the sky was not yet dark, moved over them like the beam of a searchlight. They broke apart in embarrassment as they saw Jamie and Isabel coming nearer.

"Don't bother about us," said Isabel. "Please continue—within reason."

The young man laughed. "I'm in love with her," he said. "I don't mind if everybody knows."

"I had formed that impression already," said Isabel. Then she added, "Be kind to each other."

The young couple looked at her in surprise. Then the young man said, "Yes, I will."

"He always is," said the young woman.

"Perfect," said Isabel, as they continued on their way.

CHAPTER SIX

AT BREAKFAST the following morning, Jamie asked Isabel about her plans for the day ahead. It was a question that he asked almost every day, although Isabel was not sure that he always listened to the answer. It was possible, she thought, that his asking her about what lay ahead was a form of meaningless greeting, like "How are you?," that few people answered other than with a stock response of "fine" or "good." Isabel had initially been concerned with the ascendancy of the "good" response, which she felt was misleading—to say that one was *good* implied a moral quality which was not what the questioner wanted to know about—but she was realistic and knew that these usages took hold quickly, and deeply, and there was little point in resisting them. The accusative case had similarly been under attack for years, and was on the point of raising the white flag of surrender—"They invited you and I" was about to become grammatically correct, she thought, the first stage of that victory, aural familiarity, having been long since achieved.

She answered Jamie with, "Editing to begin with and then coffee with that woman I was talking to last night."

Jamie popped a piece of bread into the toaster and depressed the lever. "Oh, yes."

He had not taken in her response, thought Isabel. I might just as well have quoted a line of Sanskrit. She was not offended—it was simple familiarity that led us not to take in everything said by those with whom we lived: We could not listen to *everything* said to us.

"And you?" she asked.

"Same old, same old," he replied.

"That's informative."

He laughed. "Well, it's true, isn't it? For most of us, life usually is the same old, same old. I'm teaching in the morning down at the Academy. Five pupils, including that boy whose parents think he's Mozart, and who isn't, I'm afraid. The parents are so proud of his playing, although I'm afraid it's not very good at all. I call them Mr. and Mrs. Salieri."

Isabel looked serious. "Of course they're proud of him. If your parents aren't proud of you, then where are you? They give you unconditional love—that's what it says in the job description. And we need it. Every one of us needs it."

Jamie did not reply. His toast had popped up and he was transferring it to a plate. He took a jar of marmalade out of a cupboard. "I enjoyed that concert last night," he said. "My part-namesake—that Jamie MacDougall—has the sort of voice I can listen to for ages. And he really makes something of those Kennedy-Fraser pieces." He paused, before sitting down at the table opposite Isabel.

"I've always liked 'The Eriskay Love Lilt,'" said Isabel. "I know that some people are sniffy about it, but I'm not. So what if it's a bit sentimental? So is a whole lot of Scottish music. I don't mind Harry Lauder—kilt and gnarly walking stick and all. 'Keep Right on to the End of the Road' is fine as far as I'm concerned."

Isabel asked why anybody would take exception to "The Eriskay Love Lilt."

Jamie gave a simple answer: "Authenticity."

"You mean they never sat about singing love lilts on Eriskay?"

Jamie grinned. "Who knows? But the point that some of the Gaelic music people make is that she embellished what she heard." He paused. "And challenges to authenticity can come in twos. She had a daughter, Patuffa, who also went round collecting songs. They were energetic, those Kennedy-Frasers."

"I suppose people were less punctilious back then. It was the early nineteen-hundreds, wasn't it?"

"Thereabouts," Jamie replied. "And nobody had heard the term *ethnomusicology* then, I imagine. Enthusiasts had no compunction in adding to what they heard. Look at Macpherson and the Ossian poems. Those were wildly popular, but the truth of the matter is that it's almost entirely bogus. So much for the Scottish Homer."

Isabel thought about this. She had tried to read some of the Ossian poems, but hadn't been able to get far with them. It was excessively dreamy stuff, she thought—all very misty and Celtic—and she had never been able to understand why people had been so keen on them. Napoleon was said to have carried Macpherson's book into battle. There had been famous paintings and opera, all based on the highly dubious folklore worked up by Macpherson and covered with swirling Highland mists. By comparison, song-collectors such as Marjorie and Patuffa Kennedy-Fraser were scrupulously discriminating.

Jamie finished his toast and marmalade. "What did you say you were doing?" he asked.

Isabel told him once again.

"She's coming here—that book-club woman?"

Isabel nodded.

Jamie said nothing. He pointed towards the upper floors of the house. "And Dawn?"

He lowered his voice, and Isabel did so too. "She's off to work. I saw her earlier on, on the stairs. She seemed to be in a hurry."

"Did she say anything?" asked Jamie.

"Not really," said Isabel. "I told her that Grace would be cleaning the top floor later today. She said something about her room being a bit untidy, but that she would deal with it when she got back from work. That was more or less it."

Jamie rose from the table. "Academy now," he said. And then added, "I wish I didn't have to work."

Isabel looked up at him. "Are you serious?"

"A bit," he said. "I wish I could sit about and read and play the piano and meet friends for lunch."

Isabel got up too. "You could, you know. I'd support you."

"You'd like me to be a kept man? Is that what you want?"

She put a hand on his shoulder. "Whatever you want—that's what I want. If you want to be kept, that's fine by me."

He smiled at her. "Temptress," he whispered playfully.

"You'd make a wonderful kept man," she said. "You might have to be a bit more louche, perhaps, but you'd do it rather well, I think."

He put his arms about her, and they embraced. He kissed her, and she returned his kisses. He ran a hand through her hair. Then, suddenly, she said, "What's that noise?"

He drew back. "Where?"

"In the hall. A noise. Something metallic. Didn't you hear it?"

He said, "A clinking sound? Yes, I did. I thought it was outside. Or the fridge. It makes odd sounds when the compressor switches on." He paused. "If it has a compressor. The thing that draws the heat out . . . the gas thing—you know what I mean."

"No, it was through there—it came from the hall."

He moved away from her and went to open the door that led from the kitchen into the hall. She followed him.

"Nothing," he said.

She glanced about her, and then pointed to a place on the floor beside the hall table.

"Are those your keys?" she asked.

He shook his head. "No."

She bent down to pick up a keyring to which a couple of keys were attached. The keyring had a plastic tag attached to it, on which the word *Rothesay* was printed. She held these up, and Jamie examined them. "Odd," he said.

"They might belong to Grace. I'll ask her."

"But they've just been dropped on the floor," Jamie pointed out. "That was the noise we heard."

Isabel looked about her. She moved closer to Jamie and whispered. "Is there somebody in the house—somebody we don't know about?"

He looked at the staircase. "Upstairs? Dawn? You said she went out to work."

"I assumed she was going to work," said Isabel. "I saw her on the stairs and made that assumption. I might be wrong. I thought she was going out—she may have been coming in."

Jamie examined the keys. Rothesay was a town on the island of Bute, in the west of Scotland. It was a favourite destination for visitors from Glasgow, taking a trip down the Firth of Clyde. "Grace wouldn't have been in Rothesay," he said. "She's scarcely ever been on that side of the country—and she doesn't like ferries. Grace doesn't do islands."

Isabel lowered her voice even further. "Why don't you go upstairs and see if Dawn's in her room? Maybe I got it wrong." She pointed to the hall table. "Leave the keys there."

Jamie nodded, and went upstairs. Isabel waited. Three or four minutes later he came back down. He shook his head as he approached Isabel. "No sign of anybody," he said. "The door was locked."

"Her bedroom door?"

"Yes. I gave her the key myself when I took her up to the room. I remember thinking that she probably wouldn't use it, but . . . well, I thought it was a courtesy. I gave her the key that was in the door when we went up there. And a front door key, too, so she could come and go as she pleased."

Isabel said that she thought that entirely reasonable. "Did you knock?" she asked.

"Yes. There was no reply."

"That means she must be out."

Jamie looked worried. "I had the impression the room was occupied," he said.

Isabel asked him why.

"I just did," he replied. "You know how sometimes you just know you're not alone. You can't necessarily say why you feel that way—you just do."

Isabel hesitated. She felt a strong sense of unease—and Jamie, she imagined, was feeling much the same thing. And yet, as she reminded herself, there was really nothing to feel uneasy about: All that had happened was that a small bunch of keys had been found on the floor and a visitor's door had been found to be locked. There was a perfectly rational explanation for both of these events. The keys had probably been dropped by Dawn on her way out of the house. She had locked her door—that was a bit odd, but not completely out of order, as Jamie himself had given her the key when she arrived. Now she looked at the bunch of keys lying on the hall table; she had not checked to see whether she recognised them.

"Is there a front door key there?" she asked Jamie.

He examined them. "No. And I don't see the key for her room either. That was one of those old ones. All the doors up at the top have their original Victorian keys."

Isabel gestured for Jamie to follow her back into the kitchen. Once inside, she closed the hall door behind them. She felt a bit foolish: This was their own house, in broad daylight, and they were behaving as if they were harbouring an intruder.

Her voice returned to its normal volume. At least she no longer felt the need to whisper. "When you said that you felt you weren't alone, why exactly did you think that?"

Jamie spread his hands in a gesture that indicated that he was unable to say more than he had already said. "I don't know," he said. "I really can't say. I suppose I felt a sort of prickly sensation at the back of my neck. You know the feeling?"

Isabel nodded. The mere mention of it was enough to make her experience it right there and then, as they stood and discussed it in the kitchen. It was the power of suggestion; it was the reason why yawns were infectious.

Jamie continued with his explanation. "There's probably a physiological reason for it. Adrenalin, or whatever. You feel scared and the body pumps out the adrenalin so that you're primed to do whatever you need to do."

Isabel asked him whether he was frightened. It had never occurred to her that Jamie would be frightened of anything. They had once discussed being afraid of the dark—Isabel occasionally felt uneasy when she went out into the garden at night alone. He had said that he never felt that way. "Are you worried about meeting Brother Fox?" he had asked, smiling at the thought. "He lurks about at night, doesn't he?"

She was not afraid of Brother Fox, she said. She had met him in the garden before when coming home late at night; he had simply looked at her as if he were about to say "Good evening" before padding off silently on his obscure, vulpine business. Foxes had their lives to lead, in their private bowers and alleyways, and we had only brief glimpses of how they ordered their affairs.

"I've never been afraid of Brother Fox," she told him. "And I don't think he's afraid of me."

"I don't think he is either," Jamie agreed. "I think he likes you. He's not so sure about me, though. I suspect he thinks that men are crueller than women. That's been the fox experience so far."

Isabel thought about this. Would foxes really make that distinction? And then she remembered a neighbour's dog. He was one of those small, yappy creatures that it was difficult to take seriously, but he was an adept at nipping male ankles. He never bit women, but he went for men with teeth bared and with hatred in his heart. This was because he was a rescue dog, the neighbour explained; he had been maltreated by a man in his previous home and he had drawn his conclusions: Creatures with deeper voices and that general look about them spelled danger.

"But women go on those hunts too," Isabel said. She was not one for the contemporary demonisation of men and the apotheosis of women: Both sexes were capable of evil, although men seemed to have the edge in that respect. "There are women who dress up in hunting pink, or whatever they call it, and chase after the poor fox on horseback. There are good reasons for fox-kind to dislike women."

"Why do they do it?" said Jamie. "What prompts people to enjoy the infliction of pain on another creature?"

"Ancient memories," said Isabel. "Ancient memories of pursuit, when hunting was pretty much all that men did."

She saw, for a moment, a flickering fire, and beyond it a group of hirsute men, each armed with a spear, preparing to traipse off in pursuit of prey. And their leader, she noticed to her surprise, was Professor Lettuce, who was haranguing a tall assistant clad in skins, who was Christopher Dove, or one of his haplogroup, if she was not mistaken.

Jamie gave her a sideways look. "Are you imagining something?"

She abandoned the Cro-Magnon Lettuce and his attendant Dove. "Men hunted together to survive," she continued. "And that memory persists. They're re-enacting old rituals that meant the difference between starvation and survival."

Unbidden, another image came to her. A fox hunt barging its way through her garden in pursuit of Brother Fox, the horses destroying her lawn with their hoofs, the braying dogs scrabbling away under the rhododendron bushes, and Brother Fox cowering under an upturned wheelbarrow while death barged past him in full cry.

Now Jamie said to her, "Do you think she has somebody up there?"

"Hiding in her room? Why?"

Jamie shrugged. "A man? Perhaps she has a new boyfriend but she doesn't feel that she can bring somebody else into our house. Guests usually can't introduce other guests, can they? What do they say on the invitations? This invitation is non-transferable?"

Isabel wondered if Dawn considered herself a guest or a lodger. "Or even a tenant," she said. "If you're a tenant in a flat that happens to be under somebody's roof, you can still treat the flat as any normal tenant would. You can have people come to see you."

Jamie was adamant that Dawn was not a tenant. "She has no lease," he insisted. "She's somebody staying in a guest room— that's all."

"A guest room with a kitchen and bathroom," said Isabel.

"Even so. She's temporary. She pays no rent. She's definitely not a tenant."

Isabel left it at that, as did Jamie. She thought: How easily frightened I am, which is shameful, as reason and observable fact should be the key-signatures of our lives—not speculation and irrational fears—disquieting stories told at the youthful sleepover, making everybody scared of the dark and the threatening things that, once the lights are turned on, it is shown not to conceal.

CHAPTER SEVEN

ROZ WAS FIFTEEN MINUTES LATE for her coffee with Isabel. The plumber, she said, had been booked in to deal with a leaking tap, but had been detained on a more urgent mission and had kept her waiting.

"He has a system of triage," she said. "He considers the calls on his time from the point of view of need. My tap was merely dripping—obviously he must deal first with those whose houses are being flooded."

"If Noah telephones," said Isabel, "the plumber must assume the call is a pressing one."

Roz looked puzzled. "Noah?"

Surely, thought Isabel, we have not forgotten Noah and . . . She realised that she did not know Noah's wife's name, or, if she had known it once, had now forgotten it. That was the difficulty with contemplating what other people had forgotten—it revealed what you yourself might be unable to remember. Of course, there were many women in history—or myth, in this case—who were not named because they were ignored or undervalued. Mrs. Noah was probably one such.

"Noah, who had the Ark," said Isabel.

"Oh, him. Yes, well . . . there wasn't much a plumber could have done to help him."

"No. I mention him just as an example of need, of course."

Roz smiled faintly. "I see. Well, our plumber is very conscientious. And he did turn up, just as he said he would."

This conversation had taken place in the hall of Isabel's house. Now she led her guest into her study, where a cafetière of coffee was waiting. They exchanged a few remarks about the traffic—there was very little—and the weather—there was a great deal—before Roz broached the subject of the book group.

"As I said last night," she began, "not everything's perfect in my book group. It started very well a few years ago now, but we've had quite a few changes in membership since then and things have become complicated."

Isabel said that she understood. "It takes only one or two disagreements to make things tricky," she said. "And then acrimony can take over. I was a member of a book group some years ago where that happened. The disagreement started over a Muriel Spark novel—I remember it well. Two members took a radically different view from one another, and insults were exchanged. Well, not exactly insults so much as doubts about the literary judgement of the other person, and that was the beginning of a long descent."

"All triggered by Muriel Spark," said Roz.

"*The Prime of Miss Jean Brodie*," Isabel explained. "One of the members wanted to defend Jean Brodie against charges of fascism . . ."

"Well, she was a bit that way inclined," interjected Roz. "And there are some teachers who are natural fascists. Not many, but some. It's one of the temptations of pedagogy. Didn't Miss Brodie admire Mussolini?"

"She did," said Isabel. She recalled the astonishing line delivered to her admiring teenage pupils: *In Italy, young girls, il Duce has abolished litter*. "It's the strong-man syndrome. There are some women who admire strong men. I knew of somebody—a misguided friend—who called her husband *Dear Leader*."

Roz winced. "Tasteless."

"Yes," conceded Isabel. "But the inner working of others' relationships is often opaque to the rest of us. Some people put up with a lot. I know somebody who calls his partner *Brain*. She seems indifferent to the implicit insult."

Roz smiled. "Unless he means it."

"He does not," said Isabel.

"Then, once again, that's a bit distasteful."

Isabel agreed. "But she seems not to mind. Although the whole thing may be a sophisticated joke. He knows that others will think he means to be sarcastic, but he isn't: He's pretending to be the sort of man who would call somebody *Brain* in that sense. And he knows that anybody who hears him will think that he means to belittle her, whereas he's really laughing at the person who thinks he would be the sort of person to speak like that about somebody—and of course he isn't." She paused. "If you see what I mean."

Roz looked thoughtful. "I wanted to tell you a bit more about the book group."

"Ah, yes, the book group . . ." Isabel had toyed with the idea of asking for time to consider the offer, but it was too late.

"I'm so pleased that you've agreed to join," Roz said quickly.

Roz's gratitude was palpable, and Isabel realised that she could not row back on her promise—if that is what it had been taken to be. And now, as if to hammer home the point, Roz continued, "I was ready to close the whole thing down, you know. That would have been a dreadful pity because in spite of everything, I suspect the members get great pleasure from reading the books we choose to talk about. In fact, I am sure that they do. They'd be very upset if we stopped. I certainly would be. If only we could deal with the undercurrents that will, I fear, tear the group apart."

Isabel asked why there couldn't be a simple clearing of the air. "Couldn't you just talk to them? Couldn't you say: Look, we need to sort out certain issues if this group is to continue? Couldn't you get people to see what the problem is and then be nice to one another?"

Roz shrugged. "How do you tell somebody that she's a complete know-all? How do you tell somebody that she's lying when she says she's read a book?"

"Well, you could have a word with anybody who seems to be making life difficult for other members."

Roz looked away. "I can't," she said. "I just can't. I tried to do something. I spoke to one of the members who's subtly needling away at one of the others. She denied everything, and I fear I exacerbated the problem. She accused me of taking sides, even though she had just told me there were no sides to take. I gave up. We need an outsider—a peacemaker."

Isabel did not argue. It was even more obvious to her now that she could not withdraw. "Tell me about the members, then," she said.

Roz sipped at the coffee that Isabel had poured for her when they entered the study. "There's me, of course. I'm the chair, although I'm actually planning to hand that position over to somebody else. I don't want to hang on to it beyond the end of next month. So, there's me, and then there's Virginia. She's been a member since day one."

"And what does Virginia do?" asked Isabel.

"She teaches English at a school in north Edinburgh. It's

rather a tough school, where a lot of the kids have had a really bad start in life. Parents on drugs. Surviving on junk food. But she's dedicated to the job. And she carries that enthusiasm over into her private life. She's ambitious for the group. She thinks book groups are meant to be educational. I suspect that if she thought the book group simply provided entertainment, she'd resign forthwith. She takes it all terribly seriously."

Even with this snippet of information, Isabel felt that a familiar picture was about to reveal itself. Most clubs, in any area of activity, were much the same. It was the personalities that created that effect: Wherever you went, people were people, with all their ambitions and failings. All book clubs would have a member like Virginia—to a greater or lesser extent—somebody with a vision of what the club might be, if only people were a little better organised, or a little bit less lazy, or more prepared to move outside the comfort zone of their habitual reading. These were the people whose shelves at home were filled with books they felt they *had* to read, rather than those they *wanted* to read. And there were some authors who benefitted greatly from the determination of such readers to be up to date with all the serious literature. Stephen Hawking had done his best to explain complicated cosmological issues to the general public, and people had responded by buying *A Brief History of Time* in their millions. And yet the realm of physics in which Professor Hawking had dwelled was firmly beyond the reach of most of the people who bought his book. Isabel herself had tried, as had Jamie, but they had both failed; in Jamie's case after page sixteen, and in Isabel's after page twenty-four. Isabel had read that *A Brief History of Time* had the distinction of being one of the most unread books in the recent history of publishing, prompting the development of the Hawking Index, which rated the percentage of a book read before the average reader gave up. It was not at the bottom of that index, but it was close to it. Its presence on so many shelves was evidence of the public's widespread desire to improve its knowledge of scientific matters, but it was also evidence of the public's failure to do just that.

Isabel could picture Virginia. There had been somebody a bit like that in the last book group she had belonged to, before she met Jamie. She had not thought about her for a long time, but now she saw her again, frowning with disapproval when another member of the group had proposed that they should read a Dick Francis novel. "They're set in the world of horse racing," she had said, "and they are terrifically exciting. How can you not enjoy a Dick Francis novel?" Some of the other members had agreed, but in one quarter, at least, there had been a discouraging silence and a counterproposal of a book, in translation, by a Danish novelist of whom nobody had heard. That novel, which was unfinished by the author, was also unfinished by most of its readers, but it continued to be bought by those who believed that buying it, if not actually reading it, was a sign of intellectual seriousness.

"So that's Virginia," said Isabel. "And what do the others think? Do they resist her attempts to improve them?"

Roz replied that the members were generally polite, but that whenever it came to a vote—and they were in the habit of voting on recommendations—Virginia's suggestions only very rarely attracted support, and that support, such as it was, came from those who felt sorry for her. She had a husband who had a reputation as one of the dullest men in Edinburgh, and people felt that the least they could do was to occasionally read one of the books she recommended, even if they never finished it.

"Poor woman," said Isabel. "It can't be easy—dealing with demanding students all day and then going back to a husband who doesn't exactly inspire."

"We all have our burdens," said Roz. "And I suppose there are worse fates in this life. Would you like me to tell you about the others?"

Isabel was beginning to enjoy herself. There was a certain fascination in hearing other people being described in a few pithy sentences, even if one might not enjoy the thought of being so described oneself. What, she wondered, would anybody say if called upon to provide a thumbnail sketch? *Claims to be a philosopher, but what does she actually do? Think? Is that a job? She's got a bit of money—but where did she get it? That's what I'd like to know, not that I'm saying anything . . .* And so on. Envy was ubiquitous. She was envied by some because of her house and her husband and her general good fortune—she knew that. And yet she never flaunted any of these things, being modest and generous of both time and money. But envy, it seemed, was indifferent to such moral efforts.

Roz went on to say something about the next member. This was Gemma, who had four children under ten, and a husband who was a senior air traffic controller. Roz explained that Gemma was quiet, unassertive and scrupulously polite. Her husband, she said, seemed very much the same. "I can't imagine him telling aeroplanes what to do, or at least not being very firm about it. I'm sure he says, *Could you possibly descend to ten thousand feet, if you wouldn't mind, that is.* And the pilots might reply, *Not just now, please. I like it up here.* That's not the way to run an air traffic control system."

Isabel laughed. "So, Gemma reads what she's told to read."

"Exactly," replied Roz. "She admires Virginia, who's her polar opposite. Whenever Virginia says something, Gemma nods in agreement. She's never disagreed with her—not once. And on the rare occasions when we accept one of Virginia's suggested titles, Gemma is virtually the only one who reads the book from cover to cover. Then she says 'profound.' That's her favourite word, *profound*." She paused. "Am I sounding uncharitable? Unkind, even? I don't want to be. I like Gemma. I even like Virginia when she's not trying to improve my mind, which is not very often, I must say. But I feel I should be truthful. I can't make this book group something it isn't. As I told you, we have problems."

Isabel asked about the other members. It would be an unusual book group where everybody posed some sort of problem, but perhaps this was one. "And the other members?" she asked. "Are they . . ." She left the question unfinished. Perhaps *trying* was the word she needed, although Gemma did not sound particularly objectionable.

Roz took up the question herself. "Are the others difficult? They're not annoying, unlike Virginia, but they have issues." She thought for a few moments. "Put it this way: If one were designing an ideal book group, one would not necessarily choose people like them, for one reason or another."

Isabel looked thoughtful. She wondered whether she now had a pretext to change her mind. It would be possible to say, "bearing in mind what you've told me about the members, I'm not sure that this club is for me." Roz might be disappointed, but she could hardly argue that Isabel had no grounds to decline her invitation.

"I'm not . . ." Isabel began, only to be cut short by Roz.

"I must tell you about Angela. It's really rather funny."

"I was thinking . . ."

Once again Roz took over. "You'd be surprised: More book groups than you might imagine have what amounts to a 'non-reading member.' We do. We have Angela."

"Who doesn't read at all?"

"Not as far as I know. She might have read in the past, but she never—and I mean never—reads the books we choose to discuss.

She doesn't admit to it, of course. She makes general comments, but what she says could apply to anything, really. And every so often she says something that provides positive proof that she hasn't read the book she's talking about."

Isabel was reminded of the Bluffers' Guides she had seen in the bookstore at Waverley Station. She had picked up *Bluff Your Way in the Classics*. She happened to know the author, who had a degree in classics, and was in a position to give readers enough hard information to enable them to talk knowledgeably about Virgil or Homer without ever having read a line of either. She had heard it suggested that Proust needed a guide like that. Most people did not have the time to read *À la recherche du temps perdu*, but might want to be in a position to talk about the great roman-fleuve.

"It's a pity," she said, "that people should feel the need to impress others like that. What's wrong with admitting ignorance?"

Roz frowned. "You can say that because you aren't ignorant. But somebody who is—well it's not always easy."

There was a note of reproach in Roz's voice, and Isabel realised that the other woman was right. "I'm sorry," she said. "I should be more understanding."

Roz continued regardless. "Then there's Fredericka. She's a bit younger than the rest of us. She's barely thirty—and very glamorous. She doesn't look bookish at all, but she's very well read. She's well liked by everyone else. And Barbara. She's a bit argumentative at times, and competitive. She likes to get in the last word if she possibly can. She dislikes Angela, but tries not to show it. It comes out, though, in the occasional barbed comment. Angela doesn't notice it, though—Barbara's too subtle. But Gemma picks it up and I think one of these days she's going to tell Angela that she's being put down, even if she hasn't noticed it."

Roz stopped, and Isabel digested the information she had been given. Then Isabel asked, "No men?"

Roz shook her head. "No. There haven't been any men wanting to join. It's a pity, isn't it? There are far fewer men in book groups than women. Men are missing out. Do you think they know it?"

"Some do, some don't," Isabel replied.

Roz asked her now whether there was anything else she needed to know. There would be a meeting of the book group the following week, and if Isabel was free, it would be a good time to come to meet the others.

"Do they have to approve me?" asked Isabel. If she were to be turned down, it would, she realised, give her the perfect way out.

"The chair chooses new members," said Roz. "And I'm the chair."

"Is that what it says in the constitution?"

Roz laughed. "There is no constitution. It's just the way things are."

"And nobody objects?"

"Nobody's said anything," said Roz.

"That's not quite the same thing," Isabel pointed out.

"Possibly," Roz conceded. "But, as I said, that's the way it is."

Isabel refreshed Roz's coffee cup. It seemed that Roz had said all she had to say about the book group. Now she glanced about Isabel's study before saying, "So you're a philosopher. Is that unusual—being a woman philosopher?"

"It used to be," said Isabel. "But no longer."

"When? Fifty years ago?"

"Yes, sixty or seventy in Britain. If you had done a head count in university philosophy departments in the nineteen-thirties, there would have been rather few women. It changed after the war. Now it doesn't make much difference, although there are still those who say that the men have been slow to let go." Glass ceilings, in spite of everything, still existed. She thought of Lettuce. She was convinced that he and Dove were suspicious of women in philosophy; men who resented women in their profession were usually concerned because they felt inadequate when faced with competition.

"What happened?" asked Roz.

"To bring about change?"

"Yes, how were the men dealt with?"

Isabel was not sure that they *had* been dealt with, as Roz put it, even if there had been change. "Some very impressive women philosophers came along immediately after the war," she said. "That happened in Oxford in particular, with people like Elizabeth Anscombe and Philippa Foot. And Iris Murdoch, too, of course."

Roz knew about her. "I've read one or two of her novels. *An Unofficial Rose.* I remember that one."

"She taught philosophy too," said Isabel. "She wrote a book called *The Sovereignty of Good.* She said that the good was like the sun. I like that metaphor. The good *is* like the sun—we feel it that way, I think."

"The sun . . . Yes, I suppose . . ." Roz found herself fascinated by Isabel. Here was a woman who lived in a street not unlike her own, who presumably went shopping in the local supermarket, just as she did, and yet who still thought about these large things. For a moment she felt defeated: She would never be able to catch up—she was destined to have a much smaller life. The book club, at least, was something; it was a connection to a world of ideas; she had that, just as so many other members of book clubs throughout the land had that to hold on to. Book clubs were a great, extended conversation, just as religion had once been, before its marginalisation in so many societies. Perhaps book clubs, now, had to do some of that work with people's souls.

"And she had many lovers," Isabel went on. "Elizabeth Anscombe, in fact, said that it would take less time for Iris to list the names of men who had *not* proposed to her than those who had."

Roz laughed. "But was their philosophy any different?"

"Yes, it was. They changed the emphasis. They were realists, for a start. They thought philosophy should help you to act in the world, not just think about what words meant. It's a complicated story." Isabel grinned. "How long have you got?"

Roz was polite, but she had to get to the fish shop before they ran out of smoked haddock. Last time she was there she just missed the final pieces and had been unable to make the kedgeree, her husband's favourite, that she had been intending to serve for dinner. She mentioned this, somewhat apologetically, to Isabel.

Brecht, thought Isabel. "Grub first, then ethics," she said, quoting the playwright's most famous aphorism. "Bertolt Brecht would say you should go to the fish shop."

Roz laughed, and then said, "Some other time, perhaps."

"All right. There are some wonderful stories about them, but, as you say, some other time. Philippa Foot, you know, was the granddaughter of Grover Cleveland, who happened to be the president of the United States."

"Really?" Perhaps the smoked haddock would have to wait.

"Yes. But let me tell you just one story right now. Elizabeth Anscombe was told at the entrance to a smart Boston restaurant that women weren't allowed to wear trousers there. Her reaction? She promptly took off the trousers she was wearing and went in without them."

"What a stylish thing to do," said Roz.

"An apocryphal thing to do, perhaps," said Isabel, a bit sadly. That story had been retold so many times that surely it could not be true. It was the sort of thing that *should* have happened, though, even if it had not.

"She was fiercely intelligent," Isabel continued. "I'm afraid that response would never occur to me—or, if it did, it would only come to mind hours afterwards. That's when the *mot juste* comes to most of us—well after the moment when it would have been just right."

Isabel was about to say something else, but she was distracted by a strange yelping sound from outside her window. Roz looked up sharply.

"That's our fox," said Isabel. "Brother Fox. I would like to think that he's laughing, but I don't think it's that. Every so often he makes that sound. It's a sort of existential howl against the conditions of his life—against being a fox, perhaps. It doesn't mean he's in physical pain."

"Poor fox," said Roz.

"Indeed," said Isabel. "Yet, in spite of the occasional howl to the moon . . ." And here it occurred to her that to a fox, the moon might well be God—*God inlunate*, perhaps. "In spite of that, I think he's happy enough on the whole. He doesn't know what it's like to be anything else." She paused. "There's a famous paper in philosophy by an American philosopher called Thomas Nagel. It's called 'What Is It Like to Be a Bat?'"

"And does he tell you?"

"No," said Isabel. "That's the whole point. We don't know, but bats know what it's like to be them. That means that consciousness is a subjective thing that cannot be explained by any objective criteria. It's an argument against reductionism."

"Oh," she said. And then she asked, "I wonder what it was

like to be Elizabeth Anscombe or any of the other people you mention."

"Philippa Foot and Iris Murdoch?"

Roz nodded. "Yes, them."

"We can infer from what they say about themselves what it's like to be them," Isabel replied. "In general terms, at least. We cannot imagine their full experience of themselves, though, simply because we aren't them."

Roz thought about this, and then said "Oh" once again. She looked at her watch. "I've taken up so much of your time. And you must have so much else to do. You can't spend hours talking to people like me about bats and consciousness and so on."

"It's what I do," said Isabel. "I decided a long time ago that I wanted to be a philosopher—and here I am. Consciousness and bats are bound to crop up. I am where I wanted to be—and I realise just how fortunate I am to be able to say that." She paused, and gave Roz an enquiring look. "Tell me, though: Are you where you want to be?"

She asked the question and immediately regretted it. Most people, she thought, would probably have to answer in the negative, and it was perfectly possible—indeed likely—that Roz was one of them. You do not ask these unsettling questions of those who come to your house for a cup of coffee and a chat about a book group.

Roz had risen to her feet. She had been ready to go, anyway, and seemed to be indifferent to any implicit challenge in what Isabel had just said. "I'll send you the details of the next meeting," she offered.

Isabel looked out of the window. The patch of sky over Scotland, beyond the maple tree, was unclouded, a lovely, unthreatening blue. There was sunlight on the lawn, a buttery yellow, warm, affirmative light. Iris Murdoch had lived so intensely, so passionately, she thought—as her published letters made so clear. Her own life was not like that at all; it was not a life lived with an eye to what a biographer might do with it; it was not a life for eventual publication. All she did was worry about how to deal with little things: if, and how, to warn Gordon that he was fundamentally misled about Cat; what to do about Dawn, who might, or might not, be harbouring somebody in her room, and in that way abusing their hospitality; whether to say anything about Lettuce's outrageous use of conference funds and his attempt to make her complicit in what amounted to fraud. Philippa Foot and Elizabeth Anscombe would not have had any trouble in deciding how to respond to any of these challenges. Their condemnation of Lettuce would have been brisk and unambiguous, and issued in the plummy tones of their time and place. They would have said that virtue should be her guide in dealing with any of these matters. And then they would have done whatever they decided was the right thing to do. And I shall do that too, Isabel told herself. I shall do what I need to do once I've decided what that is. It was often the case, though, that deciding what one should do was considerably more difficult than doing it. That was the case with getting out of bed on a cold morning, just for instance.

CHAPTER EIGHT

THE OFFICES of the Matheson Trust were in a quiet street on the edge of the Georgian New Town. It was a quarter of the city that lacked the grandeur of Heriot Row or Queen Street, or the sweeping elegance of Moray or Ainslie Place; the scale of the buildings in Albany Street was considerably more modest, as was the nature of the offices that had inserted themselves among the remaining private houses. It was not quite tattoo-parlour territory, but the accountancy and legal firms that had converted domestic premises to business offices served ordinary clients with restricted budgets. Here and there the mildly bohemian nature of that end of the New Town asserted itself, and a business sign proclaimed a shop devoted to old vinyl records, or the premises of an antiquarian map dealer. It was not far from one of Edinburgh's largest theatres, with the collection of bars and restaurants that clustered around it. From the attic windows of the buildings, craning one's neck one might see out over the Firth of Forth to the hills of Fife beyond, and be reminded of the city's romantic hinterland.

Isabel had walked along Albany Street often enough, but had never noticed the small brass plate identifying the office of the Matheson Trust. It was immediately below another plate that announced a firm of chartered accountants, and Isabel deduced that the accountants were the people who ran the trust. She had telephoned for an appointment with the chairman and had been courteously offered a meeting the next day. She had been asked what it was she wanted to discuss, but had said that it was a sensitive matter that she would prefer to raise at the meeting itself. That had brought a short silence, but the receptionist had quickly recovered and the time of Isabel's visit was confirmed.

She rang the doorbell and was admitted to an entrance hall. A woman emerged from a door at the end of the hall and welcomed her politely.

"Mr. Grant is just finishing a telephone call," she said. "He'll be no more than a minute or two."

She was offered a seat, and the receptionist made a remark about the weather. Isabel agreed: It was an unusually warm day, but rain had been forecast, had it not, and that often led to cooler winds. Those were always welcome, she said; and the receptionist agreed, although she added that too much wind was not a good thing—on the whole, that is. She did not like it when an east wind blew; it could go on, she said. It was often too cold. A cool wind was one thing—a cold wind quite another. Their eyes met in a moment of common understanding, as when those engaged in a social ritual recognise the real meaninglessness of what they are doing, but at the same time understand the reason behind their observation of the superficialities. Isabel felt an urge to break out of the necessary politeness; it would be easy enough to say to this woman whom she might never meet again: "But are you happy? Do you like your job? What do you like to read?"—anything that would enable them to say what they really felt. She sighed.

The woman heard the sigh. "Are you all right?" she asked. There was real concern in her voice.

"Yes," replied Isabel. "I am. Thank you." And then she added, "The winds must come from somewhere when they blow."

The receptionist looked puzzled. "I suppose they do," she said.

Isabel smiled. "Sorry. We were talking about winds. It's just that there's a line about that in a poem I rather like. Auden. He wrote it. He said, 'The winds must come from somewhere when they blow.' I think that's such a haunting line."

The receptionist returned Isabel's smile. "Yes, it is. It's lovely. I'd like to read more poetry. I must. I must find the time."

A door opened along a corridor, and a middle-aged man in a grey suit came out to meet her. The receptionist exchanged a glance with Isabel, who could tell that she wanted their conversation to continue, but the spell had been broken. A tiny chink in the indifference of the world had been prised open, but had to be closed. "Here he is," she said. "Mr. Grant."

Marcus Grant extended a hand for Isabel to shake. "We've never met," he said. "But I believe that my father and your father played golf together at Muirfield. A long time ago, of course. And your mother was American, wasn't she? She and my mother saw one another from time to time, I believe."

Isabel was not surprised. Edinburgh was like that; although it was a city, like so many cities it was also a village.

"My mother spoke highly of your mother," he continued.

Isabel thought, My sainted American mother.

He gestured for Isabel to follow him into his office. As he led the way, he said, "I wear more than one hat here—I'm managing partner of the accounting firm, but I'm also the chairman of the Matheson Trust. I take it that you've come to see me in that role—as chairman of the trust."

Inside his office, he invited Isabel to sit in a chair beside his desk. "Did you ever meet any of the Mathesons? Your father may have known George Matheson, but there were others. They were a Dundee family originally, and only came down to Edinburgh after he retired. But they did a lot for the arts here—the National Gallery, Scottish Opera and so on. He was very helpful to the museums."

Isabel said that she was aware of the contribution that George Matheson had made during his lifetime. "And now the trust—his good work continues."

Marcus Grant looked pleased. "We do our best. We can't support everything we get asked to take on, but we manage quite a bit. The trust's funds have been well looked after—not by me, I hasten to add—that's all handled by others. They've been careful in their investments."

"I suppose you have to be," said Isabel. "It's other people's money, after all."

She had not intended it, but it struck her that what she had just said could be interpreted as some sort of reproach. And for a moment, Marcus Grant stiffened. But then he nodded agreement. "Of course, that goes without saying."

And yet I have just said it, thought Isabel.

Marcus Grant took a piece of paper from a folder and placed it before him. He adjusted it on the large leather pad on his desk—a pad that, in days of ink, would have held a square of blotting paper, ready to record, backwards, anything dried upon it. "You told Mrs. Jamieson that you had some . . . some sensitive issue to discuss. May I . . ." He did not finish the sentence, as if the confidentiality of Isabel's business prevented it.

Isabel drew in her breath. She had not imagined that this would be easy, and she had been right. "I'm not here to make an application to the trust," she began.

Marcus Grant nodded. "I understand. We have special procedures for that—any number of forms to fill in, I'm afraid." He allowed himself a smile. "Bureaucracy, you see. We try to keep it in check, but red tape is always there, isn't it?"

"It is," agreed Isabel.

He waited for her to continue. From an adjoining office, Isabel heard a cough.

"Mrs. Jamieson has had a summer cold," Marcus Grant offered.

East winds, thought Isabel.

"These coughs can linger," he continued. "I had one recently that lasted six weeks. A bit alarming, but one shrugs these things off eventually."

Isabel went to the point. "I was shown the details of an application that I believe the trust is about to approve," she said. "There were aspects of it that I felt I needed to discuss with you."

She had been feeling tense; now, the tension drained away. She had started what she knew she had to do.

He looked immediately concerned. "Somebody else's application?"

"Yes. One that I believe is fairly far along in the approval process. It was shown to me because I am being asked to participate, so to speak."

He asked which application she was talking about. There was an edge to his voice now, and he went on to explain that he was not sure that he would be able to discuss the details of any application without the permission of the person making it. "I'm sure you'll understand why these things are treated as confidential."

She assured him that she did. "But I was brought into it, you see. I was made party to it by the applicant himself."

Marcus Grant was still doubtful. "That might enable us to talk about some aspects of it," he conceded. "But there may be details that are and must remain confidential." He paused, and went on to explain that some of the trust's grants were made to people involved in commercially sensitive research. "We give a number of grants for scientific research, you see. These are people who might be getting patents and so on. There are commercial implications there."

"I understand that," said Isabel. "But I don't think that applies in this case."

Marcus Grant frowned. "What is *this* case then? Which application are we talking about? We handle fifty or sixty a year, you know. The trustees are inundated at times."

"It's an application made by Professor Robert Lettuce."

Marcus Grant held her gaze. Then he looked down at the leather pad on his desk. He reached for a pencil, and then put it down again. Isabel watched him.

"Professor Robert Lettuce?" he said. And then, after a studied pause, "Lettuce?"

It was as if he was searching his memory, even managing to look puzzled. And yet, thought Isabel, you play bridge with him— or so Lettuce had claimed.

Marcus Grant suddenly regained his composure. "Of course. A conference, wasn't it? I remember it now. An interesting proposal, I thought. Something to do with . . ."

"Vices and virtues," interjected Isabel.

"That's right. Interesting." And then, "Not that I know much about vices and virtues myself."

It was a humorous aside, and Isabel, trying to keep the encounter civil, responded accordingly. "We don't want to know too much about the vices, attractive though some of them may seem from time to time."

"Hah!" said Marcus Grant. "Temptation? Yes, that's always lingering somewhere close at hand." He collected himself. "But what aspect of that application concerns you?"

"This is a bit awkward for me," Isabel said. "I would prefer not to be here, but I was shown the budget. I am being asked to provide publication of the papers to be delivered at the conference. I edit a journal you see."

Marcus Grant nodded. If he was the bureaucrat, he was the helpful bureaucrat now. "Of course. I remember there was something about publication in the application."

"The sums involved for that are virtually nugatory," Isabel continued. "But the honoraria proposed for the organisers are absurdly high." She paused. She felt her heart beat within her. She was nervous. "You know Professor Lettuce, of course."

Marcus Grant shook his head. "One of the other trustees met him. One of us always interviews each applicant, but we can't all see each and every one."

She swallowed hard. Marcus Grant was lying. It was as simple as that. He and Lettuce were in the same bridge club—Lettuce had said that. Unless Lettuce was lying, of course. But why would he lie about something incidental?

"I thought perhaps you knew him," Isabel said, struggling to keep her voice even.

Once again Marcus Grant shook his head, although he did not say anything.

Isabel hesitated for a moment, and then persisted. "The amount being claimed by Professor Lettuce is indefensible," she said. "I couldn't help but feel that he was, well, motivated by personal gain—for himself, and also for his assistant, a young woman who . . ."

The implication was only too clear. Marcus Grant looked at her. He was not shocked, as she thought at first; he was calculating. Then it was as if he reminded himself of how he should look, and that was reproachful.

"We allow fees for organisers of conferences," he said quietly. "There's a great deal of work involved."

"But surely these shouldn't be excessive," she protested. "I've organised conferences myself. A small honorarium is normal, yes, but not thousands of pounds."

"Views may differ as to what is normal, Miss Dalhousie."

She stared at him.

"And I do assure you," he continued, "that the trust scrutinises every item in a budget. If we have authorised a particular fee, then you may be sure that the expenditure in question is deemed reasonable."

He picked up the pencil once again and tapped it lightly on the desk. "Is there any other aspect of this application that you wish to discuss?"

Isabel rose to her feet. "I've taken up enough of your time. I've expressed my view that money that should be used elsewhere is going into private pockets. I don't see how I can make that any plainer."

Marcus Grant sat back in his chair. "I'm sorry, but I must disagree."

"Well, we disagree then." She prepared to leave.

He rose to his feet. "I'm most grateful to you for expressing your concerns," he said evenly. "And I hope I've been able to offer you at least some reassurance—even if ultimately it seems we may be in disagreement." He paused; his words, now, seemed carefully weighed. "We are a private trust, Miss Dalhousie. Your father, as a lawyer, might have explained to you that private trusts are not accountable to the general public."

Isabel felt a surge of anger well up within her. "I'm not an outsider to this," she said. "I was named in that budget. That makes me a party to it. My name was mentioned in that application without my specific consent. Professor Lettuce only told me about the project after he had submitted the application. Publication was part of it—and that is where I came in."

He remained calm. "Yes, you are a party to the conference—an incidental party, shall I say? But you are not a trustee. I hardly need point out that it is the trustees who decide how trust funds are to be spent."

"Aren't you a charity?" she asked. "Aren't charities accountable?"

Marcus Grant shook his head. "We do not have charitable status. George Matheson was adamant about keeping our independence. We are not subject to the control of the charities regulator." There was a look of triumph in his eyes now. "So, you see, we really can do what we like—as long as we operate within the scope of the deed of trust—which we do, of course."

She turned away, but, even now, the niceties were observed. "Thank you for seeing me," she said.

"The pleasure was entirely mine," said Marcus Grant. "And thank you for raising this issue with me."

Mrs. Jamieson appeared at the door. "I'll see Miss Dalhousie out," she said to Marcus Grant.

They left the room. In the corridor, Mrs. Jamieson said, "If there's anything you want to talk to me about, you may do so, you know."

Isabel turned to her. The receptionist looked anxious. Isabel wondered whether she had listened in on the conversation.

"There's one thing I would like to check up on," said Isabel. "Does Mr. Grant know Professor Lettuce?"

"Oh, they're great friends," said Mrs. Jamieson. "They go to lunch together. There's an Italian restaurant round the corner. I book the table." She gave Isabel a conspiratorial look. "I don't particularly take to the professor, I'm afraid. I don't know why."

"I know exactly why; I share your view," said Isabel.

"Of course, we women see these things, don't we?" said Mrs. Jamieson, adding, wistfully, "Sometimes it would be simpler if we didn't, but we do."

They had reached the front door. "Actually," said Mrs. Jamieson. "I should try harder to like Professor Lettuce. I really should."

"I'm not sure you need to," said Isabel.

"He's Mr. Grant's cousin, of course," said Mrs. Jamieson casually. "Did you know that?"

CHAPTER NINE

THE NEXT DAY was Saturday, a day on which Isabel and Jamie often took the boys for a walk up Craiglockhart Hill. Family walks with small boys were slow affairs, kept from being at all brisk by the limited pace that Magnus could manage at his age, and by Charlie's tendency to walk in circles. That had puzzled Isabel, and she had contemplated seeking advice on whether there was some internal compass problem. Jamie, however, assured her that it was entirely natural at that age. "There is so much to be looked at when you're that close to the ground," he said. "That's all he's doing—inspecting things. It's all relatively new to him, remember. And besides, when I was small, I think I did it myself."

Craiglockhart Hill was one of Edinburgh's seven hills, rising in the south-west of the city, not more than a mile or two from the street on which Isabel and Jamie lived. Over the years, housing had crept up to its edges, but the hill itself, with its relatively steep sides and broad, grassy top, was protected against development. To its immediate south, an encircling golf course provided a further green buffer. From the summit, looking north over the rooftops of the city, one could just make out the three bridges over the Forth—the rust-red cantilevers of the nineteenth-century railway crossing, the mid-twentieth-century road bridge, and the latest way across the firth, a construction of delicate white pillars, tiny at this distance. To the south, beyond the golf course and the final suburbs, were the Pentland Hills, the watchful beginnings of a hinterland that stretched off towards further ranges of hills and the upper reaches of the Clyde River. That way was Glasgow, and a whole different world, even if only forty miles to the west.

On the lower slopes of the hill was a large nineteenth-century building, reached by a long sweep of driveway. This was Craiglockhart House, now a university building, but until the late nineteen-hundreds an outlying part of the city's hospital system. During the First World War it had been used by the army as a place to which soldiers suffering from shell shock were sent. These damaged men, tormented by a condition that even some of those treating them refused to believe existed, dreamed their nightmares in the quiet wards of the long, low building, and in the daytime wandered round the wooded grounds of the hospital.

"I can imagine them," Jamie once said, as they made their way along the path up the hill. "I can imagine Owen and Sassoon right here, having walked over from the hospital, standing here, where we are right now, waiting for the inevitable order to go back to the trenches and to die all over again."

Isabel had looked down at the two boys and thought of how those men had once been small children, just like her two. *Was it for this the clay grew tall?* Owen had written. And it was happening, all over again, in the various places where wars were being waged, and young men were pitted against one another, to die in the same way in which they had died at Passchendaele and the Somme. It had not stopped, really; in spite of the intermittent relief of armistices, it had not stopped. Would Charlie ever wear a uniform, she wondered; would the stick that he occasionally picked up and pretended was a gun, as small boys will do despite discouragement, ever be a real one?

Now, on that Saturday morning, with the sky clear of cloud, and the boys talking excitedly at some discovery in the undergrowth, that was all very far away. It would take them the best part of an hour to reach the top of the hill, stopping at various fallen trees, which the boys would clamber over, or in the occasional tiny clearing where they would set some imaginative fantasy: a pirate café, perhaps, a bear's lair, a South American jungle patrolled by jaguars.

As they made their way along the path, Isabel and Jamie were able to talk without having to worry too much about what the boys were doing—as long as they were within sight. Jamie took her hand and gave it a comforting squeeze.

"You've had a difficult week," he said. "I can always tell."

She looked at him appreciatively. Some husbands, she believed, never seemed to feel what their wives were going through, but Jamie always did. "It hasn't been the best week of the year." She hesitated. "But still . . ." She did not like to complain. There was nothing worse than moaning about the world, particularly if the life one led in the world was so much easier than that led by so many others. After all, she had Jamie, and the boys, and the house, and the *Review of Applied Ethics*. And she reminded herself that she also had the support of Grace, who never let her down, in spite of her rather unusual views about various matters—her belief in some of the cranky notions of theosophy, for instance, and the séances she attended at the Arthur Conan Doyle Centre. Grace at least believed in something, when so many people seemed now to believe in nothing at all—other than money and washing machines and fashionable clothes.

"I can tell that you're not sure what to do," Jamie continued.

"You're . . . how do you put it? You're conflicted. Is that the right word?"

"It is," said Isabel. "I'm not sure that it was always a verb, but these things are fluid. So, yes, I'm conflicted." She smiled at him. "In simple English, I don't know what to do."

"About what?"

"About Robert Lettuce, for one thing. And about Gordon and Cat. And then there's Dawn—I don't know what to do about her."

Jamie looked thoughtful. "Dawn's my fault," he said.

She resisted this. "No, I made the offer. I invited her."

"Only because I mentioned her in the first place."

She shrugged. "I suppose she's not top of my list. Going to see Marcus Grant yesterday has created a much more pressing problem."

He asked her to tell him more about it. "You said that he confirmed that they approved Lettuce's questionable budget?"

"Questionable?" Isabel snorted. "Outrageous, more likely."

Jamie asked about Marcus Grant. Had he been simply careless in waving Lettuce's proposals through, or was there something more sinister going on?

Isabel was in no doubt about her answer. "It's corruption, I'd say. Lettuce is his cousin. He should have recused himself from any decision. You don't give large grants to your cousin."

Jamie considered this. "Even if it's an entirely private trust?"

"It may be a private trust, but the money's not his. He has to administer it along the lines set out by the person who set up the trust—in this case, George Matheson. He may have been a bit eccentric, but he was entitled to expect that his trustees would carry out his wishes."

"And those would not have been that the money should be given to the trustees' cousins."

"Exactly," Isabel agreed. "And Marcus Grant knows that. Remember, he lied to me when he claimed not to know Lettuce. He knows he's in the wrong. He's crooked—it's as simple as that."

From the path ahead of them there came raised childish voices. The boys were crouched over a muddy patch of earth, poking at it with twigs they had picked up. Now Charlie flicked mud over his younger brother and laughed with delight.

"Charlie!" Jamie remonstrated. "We don't cover our brother with mud."

Isabel smiled. The writ of comity ran so tenuously down there among the children—almost as weakly as it sometimes ran in international affairs. "Sometimes we do," she muttered.

Jamie grinned. "Party line, please," he whispered to her, and then, bending down to address Charlie face to face, he scolded, "Stop it right now, and say sorry to your brother."

A mumbled apology brought peace, and the boys abandoned the mud. Jamie turned back to Isabel. "I remember loving mud. I think it's more a boy-thing than a girl-thing."

"Chromosomes," said Isabel. "They tend to assert themselves in spite of the best efforts of androgyny." She paused. "Playing with mud is harmless, of course. Playing with guns, though . . ."

Jamie agreed. Toy guns were banned in the house, and he discouraged the boys from picking up sticks and using them as pistols. At the same time, one had to be careful: The forbidden could exert a powerful attraction, and sometimes it was best just to ignore that of which one disapproved.

"We used to play Cowboys and Indians," he remarked. "It's embarrassing to think of these things, isn't it? It never occurred to us that the cowboys were engaged in a land grab."

Isabel sighed. "The history of humanity is one long land grab, don't you think? There are very few people with an original, unsul-

lied title to their place. Where are today's Scots from? Or the English? Who are they? French invaders? Germans? People have
always moved in large numbers, and they are still moving."

"Climate change?"

"Exactly," said Isabel. "People hear of better grazing over the
next hill, and go for it. Then somebody like Columbus comes
along and decides that there's gold to be had if you sail westwards,
and suddenly you have a New World."

"Which was already populated . . ."

"Of course. *Terra nullius* was the biggest lie of the lot. Everywhere belonged to somebody." Isabel looked up at the sky that had
witnessed so many lies, so many acts of cruelty, committed under
it. Nothing shocked the sky. She turned to Jamie. "New Zealand,
of course, is an exception. There's no evidence of any human set-
tlement before the Māori arrived from Polynesia. Suggestions that
there were others before them tend to be politically motivated. So
Māori claims to be the original inhabitants are pretty strong. New
Zealand really was *terra nullius*, it seems, when the first Māori
people arrived."

Jamie shrugged. "Then that settles that. It was theirs first. No
argument."

There was a question that had often bothered Isabel. "Yes.
But at the same time the claim of some people to having deeper
roots in a place shouldn't of itself weaken the claims of those who
came later. I don't think it's right to disenfranchise people who
are born in a place simply because their grandparents were born
elsewhere. Should you give such people second-rate status? Do
you say to the children of immigrants: You don't count as much as
those who go back further? Where's the justice in that?"

"There's none," said Jamie.

"And that's a sure-fire recipe for resentment," Isabel went on.

"If you treat people as being second-class citizens, that's the way they'll behave—as second-class citizens. Auden said something about that in "September 1, 1939." He put it so well: 'I and the public know/What all schoolchildren learn/Those to whom evil is done/Do evil in return.' What can you say to that except *Yes, yes, exactly?*"

"Yes."

"And look at all those people," Isabel said, "who are stranded as a result of the withdrawal of empires. Millions of them. Russians, for instance, on the wrong side of the borders that sprang up after the dissolution of the USSR. Most of them were born where they happened to live, but then may find themselves in another country altogether. They have the right to call their place home just as much as anybody else. But I'm not sure they always feel welcome."

Jamie agreed, but he pointed out that they had to accept that they were part of another polity—and were a minority. "Minorities can't have everything their own way," he said. "They may have to compromise. If they do that, then of course they should have the same rights as others."

"Which they don't always have," said Isabel. "People like that may find that there are no jobs for them, fewer educational possibilities, all sorts of discrimination. They call it nativism."

"That's true," said Jamie. "And yet the people who are already there, who have built the place, could argue that they are entitled to the fruits of what they've created, and new arrivals aren't. That may sound selfish, but you can see the argument. If I pay taxes for years for some sort of benefit, why should a complete newcomer have the same rights?"

"Because it's about membership," Isabel suggested. "If you become a member of something, there are good reasons for treating you the same as everybody else." And there was something else, now that she came to think of it. "The newcomer is going to make a prospective contribution. That gives some entitlement, surely."

Jamie sighed. "You're right. It does. I wouldn't want to exclude newcomers from what the rest of us enjoy. That's bad hospitality, I think."

Isabel shared that view. But these issues, she thought, were not always determined completely rationally.

"We must remember," she pointed out, "that the appeal of the *we got here first* mantra is always going to be very strong. Anybody who comes after you is going to be called a settler. But that's deeply illiberal. A person's civic status shouldn't depend on their origins. If they are a citizen, then they're a citizen—no ifs or buts." She sighed. The world was not always rational—and very rarely fair. "It's ownership, isn't it?" she continued. "Ownership is the trump card that beats everything else. Ownership is powerful magic. *It was mine before you came along.* It's hard for people to argue against that. That belief is instilled when we're two or three. Charlie has it; Magnus has it. Remember how Charlie hung on to his toys when Magnus arrived: He wanted us to lock the cupboard to prevent Magnus getting a look-in. Adults feel like that too."

Talking to Isabel, Jamie reminded himself, was like taking a dog for a walk in a field. At any moment the dog may scent a rabbit and disappear down a burrow. Now he returned to the subject they were discussing before this discussion of entitlement. "What are you going to do?"

She was not sure what he meant. "About?"

"About Lettuce." He paused, and fixed Isabel with a quizzical look. "You don't want him to get away with this, do you?"

She did not. But it was one thing to hope that somebody would not get away with wrongdoing, and another thing altogether to interfere actively in a situation which ultimately was not her concern.

"I don't want Lettuce to get away with any of it," she said. "He's . . ." She broke off, overcome by the strength of her antipathy. And that alarmed her, as part of her told her that it was, quite simply, wrong to feel quite so intensely hostile towards another. Dislike of that nature was disfiguring. She swallowed hard. "He's not a good man."

It sounded so tame that she almost laughed. Jamie found it amusing too. "Oh really?" he said, in mock surprise. "Not a good man?"

Isabel grinned. "You know what I mean. It's just that I find it difficult to describe the length and depth and breadth of his . . ." Again, she struggled to find the right word.

"Self-centredness?" suggested Jamie. "Pomposity? Vanity?"

"Yes, all of those."

Isabel was briefly silent. Then she said, "I know I shouldn't feel the way I do. I know that I should rise above my distaste for Lettuce and Dove. They're dreadful, yes, but I shouldn't let them make me uncharitable. I suppose I should forgive them their failings."

Jamie looked surprised. "Why? Why should you forgive them? What have they done to deserve forgiveness?"

"Nothing," said Isabel. "But that's the point about forgiveness— it's often one-sided. You forgive somebody even if they've not done anything to atone. Forgiving is like priming the pump—the flow doesn't start until somebody puts some water into the system. Somebody has to take the first step."

Charlie and Magnus were a few steps ahead, stopping now and then to pick up something from the path, or running off to investigate something in the undergrowth. But now Charlie stopped in his tracks and turned to stare at his parents. "Pofessor Lettuce stinks," he announced. The title *Pofessor*, Isabel thought, was strangely apt. Lettuce was a *pofessor* rather than a *professor*— of course he was. What a difference the omission of an *r* made.

Jamie exchanged an astonished glance with Isabel. She could see that he was struggling to keep a straight face. But there was a parental position to defend, and so she said, "You mustn't say unkind things, Charlie. It's not nice to say that people stink."

"But he does stink," insisted Charlie. "You just said so. You said that to Daddy. Daddy thinks so too, don't you, Daddy? You think Pofessor Lettuce stinks. You said so too."

"Stinks!" echoed Magnus, in a high-pitched squeak. "Stinks! Stinks!"

"I didn't say anybody stinks," said Jamie. "And Mummy's right, boys: You mustn't say that people stink."

"I heard you," insisted Charlie. "I heard you say you didn't like him. You said he was bad. Bad people stink."

"I said that I wasn't very fond of Professor Lettuce," said Isabel. "But perhaps I was being a bit unkind—and now I'm sorry. All of us have our bad points—every one of us. We should try to be nice to people even if they're . . ." She looked to Jamie for help, but he simply grinned.

"Even if they're a bit bad," Isabel concluded.

"I still say he stinks," said Charlie. "But I'm hungry. Can we have an ice cream on the way back?"

It was a neat solution, and Isabel quickly agreed. "If there's no more unkind talk about poor Professor Lettuce," she said, "we can go to Luca's on the way back and get an ice cream."

"With chocolate?" asked Charlie.

"With chocolate," confirmed Isabel. Was this a bribe, she wondered.

Charlie looked thoughtful. "Pofessor Lettuce is okay," he said.

"That's kind of you," said Isabel. "It feels better to say something like that rather than something nasty, don't you think?"

Charlie hesitated. "Maybe," he said.

He did not sound convinced.

Jamie burst out laughing. "Oh well," he said. "Ice cream first, then ethics." And then, sotto voce to Isabel, "They hear things, don't they? They listen in from down there—down at your feet. They don't miss a thing. We need to be careful. We need to turn a tap on when we talk freely. We need to think: East Germany and the Stasi—be careful what you say."

They made their way back along the path they had been following. With the boys out of earshot, Jamie asked Isabel what she was going to do. "Can you go to the police?" he said.

Isabel replied that she could not imagine the police taking an interest. "They'd probably say there's no offence here. Overcharging for something is not criminal—strictly speaking. We might call it criminal, but it doesn't really fit. It's not theft. There are no fraudulent statements to get a benefit. It's just a bad use of something by people who are so placed as to be able to take advantage of their position."

Jamie wondered about the other trustees. "Presumably our friend Marcus is not the only trustee."

"No, he's not. I saw their leaflet. There are six of them." Isabel pointed out that the others must have approved Lettuce's budget when they saw the application.

"But did they know that Lettuce and Marcus are cousins? Would they have had a closer look if they knew that?"

The question hung in the air. It was exactly the right question to ask, thought Isabel.

"I think you've identified exactly what I have to do," she said.

"Write an anonymous letter to the other trustees? Tell them that their chairman is crooked? Signed *a friend*, like all such letters."

Isabel laughed. "No, something much more effective than that. And no need for anonymity—which is wrong anyway."

"Oh, yes?"

"I could let them do the putting together of two and two," Isabel said. "People are much readier to experience outrage if they discover the cause for outrage themselves."

They finished the walk and bundled the boys into the car. Stopping outside the popular ice-cream parlour at Holy Corner, Jamie took the boys inside to collect their ice-cream cones. Soon there was chocolate ice cream on every nearby surface: on the boys' faces, on their clothing, on the white leather seats of Isabel's green Swedish car. Isabel sighed. Life was messy, in every sense.

CHAPTER TEN

THE BOOK CLUB met the following evening at Roz's house. Roz had explained that unlike most book clubs, in which meetings were hosted by members in turn, hers had never met anywhere but in her large living room. "It started that way," she said, "and somehow we never considered any other option. Some book clubs are conservative, I suppose. They do things a certain way, and the members don't like change."

Isabel had not intended to be the first to arrive, but when Roz opened the front door to her at seven-thirty that night, none of the other members was present.

"They arrive in dribs and drabs," said Roz. "But we always start by eight. They like to chat before we get down to business."

Isabel said that she understood. Book groups were not only about books, but about friendship too, and friendship thrived on casual conversation.

Roz agreed, but said that she sometimes struggled to get the discussion back on the rails. "One or two of our members need little encouragement to go on at length—about anything and everything. I try to steer them back to the book we're talking about, but it doesn't always work."

"Better than long silences," said Isabel. "I heard of a book group where nobody said anything. The only person who spoke was the organiser—the rest remained silent."

Roz laughed. "What was the point?"

"I suppose they got something from simply being with other people," Isabel suggested. "Have you ever been to a Quaker meeting? That's what they do. They sit there until somebody is moved to say something. They can sit for a long time, I'm told."

Roz took Isabel into the living room. "I'd introduce you to my husband," she said. "But he isn't here. Eric belongs to a wild swimming club, and he often goes wild swimming on my book-club nights. Lochs. The sea. Only in the summer, of course, although some of them like to do the Loony Dook on New Year's Day each year."

Isabel grimaced. The Loony Dook was an annual event in which hundreds of swimmers braved the water of the Firth of Forth on the first of January, irrespective of the weather. There were occasions in which they had taken to the water in a snowstorm—to the delight of shivering spectators.

The bell rang, and Roz went to the front door. When she returned to the living room, she was accompanied by two women in their late thirties or early forties. These were Virginia and Gemma. Virginia was elegantly dressed in a dark green trouser suit, while Gemma had a more homely appearance. Both gave Isabel an inquisitive look. Virginia smiled; Gemma seemed more unsure of herself and her expression remained passive. Isabel remembered what Roz had said: Virginia was the leader here—and Gemma followed.

Roz introduced them. "Isabel," she said, "has very kindly agreed to join our group. She has been in a book group before, but not for some time."

She looked to Isabel for confirmation, and Isabel nodded. "I was a member of one a few years back. It eventually fell apart."

Gemma looked anxiously in Virginia's direction. It was clear to Isabel that Gemma was concerned that this group was facing a similar fate, and that she did not want this to happen.

Virginia smiled. "That happens. People get new interests. They move on. That's why . . ." She did not complete the sentence. Roz looked at her sharply. Gemma looked away.

"I know that you worry about these things," said Roz suddenly. "I know that you're concerned."

"I just think that it's important we don't drown ourselves in trivia," said Virginia. "Some of these clubs spend their time reading popular stuff and then discover that they've suffocated themselves with the superficial and the irrelevant."

Gemma nodded solemnly. "That's right," she said. "Romantic novels, for instance."

Roz was about to say something, but was beaten to it by Virginia.

"I will not read a romantic novel," she said firmly. "I categorically refuse."

"Nobody has suggested a romantic novel," said Roz, evenly. "Or at least, I haven't heard anybody say they wanted us to read one."

Virginia looked doubtful. "Not openly," she said. "But I think I know who might try to slip one in—under the radar, so to speak."

"Doesn't it depend on how you define a romantic novel?" said Isabel. "There are some great novels that are unashamedly romantic."

"I think Virginia means those novels you can buy at the railway station," said Gemma. "Bodice rippers—or whatever they're called. Or even chick-lit."

Virginia rolled her eyes. "You can tell by the cover. It usually reveals what's inside. And romantic novels have good-looking men embracing receptive young women. In profile. Against a sunset, perhaps, or a Mediterranean backdrop."

Roz said that nobody had ever suggested anything of that sort. "I agree with you, Virginia. If somebody proposed one of those, I'd simply say no. We aren't that sort of book group."

"Thank heavens," said Virginia. "If we were, I, for one, wouldn't be a member."

Isabel looked at Roz. They had been together for no more than a few minutes, but already Virginia seemed to be identifying the high moral ground for her to scale. Roz caught Isabel's look, and smiled weakly.

"I don't think we should worry too much about that," Roz said. "Although I might point out that Walter Scott was a romantic novelist—in the broad sense—and I shouldn't want to exclude him on those grounds alone."

"I find him a bit hard to read," said Gemma, almost apologetically. "I've tried, but . . . well, I gave up on *Rob Roy.*"

"Scott's not for everyone," said Virginia. "His stories go on and on and don't have a great deal of psychological insight, as far as I can see."

Isabel frowned. "Did psychology exist in Scott's day?" she asked.

The other three women looked at her.

Isabel explained what she meant. "As an identifiable discipline—or perspective. That's what I wondered. Scott's understanding of human nature would have been very different from our own."

Isabel looked at Roz, who was smiling. "Nobody has recommended Scott yet," she said. "But if they do, then . . ."

"I definitely don't want to read Walter Scott," Virginia interjected. "Walter Scott is *not* what this book group is about."

Isabel was not surprised by this statement, in view of what she had heard about Virginia, but she took the opportunity to probe. "I'm obviously the newcomer," she said. "Tell me: What *is* it about?"

Virginia hesitated. She glanced at Roz. "It's about literature," she said. "It's about how books can enrich our lives." She gave Isabel a brief, apologetic look. "I'm sorry if that sounds a bit pompous, but that really is what books mean, in my view at least."

Gemma was nodding. "That's right," she said. "I used to read anything I came across. I don't do that any longer."

"There you are," said Virginia. "Books, you see. That's why we're careful about what we choose to read."

They were disturbed by the ringing of the doorbell. Roz left the room.

"Fredericka is always late," said Gemma. "And she always makes the same excuse. Traffic. But the truth of the matter is that there isn't all that much traffic—it's her."

Virginia gave Gemma a discouraging look. She pursed her lips. "Doesn't matter," she said.

Now Roz came back into the room with Fredericka and another woman whom Roz introduced to Isabel as Linda. The two new arrivals smiled at Isabel. "I'm so glad that you're joining us," said Fredericka. "We need to keep numbers up."

Linda agreed. "You don't want a book group to get too big," she said. "We were getting slightly on the small side. A few new members would help."

Virginia frowned. "Not too many," she said.

Isabel looked at Fredericka. She did not want to stare, particularly as she could see that Fredericka was casting glances in her direction too. The two women were evaluating each other, as people will do on introduction—and yet such evaluation tended, as now, to be discreet and tangential. Isabel was struck by the other woman's appearance, by the calm, almost melancholic beauty of her face. This was somebody, she thought, whom it would be impossible to ignore should one meet her in the proverbial crowded room. She was tall, perhaps even slightly willowy, and was wearing a russet shawl draped casually about her shoulders. Isabel found herself thinking: *I want that shawl*. She stole another glance, and then looked away quickly. Fredericka, she realised, was used to this: Attention was nothing new to her.

Roz invited everybody to sit down. "We're quorate," she said. "And since this is Isabel's first time, I suggest we launch straight into the book. We can catch up over tea later on."

There were murmurs of agreement as they sat down. Then Roz introduced the book. "I must say at the outset that I didn't enjoy this one. I'm not saying that it's totally without merit, but I was very pleased when I reached the end."

This verdict took a short while to be digested. Virginia spoke next. "I'm afraid that I'm inclined to disagree. I thought this was one of the most interesting novels I've read this year. I thought it was exceptional."

Gemma looked up. "It was superb," she said. "Really superb."

Roz shook her head. "I wouldn't call it that at all. I don't think this woman can write."

"Of course she can write," snapped Virginia. "It's four hundred and twenty pages. You can't produce four hundred and twenty pages unless you can write."

"Plenty of people who can't write do just that," Roz retorted. "Style is pretty much discredited these days. It's content that people pay attention to."

Angela raised her hand, almost as if she were in a classroom. "Surely the point is simply this: Does the author make her case? That's the issue, in my view. Does she do what she sets out to do?"

Isabel noticed that Roz's lips seemed fixed in a rigid smile. This had been triggered by Angela's intervention. That was interesting. Was it impatience? She looked at Fredericka, who had turned her head away, and was fidgeting with the fringe of her shawl. She, too, seemed irritated—or was she amused?

Fredericka turned her head back. She was staring at Angela. She stopped fingering the shawl and adjusted it over her shoulders. "That's interesting, Angela," she said. "What do you think the case is?"

Angela returned Fredericka's stare. "Well, it's pretty evident, isn't it? Her central point is right there. She doesn't hide it."

Gemma frowned. She was struggling to make sense of this, thought Isabel. Perhaps Gemma was not as intellectually nimble as the others. Fredericka was quick—Isabel had picked that up immediately—and Gemma must know that. Her loyalty, of course, was to Virginia—Roz had made that clear, and Isabel could see it in Gemma's body language. She *worshipped* Virginia; that was the word. Or *adored* her—that was another possible word.

It was Roz who broke the silence that followed Angela's comment. "I think we should find out who actually enjoyed this book. Then we can ask ourselves why."

Fredericka now addressed Isabel. "We don't vote in this group," she explained. "Some book groups have a rating system—you know, six out of ten, seven out of ten—that sort of thing. We've never done that."

"We should," said Angela. "I've always thought that would be helpful. I can't understand why we don't do it."

"Because it's far too simple," Fredericka retorted.

Angela raised an eyebrow. "What's simple about a rating sys-tem? And, anyway, what's wrong with simplicity?"

Fredericka shrugged. "It's the way they do it on television real-ity shows—the dancing shows—that sort of thing. Or that ghastly song competition, where they give points to trashy music. No thank you."

Roz intervened. "I think we get a clear enough idea of people's feelings, even without an actual rating. But who liked this book? Just a general response—no out-of-tens."

Hands went up. Angela hesitated, then decided that she had enjoyed the book after all. Perhaps she had enjoyed *not* reading it, thought Isabel, and she smiled at the thought. But then she cor-rected herself: She did not know for certain that Angela had not read the book, and she should not simply rely on Roz's accusation to that effect. And, by a stretch of the imagination, there were per-fectly legitimate reasons for not liking a book, even if one had not read it. One could dislike a book based on the report of others— on the basis of the book's reputation among people whose views one respected. Isabel could think of several books that she dis-liked because she had a good idea of what was in them. That was a defensible position, she thought. It was not all that different from disliking a person you had never met, but who had been shown to be grossly offensive; there was good reason for your dislike, even if your paths had never crossed. That was a concomitant of being a public figure: You could be disliked by legions, few of whom would ever have met you personally.

The discussion of the book continued for half an hour or so. Then Roz rose to make tea, and the members chatted among themselves. Isabel felt slightly excluded, as there was some dis-cussion of a local man she did not know but whose doings were the subject of local scandal. He had built a garage extension without getting planning permission from the city council. "It should be razed to the ground," Virginia said, adding "at his expense, of course." Gemma, unsurprisingly, had agreed with that, but Angela said that planning requirements were so stringent that it was perfectly understandable if people ended up building unauthorised extensions. Virginia remarked that if that view were generally held, then life in society would become all but impossible. "Remember your Hobbes," she said pointedly, shaking a finger at Angela in mock reproach. They really don't like one another, thought Isabel.

Roz returned with a large tea tray. Once she had poured everybody a cup, she raised the question of membership. "One of you has asked me in confidence," she began, "whether we might open membership to men. Just a few men," she added quickly. "And the right sort of men, of course."

Virginia burst out laughing. "The right sort of men? Are you serious, Roz? Nobody talks about the right sort of *anybody* these days. The zeitgeist is dead set against that sort of non-inclusive language."

Roz defended herself. "I don't care what the zeitgeist says. There are some men who are clearly not the right sort. You know that as well as I do, Virginia."

Virginia glared at her. "Do I? Perhaps you could enlighten me, Roz. What do I know about the right sort of men?"

Roz looked up at the ceiling. She spoke now as if explaining an elementary truth to somebody who might have difficulty in grasping it.

"Overbearing men," she said. "Men who won't let anybody else have their say. Pushy men. You know the sort."

"Alpha males?" suggested Fredericka.

"Precisely," said Roz. "You know what they're like. They'd inhibit our discussion because they'd behave as if their views carried more weight than ours."

Gemma looked interested. "I'm not sure that I know any alpha males. Or at least I'm not sure that I would know how to recognise them."

"Oh, you'll have encountered them all right," said Virginia. "They will be the men who have taken the things that might otherwise have come to you—the opportunities, the encouragement, the praise. You may not have realised at the time that they were alpha males, but that's what they would have been."

Isabel found herself wondering about Virginia's husband. Roz had said that he was the dullest of men, and so he would hardly be an alpha male. Was there such a thing as a beta male? That, perhaps, was not quite the right term, because the term *beta* was used to describe a prototype of something that was still being developed, and one could hardly apply it to men. Perhaps *omega male* was a better description of dull men, as that was at the other end of the Greek alphabet from *alpha*. For a moment, she pictured Virginia's husband in his domestic setting, wearing carpet slippers, perhaps, and a beige-coloured sweater with faux-leather buttons up the front. He would be sitting in an armchair reading the *Edinburgh Evening News* impassively until he put down the paper with a sigh and began to stare into space, or watch football, which was much the same thing, Isabel thought. Or he would be in his garage, painstakingly working on a home carpentry project—a three-legged stool—that will have occupied him for at least several weeks, and that would never be stable enough to sit upon. Roz was right, she thought: Virginia's husband was very dull.

She imagined him walking the dog in Morningside, and the dog would be a very plain animal indeed—a dispirited-looking creature of unidentifiable breed—neither large nor small, just immensely dull: a defeated dog. That was Virginia's omega-male husband—poor woman. Of course, he would be happy enough, her dull man in his cardigan, because he would have no idea of what he was missing. There would be no passion there, no despair over the state of the world, no enthusiasm. He would not be open to anything new and would remain quiet about the great issues of the day, voting for the least offensive, the least radical option, desperate to avoid rocking any of the boats in which he might find himself. His life would run narrowly and correctly to the grave. How many women were married to men like that, and secretly longed for some spark that would ignite their lives?

But then she thought, who am I to disparage such people? The world *needed* men like Virginia's husband, because they uncomplainingly did what they had to do. Not much happened to them, but they plodded away, going into their offices or factories every day, week upon week, month upon month, year upon year, while more adventurous people diverted themselves with interesting, challenging things. We should not condescend to such people, she reminded herself. They were the bedrock of any society. If she ever met him, perhaps she should go up to him and whisper, "Well done! It's people like you who keep us going! Thank you!" And he would look at her in puzzlement, but she would be able to see that he was pleased because nobody else would ever have said something like that to him. And he would respond with, "Do you really think so?" And she would reply, "Yes, I do. And don't listen to anybody who tells you that you're dull." Of course, that might not be quite the right thing to say, but still . . .

SHE WALKED BACK HOME after the book group ended. She did not have far to go—no more than a few blocks of quiet houses tucked up for the night in their leafy gardens. Summer evenings in Scotland were long ones: Edinburgh, at fifty-six degrees latitude, was still bathed in an attenuated, lambent light, gentle and failing, but still there. A small group of students, three girls and a boy, were walking in the same direction as Isabel, but more slowly, and she overtook them. They moved aside politely to let her pass, and she said, "Good evening." The boy smiled and said "Good evening" in return, but once Isabel was some distance away, she heard sniggering. One of the girls intoned "Good evening" in exaggerated tones, and Isabel was unsure whether the mockery was directed at her or at the boy, who might be being accused by his companions of good manners. She almost turned to send a glance in their direction, but stopped herself. They were young—nineteen, perhaps—and when you are nineteen it's just you, really, and nobody else matters very much. They would not be nineteen for ever, but for the time being they should be allowed as much self-absorption as they needed.

She paused at her gate, and looked up at the façade of her house, set back from the shrubbery that dominated the front garden. It had been built in the late eighteen-eighties, with the reddish-pink stone from one of the quarries that had been used for the building of the southern suburbs of the city. The land here, although less than two miles from the castle, at the heart of the city, had been farmyard until a speculative builder had acquired it. This now forgotten developer had conceived of houses for a certain sort of person, and had not been embarrassed to specify in the original title deeds that the house, and those around it, were to be exclusively for "bank managers and above." Isabel had hooted with laughter when her lawyers had drawn her attention to the unenforceable condition. "Such complete confidence," she said. "Even in Scotland, where school-children read Burns's 'A Man's a Man for a' That'? Yes, but . . ." She sighed. "Such a pity."

"A pity?" asked the lawyer.

"For all those who weren't quite bank managers—for those who were at the bottom of the heap."

The lawyer agreed. "Social stratification is an absurd thing," he said.

"And yet," mused Isabel, "can you name one society—just one—where it doesn't exist?"

The lawyer thought. "The United States?"

Isabel shook her head. "The Americans have a class system—it's just that they don't like to admit to it. Money determines where you are—and, to an extent, which college you went to. You buy your way into a particular level of society when you pay your tuition fees." She paused. "And then geography enforces it. Not everybody can live in Santa Barbara or the Hamptons."

The lawyer tried again. "Communist countries? The Soviet Union—when it was still in business?"

Isabel looked at him in astonishment. "Are you serious? Class was inherited there, just as it could be everywhere else, the only difference being that in Soviet Russia it was immutable: If your origins were bourgeois you were at a considerable disadvantage—all your life. And what about the *nomenklatura*? If you were a high-ranking Party official, regular access to caviar was assured. Just as it was to smoked salmon, lobster and Scotch whisky. No, you'll have to think again, I'm afraid."

He made a last attempt. "Australia?"

Isabel considered this. There was an egalitarianism to Australian society that had always appealed to her, but for a long time it had major limitations: Not everybody was equal. There had been many who were altogether excluded. But at least they were doing something to acknowledge and make up for that. So, she said, "To an extent, yes."

Now she opened the gate and began to make her way up the

path to the front door. There were no lights in the windows, but Jamie, she imagined, would be in the music room at the back of the house. There was Dawn, of course—she suddenly remembered her—but her room, on its attic floor, was also at the back. She did not want to think about Dawn—her life was quite complicated enough without adding to it any concerns about her strange tenant.

There was a movement, barely perceptible in the rhododendrons on one side of the path. It was nothing much—perhaps no more than a slight stirring of the sort that a breeze might cause—but then she heard a rustling noise, as of leaves being disturbed in the undergrowth. Like the movement, it was brief and was followed by silence. She stopped, and gazed into the dark space beneath the plant's spreading foliage.

"Brother Fox?"

Her voice a whisper. Somewhere in the distance, a siren sounded for a second or two, a faint whistle of emergency.

"Brother Fox?"

What do I expect? An answer?

She moved very gingerly towards the plant and lowered herself to her haunches. He would take fright, she thought; this was not the way to gain the confidence of a fox: Putting distance between them would be a surer sign of pacific intention. And who could blame him for being wary, given the long war between our species and his; given the atrocities we had visited on his kind? But surely, she told herself, he knows by now that I am no threat to him—that I am a non-combatant in that war.

Her eyes accustomed themselves to the relative darkness. Now she could make out his shape against the background of leaf and branch; the head, the ears, the curve of the spine, the long sweep of the tail. And the eyes, too, for a shard of light from somewhere, one of the streetlights perhaps, was reflected in a small, dark well.

He moved his head, and she saw him more clearly now. He was staring at her. He could have turned tail and slunk away, but he did not. He took a hesitant step forward, and she thought for a moment that he might come out to meet her; that she might extend a hand and he would nuzzle at it, just as a dog might do.

"Oh, my darling," she whispered. "My darling friend."

He looked at her inquisitively, as if awaiting her next move. But she had nothing to offer him. She thought of the fridge in the kitchen and its contents. There was half a Melton Mowbray pie, which he would adore, because what fox would not like pork? But if she went inside to fetch it, he would almost certainly be away by the time she returned. And even now, he was beginning to move again. He had to leave—the night was just starting for him, there was so much else for him to do.

She stood up again, because she had been uncomfortable crouching down. There was a further rustling sound, and he was gone.

JAMIE HAD DECIDED on an early night and was already in bed by the time she returned. He had switched off his bedside light but had left hers on. His clothes were draped across the chair on his side of the room—his favourite shirt, a Bengal stripe from Thomas Pink; his olive chinos, loved so much that they were now almost threadbare and would have to be replaced soon; the bamboo socks that he said were cooler than wool and more sustainable. The distress signals from the planet were getting through, Isabel had remarked, when men were beginning to insist on sustainable socks. She glanced at their bed, at his head upon the pillow, at his bare shoulders, for it was a warm night and he had never liked pyjamas. He is mine, she thought; he is the centre of my world, mine.

He had not yet gone to sleep, although his voice, when he spoke, was drowsy.

"The book group," he muttered.

"Interesting," she said.

He moved his head on the pillow. "I did nothing much." He was on the verges of sleep, and his words faded away.

"You can go back to sleep," said Isabel, crossing the room. "We can talk tomorrow."

He took a little while to respond, and she thought he might have drifted off. But he had not. "I wasn't asleep yet. Tell me about it."

Isabel sat down on the edge of the bed. She reached out and took his hand. He felt so warm; was that because she was cold, having just some in from outside?

"I saw Brother Fox," she said.

"Under the rhododendrons?" asked Jamie.

"Yes. He looked at me. I thought he was coming out to say hello."

"He loves you," said Jamie. "He told me so himself. He said: *I don't trust you, but I like the woman.* Those were his exact words."

She laughed. "Flatterer."

"No, I'm not making it up. Foxes are good judges of character. You can't fool a fox." He turned his head on the pillow to look directly at her. "What were they like—the book-group ladies?"

Isabel thought for a few moments about how she might answer the question. The meeting had been more or less as she imagined it might be. "I was forewarned," she replied. "They don't like one another. That's the basic problem."

Jamie smiled. "Then what's the point?"

"I'm inclined to agree," said Isabel.

"I don't see what you can do," said Jamie.

"I don't either," sighed Isabel.

"Tell her that," Jamie said. "Just tell this Roz person that you can't wave a magic wand and make everything better."

She stood up and began to prepare for bed. She opened a curtain. She liked the room not to be entirely dark, a legacy of childhood fears. The last of the evening glow had faded, and there was a pale, almost full moon, suspended in the sky like a giant night-light.

"Tell her tomorrow," said Jamie, his voice once again drowsy. "Tell her that you can't do anything."

"I shall," said Isabel.

"Promise?"

"No," she said. "Or, maybe. Possibly."

She was tired too, just as he was. But in her mind she heard the line about promises and sleep. Who was it who had promises to keep and miles to go before he slept? Yes, it was Robert Frost. He had said that, in that poem about snow and his little horse, and woods of uncertain ownership.

Jamie's breathing became deeper and more regular. Sleep, she thought, our nightly adventure. She wondered about his dreams and whether she featured in them. He had never said anything about that, and, for her own part, she was not sure he featured in hers. Dreams were parallel, private lives, and those with whom one spent the day could well be excluded from them.

She puzzled over that for a few minutes, and then her thoughts drifted to the events earlier in the evening. Now she pictured the members of the book club sitting in a circle. She saw herself addressing them, their doleful eyes fixed on her. *You are a most unedifying group of people*, she might say. *You should be ashamed of yourselves.*

They stared back at her, each a wraith that slowly disappeared as sleep embraced her. The image of Roz came to her, looking at her pleadingly. "You have to help us," she said. "You have to."

She resisted. "Why? Why ask me to do this for you?"

Roz answered as if it was completely obvious. "Because that's what you do, isn't it? You help people." And then, after a short pause, and almost as an accusation, "It's your job, I believe."

It seemed to Isabel to be grossly unfair that she should shoulder the burdens of so many other people—Dawn, Roz and her squabbling cohort, Gordon, Cat, Eddie, Professor Lettuce, even Brother Fox—who was most undemanding when compared with the others. Why did people expect her to sort out all these things? *I am not a one-woman United Nations . . .*

John Donne . . . John Donne. *No woman is an island . . .* The change in gender sounded quite natural now: It was about time that the great statements were amended. *No woman is an island . . . If a clod be washed away by the sea, Europe is the less . . . Any man's death diminishes me . . .* But clods *were* being washed away by our rising seas, thought Isabel, and we are diminished as a result. We might remember Canute and the tide, she thought . . .

"I can't," Isabel whispered. She was imagining herself saying this, but she spoke it out loud. But not enough to wake Jamie.

CHAPTER ELEVEN

ISABEL SAT IN HER OFFICE, contemplating the in-tray on her desk. A consequence of thinking of other things, she told herself, was plain to see. An in-tray was a barometer, revealing the level of attention one gave to things that needed to be done. And just as one ignored the barometer at one's peril, so too did overflowing in-trays presage looming angst.

It was not that Isabel was overworked: Her editorial job was not unduly onerous, and could be performed easily enough by one person. The problem, though, was the deadlines that marked out the stages by which particular steps must be taken. Manuscripts sent in by their authors had to be submitted to members of the editorial board—a collection of helpful readers with expertise in the journal's main areas of concern. Their comments, ranging from minor suggestions to proposals for extensive rewrites, had to be sent back to the authors, some of whom might object to what they saw as unwarranted interference. That required tact and occasional firmness, but, most of all, it needed time.

Then there was the copy-editing, a task farmed out to free-lancers, who would return the manuscript adorned with directions to the typesetters. After that came proofs, of which several sets were currently sitting accusingly on her desk. These were dispatched to the author and a proof-reader, as well as being read by herself. Finally, everything would be sent to the printer to allow the presses to roll. That process—the printing of the pages— happened at a time agreed with the printer, and if there was editorial delay, the slot could be lost to other clients. As all printers knew, every client's order was urgent and could not be delayed.

So now, as she sat at her desk that morning, Isabel knew that she would simply have to tackle the backlog of work head-on if the schedule for the next issue of the *Review* was not to be delayed. She had been putting it off over the last few days, but now the wells of denial had run dry and she would have to begin. She picked up a manuscript that had completed the review process and was ready for the next stage. "Responsibility for corporate wrongdoing," read the title, followed by a sub-title that neatly revealed the author's position: "How to get directors into jail without passing Go." At least retribution was accompanied here by humour, Isabel thought. Her eye ran to the first footnote, in which the author acknowledged indebtedness. At the foot of the usual acknowledgements of the assistance of various institutions came the poignant line *In memory of Aunt Norah, a victim of negligence.* For some reason, Isabel thought: run over. It would have been a small tragedy in the scale of things, but a big one for the late Aunt Norah, and one should not make light of such things, but she wondered how it had happened. She thought, again for no particular reason, of a tram. There had recently been a near miss between an Edinburgh tram and a pedestrian; had that been Aunt Norah's misfortune? The unfortunate lines came to her: "Oh look Mama, what is that there?/That looks like strawberry jam?/Hush, hush, my dear, it's poor Papa/Run over by a tram." She stopped herself. The mind could be uncharitable, indeed cruel.

She came back to the paper. There was often a reason why people did the work they did—a reason in personal biography—and the spur behind the quest for corporate accountability in this case was an obvious one. Her smile flickered and then faded as she began the task of preparing the manuscript for the copy-editor.

And then Grace knocked at the door, waited a second or two, and came in. She bore a tray on which a pot of coffee, a jug of hot milk, and two cups were placed.

"I know you're busy," said Grace, putting the tray down on the table beside Isabel's desk. "I told her that you wouldn't want to be disturbed, but she insisted. I've put on an extra cup for her."

Isabel sighed. "And she is?"

Grace tried to remember. "Gloria Something. I didn't catch the name. She's a redhead."

Isabel frowned. "And did she say why she wanted to see me?"

"I asked her," replied Grace. "I asked her twice, and she said that she'd prefer not to say. She wouldn't go away."

"Oh well, I suppose I'll have to see her. I'm very busy, though . . ."

"I told her that," said Grace. "I said that you were up to your eyes." She pointed to the in-tray. "Show her that."

Isabel asked Grace to bring her visitor in. She put aside the manuscript she had been working on and made a quick effort to tidy her desk: Grace had already looked disapprovingly at the clutter and she did not want this uninvited caller to do the same.

Isabel was fairly tall herself, but Gloria was a good few inches taller. She was a young woman, probably in her early twenties, Isabel guessed; a redhead, as Grace had announced; and dressed casually in jeans and an olive-green top. There was a certain elegance in her clothing and her manner—and a poise that Isabel recognised as typical of an expensively educated postgraduate student.

"I'm Gloria MacFarlane," she announced, stepping forward to shake Isabel's hand. "We haven't met."

"No," said Isabel. "I don't think we have." *MacFarlane?* The name was familiar; she had seen it recently, but could not recall where. *MacFarlane?* Then it came back to her: This was Lettuce's assistant.

She invited Gloria to sit down.

"I know you're busy," Gloria said. "Your . . ." She gestured towards the door behind her.

"Grace," said Isabel.

"Yes, Grace told me that you were snowed under with work."

Isabel gestured to the papers on her desk—to the piled-up in-tray. "You know how it is," she said apologetically. "I try to keep on top of things."

Gloria smiled. "I don't want to take up too much of your time, but I really wanted to speak to you about something that's . . ." She paused. "Something that's worrying me."

Isabel nodded. "I saw your name on a grant proposal," she said. "I take it that's you."

"Yes," said Gloria. "I'm Professor Lettuce's assistant. I'm actually a postgraduate student—I'm doing a PhD but I have this small job helping him—and Dr. Dove."

Isabel let her continue.

"Professor Lettuce has been very helpful to me," said Gloria. "In all sorts of ways. He asked me to index a volume of essays he was putting together. And Christopher has also done a lot. I'm very grateful to them."

Isabel inclined her head. "It's so important to have senior people who'll give you a helping hand," she said. "I had a lot of help when I was starting off."

"Yes. Professor Lettuce has helped get a paper I wrote

accepted for publication in *The Philosophical Quarterly*. It comes out next year."

Isabel offered her congratulations. "Your first publication, I take it?"

Gloria beamed with pleasure. "Yes. I know it won't seem all that much to somebody like you, but it's important for me."

"Of course it is."

Gloria's hands were clasped together as she spoke. "You said that you saw the proposal that Professor Lettuce put to the Matheson Trust?"

Isabel said that she had seen it. She said nothing about the figures it contained. "Robert Lettuce is keen for me to publish the papers from the conference. You know that, don't you?"

"Yes," said Gloria. "I was pleased by that. It's a pity when these conferences take place and then nobody hears anything more of the papers. It's such a waste."

"I agree," said Isabel patiently. She wondered when Gloria would get to the point. There was tension in the air, and she was now fairly sure what its focus would be.

Gloria fixed Isabel with a searching gaze. "You saw the budget?" she asked.

"I did."

"You saw the amount that was going to be paid to various people?"

Isabel waited a moment. Her reply was measured. "Yes, I did see that."

Gloria waited for her to say something more, but Isabel was silent.

"It's a lot of money," Gloria said eventually. "The overall budget is high, anyway, but the amount that is going in fees seems . . . well, it seems excessive, in my opinion." She looked at Isabel apologetically—as if she had overstepped some mark. After all, who was she, a person on the lowest rung of the academic ladder, to question the proposals of somebody as senior as Professor Lettuce?

Isabel felt sorry for Gloria. It was now clear to her that this was a whistleblowing visit, and she felt a rush of sympathy for this young woman. She leaned forward at her desk. "Gloria, listen, I agree with you one hundred per cent. That budget is frankly ridiculous."

Gloria's relief was evident. "Oh, thank you for saying that. I was worried that I was sticking my nose into matters that don't concern me. I was worried that you would consider it a bit of a cheek."

Isabel reassured her that there was no danger of that. But then she went on to raise the issue of the payment to Gloria herself. "I noticed that there was to be a large payment to you," she said. "It's not just Professor Lettuce and Dr. Christopher Dove—you profit too. Eight thousand pounds, I seem to recall."

Gloria winced. "I never asked for that," she blurted out. "I'd never ask for that much. I had no idea."

Isabel watched her. Gloria's discomfort, and the outrage she now showed, struck her as being entirely genuine. She liked this young woman—she was telling the truth, she thought. "Perhaps you'd like to tell me what happened," Isabel suggested. "What exactly did Professor Lettuce say to you about this payment?"

Gloria was fiddling with a handkerchief as she spoke. She was clearly under considerable strain.

"You don't have to worry about me," said Isabel, "I'm on your side on this. And anything you say to me I promise to keep confidential. You have no need to worry."

"Those figures are imaginary," Gloria blurted out. "Nobody's getting anything near that amount. I'm going to get two hundred pounds for my work, and Professor Lettuce says that he's going to get nothing at all. He's not doing this for the money."

Isabel struggled to contain her surprise. "So you're saying that he's not claiming twenty thousand pounds?"

"No. That's . . . that's all theoretical."

"You've lost me," said Isabel. "Twenty thousand pounds is twenty thousand pounds—unless he's not going to get any of it."

"He won't," said Gloria. "Not a penny, apparently." She paused. "There's something going on. That's why I decided to come and see you."

Isabel held up a hand. "Let's have something to drink. Tell me all about it over a cup of coffee."

She reached for the coffee pot and poured a cup for Gloria, and one for herself.

Gloria wrinkled her nose. "I adore the smell of coffee," she said. "It takes me back to when I was a student in Siena. I did a six-month exchange there as part of my first degree. There was a coffee bar next door to the student hall I was staying in. The smell drifted through my window when I opened it. They served squares of pizza on greaseproof paper first thing in the morning. Workmen went in and washed these squares down with red wine. At seven a.m."

"Smells are so evocative," said Isabel. "Gauloises cigarettes: France. Cinnamon buns: America. Thyme: Greece."

"And Scotland?" asked Gloria.

Isabel looked thoughtful. That depended. In Gloria's voice she detected a note of the west of Scotland, even the Highlands. "Seaweed?" she suggested. "Which is a sort of iodine smell, isn't it?"

Gloria smiled. "I spent part of my childhood in the Western Highlands," she said.

"That possibility crossed my mind," said Isabel.

"I can't go back there," Gloria went on. "I cry too much."

Isabel waited. "Nostalgia?"

"Yes. Nostalgia. Because everything was simpler then—far simpler."

Isabel knew exactly what she meant. "Please tell me about the grant application. You were going to explain."

"I would do anything for Professor Lettuce," Gloria began.

Isabel had not intended to say anything, but it slipped out. "I wouldn't."

Gloria looked up in surprise. "But Professor Lettuce . . ."

Isabel did not allow her to finish. "I'm sorry," she said quickly. "I didn't mean to sound like that. I suppose it's just that I would never give anybody *complete* support. I'd always want to be able to dissent."

Gloria looked relieved. "I thought you were going to say you didn't like him."

Isabel was impassive. "Those payments?" she prompted.

"When Professor Lettuce first showed them to me," she said, "I was completely astonished—especially over the eight thousand for me. But before I could say anything, he laughed and said that they were just figures on paper and the real payment would be much smaller. He said that he was sorry to disappoint me, but there was an accounting issue that had to be put right, and that this was the way the trust wanted to do it.

"I suppose I looked suspicious, because he went on quickly to ask me if I could keep a confidence. He said that there was nothing illegal about what was going on and that it was being done to protect the chairman of the trust from embarrassment. He was being helpful in supporting the conference, and in return we should do something for him."

"I think I continued to look doubtful because he was a bit reluctant to explain further, but eventually he did. He said that

Marcus Grant had made a bad mistake in investing some of the trust funds in a company that the other trustees had advised him to avoid. He was convinced that it would do well, but it turned out that it had encountered a serious problem—the company had been hit by a tax bill that it should have avoided. As a result, it declared no dividend that year. That meant that trust income was down. He said that if the loss were to be disguised as grant payments, then the other trustees would be none the wiser. So rather than give that money to Professor Lettuce and Christopher Dove—and me, I suppose—it would simply be put back into the black hole that had appeared in the accounts."

Isabel took a deep breath. Surely this was dishonest, at best, and possibly even criminal. Gloria sensed her reservations, and went on, "Nobody's stealing anything, you know. All that is happening is that information is being withheld from the other trustees. Nobody is any the worse off. We don't get any money, of course, but we weren't really entitled to it. So, by pretending that we have received the grant—or our bit of it—we save Marcus Grant from being embarrassed by his bad choice of investment."

Isabel shook her head. "I don't like the sound of that at all," she said. "Who are the victims here? The other trustees, surely. They are effectively being hoodwinked. That may not be illegal—as far as I know, of course, and I may be mistaken—but it's definitely wrong. Professor Lettuce isn't profiting by it—I'll give him that—but he's party to a deception. It's flagrant dishonesty in my view."

Gloria sighed. "That's what I've decided," she said. "At first I agreed to it because I thought Professor Lettuce wouldn't approve of anything underhand, but then I started to think more about it and I realised that it was, as you say, a scheme intended to deceive others. And then I started to worry."

She looked at Isabel in mute appeal.

"You've done the right thing," Isabel reassured her. "You've decided not to be a part of it."

"But what do I do next? You're the only person I've told about this."

Isabel drew in her breath. The burden now fell upon her: She was older than Gloria and she was implicated because of her being part of the conference project. This was quite different from the book-club problem, where she was an outsider being drawn into a problem: She was part of this one.

She met Gloria's gaze. "I'll deal with this," she said. "You needn't worry."

"What will you do?"

"I'm not sure," said Isabel. "Sometimes solutions take some time to suggest themselves."

"You won't tell Professor Lettuce I came to see you?" asked Gloria.

"I won't," said Isabel. "I won't even mention you."

"I don't want him to be angry with me, you see. My job . . ."

"Of course, I understand. And you mustn't worry. All that I would say is that in future, you might perhaps be a little careful about Robert Lettuce. I don't want to discourage you too much— and he's clearly been very helpful to you. But there are some people who have—how shall we put it?—flaws. I'm not saying that they don't have good qualities—they do—but at the same time they may have fairly significant flaws. Professor Lettuce may be one of these. I'm not suggesting that he is; I'm merely raising the possibility that he may be."

Gloria sat back in her chair. "Will the conference take place, do you think?"

Isabel hesitated. It would have been an interesting meeting, and she would have enjoyed publishing the papers. But she doubted now whether there would be much enthusiasm on the part of Marcus Grant—particularly in view of his impending resignation from any involvement in the affairs of the Matheson Trust, which she was confident would shortly come. He would submit his resignation, she thought, after her conversation with him, which would be a frank one. And as for Professor Lettuce, she imagined that he would be withdrawing his application to the trust in its entirety after receiving a letter that Isabel proposed to write to him that evening, at the latest.

"I don't think that this conference will go ahead," said Isabel. "But here's an idea—we could hold a small conference ourselves—under the auspices of the *Review*. It would be on a much smaller scale, of course—just a day of meetings in one of the smaller venues at the university. But it could be worthwhile. Same subject, of course: the virtues and vices brought up to date."

Gloria smiled. "Can I help you with it?"

"Of course you can," said Isabel. "And the *Review* will pay you—in real money this time."

"Thank you."

"But not eight thousand pounds," Isabel added quickly. "Two hundred, perhaps."

"That'll be fine," said Gloria. "That's about right, I think." She swept her hair back from her forehead as she spoke. It was beautiful hair: russet in shade, not ginger, and it had a sheen to it that such hair can sometimes have. Isabel thought: If one had hair like that, would one feel the need to do *anything*? One might just sit all day and let people admire one's hair. Or brush it endlessly. And she remembered the russet-coloured shawl that Fredricka had worn at the book-group meeting. That would go so well with this Gloria's hair. It would create a symphony. There is still beauty in the world, thought Isabel—and that is a great consolation. There is hardship and mistrust and all the things that go with those, but there is still beauty.

"Smaller things—and smaller amounts—are almost always about right," said Isabel. I've coined an aphorism, she thought—not a particularly good one, but one that fitted the circumstances rather well. But was it true? She was not sure: largeness of spirit, generosity of gesture—these were usually better than their meaner equivalents. But then it occurred to her that aphorisms might not have to be true: A pithy observation might be wrong and still have an aphoristic quality to it. The essence of an aphorism was that it made a general observation within a very small compass. If the observation were to be flawed, would that be a *false aphorism* or a *misleading aphorism?* She would have to think about that. But not now.

CHAPTER TWELVE

GLORIA MACFARLANE'S ARRIVAL had disrupted Isabel's work that morning but its overall effect was beneficial. After Gloria had left, the anxiety that Isabel had felt over the Lettuce affair faded away almost completely. What had happened was strange, but it made sense, and, moreover, the way out of a potentially awkward situation was now quite clear. She was relieved to discover that Professor Lettuce had not been involved in a criminal scheme to enrich himself. Although she did not have a great deal of time for Lettuce, she did not want him to be shamed or humiliated. Lettuce was pompous and irritating, but he was not in any way despicable, and Isabel even felt a sneaking fondness for his misguided ways. Without Lettuce, the world of academic philosophy would be, she thought, a great deal duller: Lettuce provided entertainment, as did Christopher Dove, who was a splendid pantomime villain, Isabel thought. She imagined Dove arriving to deliver a lecture and being greeted with hissing from the audience—the same audience reaction that always greets Captain Hook in *Peter Pan*, or the Ugly Sisters in *Cinderella*.

Her lighter mood enabled her to get through the day's work remarkably quickly. By three o'clock in the afternoon, the towering pile in the in-tray had more or less disappeared, and by five it was completely cleared. Grace had gone to collect the boys from school, and Isabel was now able to take over their dinner and bath-time. Charlie was full of stories from school: One of the girls had pulled the hair of another girl and had been made to sit by herself until she made a full apology. One of the boys had been sick over the teacher's shoes, and the stick insects that the class had been keeping in a small terrarium had all escaped and could not be found. Isabel listened to this with interest, as did Magnus who, not wishing to be upstaged by his older brother, reported that half his class had died before ten o'clock. Their lunch, he said, had been given to somebody else. Isabel received this news with appropriate solemnity and had then gently reminded Magnus that it was important not to tell lies, even if to do so was at times very tempting.

Charlie had administered his own warning. "You'll get lockjaw if you tell fibs," he had advised. "And your nose will grow longer. So you better watch out, Magnus."

Isabel was intrigued. Lockjaw must have been mentioned at school, as she had no recollection of mentioning it herself in the boys' hearing. It was a condition well suited to the childish imagination, with its threat of jaws clamped tight in agonising grimace.

"That's not true, Charlie," she said. "You mustn't tell lies, but that's nothing to do with lockjaw."

Charlie looked doubtful. "Or lightning," he said. "If you tell lies you get struck by lightning."

"No, that's not true either," said Isabel. And sighed. Childhood could be a dark and frightening time, with all these threats. As a young child she herself had believed that treading on the lines in the pavement would lead inexorably to an attack by bears. That there were no bears in Scotland was beside the point: Bears had ways of getting you anyway. And then there had been that copy of *Struwwelpeter* that a cousin had shown her when she was seven. She had read with horror of the Suckathumb Man, that wild-eyed figure with his great tailor's scissors who would cut off the thumbs of children who sucked their thumbs. The illustrations accompanying this salutary tale had been vivid: the blood a bright red, the terror in the victim's face unmistakeable. Generations of German children had been frightened by that book and it was still in print, she believed. Concealed in the horrifying stories were moral lessons, but that was not the way she wanted to teach Charlie and Magnus how to behave.

The boys were put to bed, and then Isabel went into the kitchen to prepare dinner. Jamie would be home late, he had said, as he was playing in an early-evening concert in Glasgow and would not get back to Haymarket Station until at least eight-thirty.

Isabel looked out the ingredients for a mushroom risotto, brought the arborio rice to the boil, and prepared the mushrooms. Then, with the pot tucked away in the oven, she sat down at the kitchen table and flicked through a music magazine that Jamie had left in the kitchen. The magazine was full of news of musicians who meant nothing to her, although here and there she saw a familiar name. An article about Arvo Pärt caught her attention, but it rapidly became too technical for Isabel to understand. Jamie had introduced her to Pärt's music, and she had developed a taste for it, but the musical analysis of Pärt's *tintinnabuli*, into which the article soon delved, was beyond her.

The key to it was that Pärt liked the sound of bells, and that a bell usually sounded a single note encased in harmonics. Isabel understood that, but further technicalities of chords and inversions escaped her. The article said that Pärt composed silences, that he set great store by the quiet on either side of the note; there was as much silence in his works as there was sound. She put the magazine down and gazed up at the ceiling. Surrounding silences were important in human speech just as they were in music, she thought: The silence that preceded a word could be laden with meaning, as could the silence that followed it.

She heard the doorbell ring, and it broke her chain of thought. She wondered whether it was Jamie, and that he had forgotten his key, but when she looked at her watch she saw that it was too early for him to have returned from Glasgow. She got up from the table and made her way through the hall.

Cat stood on the doorstep.

"I'd like to come in."

Isabel moved aside. "Of course." She sensed that something was wrong. Cat usually telephoned before dropping in; there had been no call.

They went into the kitchen.

"I'm making risotto," Isabel said. "There'll be enough for the three of us, if you've no other plans."

"Where's Jamie?" Cat asked.

Isabel explained that he was playing in an early concert in Glasgow. Cat half listened to this, but did not seem interested. "I can't stay for dinner," she said.

"Suit yourself," said Isabel. "I just thought that if you hadn't eaten . . ."

Cat spun round to face her. "Gordon's gone," she said.

Isabel caught her breath. There was a certain familiarity to this conversation; it was Gordon this time, but not long ago it had been Leo who had gone, and others before him. But Gordon, she felt, was different: Gordon had seemed so suitable. He had been talking about marrying Cat, after all, and that had only been a few days ago. What could possibly have caused his sudden departure?

Isabel invited Cat to sit down. She poured her a glass of white wine—the New Zealand white that Isabel liked and that she knew Cat enjoyed too. "Tell me what happened," she said.

"He left a note," said Cat. "He didn't even tell me to my face."

Isabel sighed. "When did this happen?"

"This morning," said Cat. "He got up early. He said he was going to go for a run. I stayed in bed. Then, when I went into the kitchen, there was a note on the table. Just like that."

Isabel made a sympathetic noise. "I'm so sorry, Cat. This is . . . well, it's awful. It is really awful." She paused. "What did he say in the note? Do you want to tell me?"

"He said that he didn't think it was going to work," said Cat. "He said that when you feel that way, it's best to make a clean break. He said that he hoped I didn't mind his leaving without telling me about it, but he said that he would find it too upsetting."

"And you're not meant to be upset?" said Isabel, a note of anger creeping into her voice.

"He said that he felt that neither of us owed the other anything. He said that it had been an important time in his life, but that ultimately it wasn't right—for either of us."

Isabel took a sip of wine. She sensed that she was on perilous ground. Cat did not take criticism well, and if she said anything that could be interpreted as questioning her judgement when it came to men, then the situation could quickly become fraught. So she was cautious. "It's possible that he just couldn't face commitment," she began. "I thought Gordon was very suitable, but some men are like that, you know. I'm not suggesting there was anything wrong with him, but they take fright and then . . ."

Cat cut her short. "I think that he heard something about me."

Isabel trod gently. "But what could he have heard?"

Cat was looking at her accusingly. "He might have heard that

I . . . well, that I have had a few boyfriends. He was odd about that, you see. I got the impression that he wanted to put me on a bit of a pedestal." She looked away. "Who doesn't have a romantic past these days? Everybody has relationships."

Isabel answered quickly. "You're right. The days of . . ." She almost said *chastity*, but stopped herself just in time, and said *uninvolvement* instead. Then she continued, "I imagine that the Temple of the Vestal Virgins would be hard put to recruit these days."

It was a light-hearted aside, of course, but Cat neither took the reference nor thought it amusing. She turned to face Isabel again. "You spoke to him a few days ago, didn't you?"

Isabel could see where this was leading. She struggled to remain calm. "I did. Yes, I spoke to him."

"And did you talk about me?" Cat pressed, her voice rising.

Isabel liked to tell the truth. She disliked lies, and found it inordinately hard to tell them. "Of course we spoke about you. Would you expect otherwise?"

Cat drew in her breath. "And what did you talk about?"

Isabel hesitated. Cat had no business interrogating her about a private conversation she had had with somebody else. Surely she understood that: It was a rule of everyday protocol, really—the same rule, applied at a much lower level, that prevents you from revealing what the president of the United States or the Pope says to you when you are admitted to a tête-à-tête. You don't say "The Pope told me that he can't stand . . ." and then give the name of one of the many people of whom one imagines the Pope must disapprove. So Isabel said, "It was a private chat. I wouldn't ask you what you said to one of your friends if you had a private chat with her. So, I really don't think you should ask me what I said to Gordon or what Gordon said to me."

It was a perfectly reasonable response, but also a perfectly wrong one in the particular circumstances.

"You must have told him about my previous boyfriends," Cat challenged. "Did you?"

Isabel gave an honest answer. "Not really. No, I wouldn't do that."

"So what did you talk about then?" snapped Cat.

There was a question of principle, Isabel thought. "I told you: It was a private conversation."

"Then I take it that you did talk about my love life."

It sounded a curiously old-fashioned expression, coming from Cat. But it was clear enough what Cat meant.

"Your love life?" Isabel decided to give in. "Actually, we talked about his relationship with you. It was that way round. He started the conversation, as it happened. He told me how much he appreciated you. He was quite frank with me that he was very much in love."

Cat was silent, caught, Isabel felt, between disbelief and surprise.

"And another thing," Isabel continued. "He made it clear he thought that you hadn't had many relationships before this one. He thinks of you as . . . well, as an innocent, so to speak. In a nice sense, of course."

Cat suddenly shook her head. "I find this very difficult to believe. Sorry, but I do."

Isabel was taken aback by the directness of Cat's response. Cat was her niece, and even if there was a relatively small age gap between them, you did not expect a close relative to accuse you of lying. She gave Cat a reproachful look. "Are you saying that I'm making this up?"

Cat avoided her gaze. She looked uncomfortable, but she

seemed to be sticking to her insinuation. "I think you probably said something about me that has put him off. That's the only conclusion I can reach." She paused. "I'm sorry if you don't like that, but it's the way I feel. I think you've put him off."

Isabel felt her heart beat more vigorously. Her neck felt warm. This was what it was like to be disbelieved. This is how the innocent must feel when accused of a crime they have not committed.

"You're completely wrong," she said. "I would never lie to you, Cat. Surely you know that?"

Cat had risen to her feet. "I'm going," she said.

"I don't want us to part on these terms," said Isabel. "Please, Cat. Please don't leave things like this."

Cat hesitated, but only briefly. "Sorry," she said. "I really have to go."

Isabel made a final effort. She reached out and took Cat's arm, but she was quickly shrugged off. She did not follow Cat to the front door, but left her to let herself out. Then she returned to the kitchen and sat down at the table again. The evening had started so differently, with her pleasure over the resolution of the Lettuce affair. But the effect of that was to be short-lived: Now she felt a flat despair embrace her. Cat was mercurial—she always had been—but this was a serious breach, and she wondered whether their relationship would weather it. It would, she decided: Cat had been in a huff before, but that did not make the experience any more bearable. She wanted Jamie to return; she wanted a shoulder to cry on, and there was no shoulder on which she would more readily and therapeutically cry than his.

CHAPTER THIRTEEN

Jamie did not get home until shortly before midnight, by which time Isabel had gone to bed. He had telephoned from Glasgow after the concert to say that he had met a friend from the Conservatoire, Alastair Brown, who had invited him to go out for a drink. Would she mind if he was late? She wanted to say that she would. She was about to say that she was sitting in the kitchen, by herself, thinking of how problematic her life had suddenly become, and wanting nothing more than for him to put his arms about her and comfort her. She could easily have said that, and he would have responded accordingly, but she did not.

"Of course," she said. "So what's Alastair doing?"

She was not really interested in his answer. Alastair was always doing something peculiar, in her opinion. The last time that Jamie had mentioned him, he had acquired an Irish wolfhound from a tuba player whose wife had thrown both him and the dog out of the flat. Alastair had come to the rescue, but the dog had been stolen from under his nose by a taxi driver who stopped his cab, snatched the dog, and disappeared before Alastair could do anything but remonstrate.

"You wouldn't believe half the things that happen to Alastair," Jamie had said, when he told Isabel about this.

And now Alastair had bought a boat, Jamie said. The boat was in the garage of his house in Bearsden and he was restoring it. He wanted to show Jamie the progress that he had made with that, and would run him to the station afterwards. Was that all right with Isabel?

"Isabel? Are you still there?"

She struggled not to cry. "Yes, I am. I was thinking."

Jamie laughed. "Nothing unusual there. Are you sure you don't mind if I go round to Alastair's place?"

"I don't mind." She did. "But don't miss the last train."

"That's very late. I'll be back by midnight. Promise." He paused. "Is Dawn in, or is she working?"

Isabel had not thought about Dawn. They rarely saw her, and in some respects she was the perfect guest: invisible and inaudible, even if she kept her door locked, which worried Grace, in particular, and is something that would have to be addressed at some time or another. But not now, with Cat and the book group and Lettuce all weighing on her mind.

"I don't know," said Isabel. "I haven't seen her."

"Are you sure everything's okay?"

She reassured him that it was, and they rang off. She took the risotto out of the oven and ate a portion, saving the rest for Jamie's lunch the following day. She looked at her watch. She could always go back into her study and do some work, but the thought did not appeal. She could watch television, which was something she very rarely did and which seemed a particularly unattractive prospect at that moment. Television was noise, and people being confrontational; it was people shooting one another or finding bodies, or dancing about on the stage in glittery costumes. Television was a cleverly packaged anodyne, Huxley's soma in some respects, but it was not what she needed.

She would do some work in her study and then, later on, would make herself a cup of warm milk and honey. She would take that up to bed with her, along with a book. She would read something that went with milk and honey—perhaps Barbara Pym or even Eliot's *Four Quartets*, which she sometimes turned to when she wanted something calm and measured. There was nothing wrong with going to bed early with milk and honey and *Four Quartets*: There was nothing to be ashamed about in that. The thought made her smile, which helped slightly. *What did you do?* I went to bed with a cup of warm milk and read *Four Quartets*. *Why did you do that?* Because there are times when the world is frankly too much, and Eliot's voice has this particular feel to it. *You mean soporific?* No, I don't mean that. I can't explain it really; there are times when what you just feel like doing is exactly the right thing to do.

She had gone upstairs and checked on the boys, who were sleeping soundly in their shared bedroom, surrounded by the images and things of boyhood: their pillows with spaceships printed on them, their half-finished wooden rail-track snaking away under a bed, their plastic superheroes frozen in mid-drama on the shelf.

She still wanted to cry, or half wanted, she thought. There was a state of mind that was made up of half-wants, Isabel felt; it was a useful concept to cover those situations where we were on the verge of doing something, but were dissuaded from doing it or decided ourselves to do otherwise. But it would be difficult to cry and drink hot milk and honey at the same time, and so she got into bed, sipped the hot milk, and felt immediately better. She was tired—perhaps more tired than she realised. Many women, she thought, are tired—tired to the bone, because they have to keep so much going. Her life was so much easier than the lives of many others—she never forgot that—but she might still be allowed to be tired because she had all these issues to deal with.

She felt drowsy. She took a last sip of milk. *Four Quartets* lay unopened. She switched off the light and lay there in the darkness, her tiredness about her like a blanket. Half awake, half asleep, she heard footsteps on the landing outside the bedroom door. The boys, she told herself; sometimes they woke up and padded through to their parents' room for comfort. But this was different. Another footstep. She thought: Dawn. It's just Dawn coming home after one of her shifts at the hospital. But then she imagined that she heard a voice. Or was it something else? Sleep was winning the battle now and she was drifting. It was nothing to worry about: I can't worry about everything; I have to let things be. The noise stopped. The footsteps, if they had been footsteps, had faded. There was nothing now, other than the tiny, almost inaudible sounds that any house makes at night, for houses breathed, in their particular, creaking way, and one could hear them if one stayed quite still and listened.

She was only dimly aware of Jamie's return, half surfacing from sleep, registering that his bedside light was on. She struggled to say something, but she had no clear idea of what it was that she wanted to say, and the muttered words, unintelligible anyway, died upon her lips. She did not hear him say, "Go back to sleep, Isabel," nor did she feel his light kiss upon her cheek, and then it was morning, and she heard a gull mewing as it glided past the house on the noisy business that seabirds pursue when they wander inland. Jamie was already dressed and standing at her side of the bed, holding out a cup of tea.

"You were out for the count. You must have been tired."

She looked up at him, and felt a sudden rush of gratitude. Its strength and unexpectedness surprised her. I'm so fortunate, she thought, and, like everybody else, for most of the time I take what I have for granted. At the heart of her good fortune, she realised. was the simple fact of being alive: When you looked at where we were, in our brief moment, in a vast universe of billions of stars, when you did that and then reflected on the tiny, passing spark that is our lifetime, then how could you feel anything but immensely grateful for consciousness—irrespective of what your circumstances were.

Jamie smiled at her. "You didn't make much sense when I came in."

She reached out for the cup of tea. "I'm sure I didn't."

She took a sip. "And Glasgow? Alastair?"

Jamie sat down on the edge of the bed. "He showed me his boat. He went on and on about it. He wants to sail to St. Kilda one day."

Isabel said that she thought that most people in Scotland who had boats wanted to get to St. Kilda at some point. Few managed it.

"No," said Jamie. "It's not easy. You can only land if the wind is in a certain direction, and it very rarely is. Alastair will never get to St. Kilda. His boat looks far too decrepit. It's going to take him years to get it into seaworthy condition. Poor Alastair." He paused. "What happened here? Anything?"

"Nothing." She looked at her watch. "Has Grace walked the boys to school?"

"She has. I offered, but she arrived early and wanted to do it. I told her you were sleeping in."

Isabel finished her tea, which was already lukewarm. Jamie said, "I'm sorry, the tea's probably gone cold. I can make you another cup."

She shook her head. "I was reading about another thing we shouldn't do—drink very hot liquids. Apparently it raises the risk of oesophageal cancer."

Jamie stood up and stretched. "Virtually everything's risky," he said. "Including life."

"Yes, but . . ."

Jamie interrupted her. "Grace was a bit preoccupied this morning. You can always tell when something's biting her."

"Yes, you can. What is it this time?"

Jamie lowered his voice as he pointed upstairs. "Her," he said. "Dawn."

Isabel sighed. "Grace doesn't approve. She's made that pretty clear. She wants her out."

"I know, but . . ."

Isabel sighed again. "We can't chuck the poor woman out just because Grace has taken against her. This is *our* house, after all."

Jamie said that he understood that, but Grace was almost a member of the family and if you were almost a member of the family you almost had certain rights.

"But what can we do?" Isabel asked. "Should we talk to Dawn? Should we explain that Grace is unhappy and say that much as we'd like to go on helping her, we feel that . . ."

Jamie interrupted her. "It's the locking of the door that's really got up Grace's nose," he said. "She says that it's an insult to her."

"An insult?"

"Yes, it implies that Dawn thinks that Grace might steal some of her stuff."

Isabel made a gesture of despair. "Oh, really, that's utterly ridiculous. Dawn probably just wants privacy. Who doesn't?"

"Yes," conceded Jamie. "Everybody wants privacy, but when you're staying with people, then I think I agree with Grace: You shouldn't lock your door."

That was right, thought Isabel; a guest's door should definitely not be locked. But she wondered whether what she and Jamie had said about everyone wanting privacy remained true in the age of social media. Privacy, she thought, might rapidly be becoming an outdated value, like modesty, viewed as almost quaint in the eyes of a generation used to revealing their lives in internet posts. That others, potentially millions of others, should know what one liked to have for breakfast, what music one listened to, what one thought about political or other causes was striking enough, but when such disclosures became more intimate, and included details of dreams and fantasies and friendships, then what room was left for privacy? And yet, Isabel told herself, perhaps it was healthier to be open about oneself; perhaps concern for privacy encouraged dark corners, dishonesty, even shame. Light was antiseptic in its properties, and if it were to be shone into our lives like this, then it might be beneficial rather than harmful. To have no secrets from others might be a sign of trust rather than of emotional promiscuity.

Isabel reached for her dressing gown as she got out of bed. "Is she in at the moment?"

Jamie shrugged. "I have no idea. She works those odd hours. She may be."

"Let's go up?"

Jamie looked doubtful. "Now?"

"Yes, let's go up and see whether her door's locked."

"And if it isn't?"

"Then, if she's in, we can talk to her. What do the psychologists say? Verbalisation precedes resolution."

Isabel had quoted that to Jamie before, and he thought it was, on the whole, true. But there were some situations when it was difficult to decide exactly what to put into words.

THEY MADE THEIR WAY up to the attic floor. As they reached the landing at the top of the last flight of stairs, they stopped and looked at one another. Jamie pointed to the door, and mouthed the word "closed." Isabel put a finger to her lips to discourage him, but he leaned forward and whispered, mischievously, "We're like a couple of ten-year-olds looking for a mystery." She did not reply, but took a step forward to try the door. She turned the handle gently. It was locked. She bent down and peered into the keyhole. Then she stood up and turned to face Jamie.

"The key's in the lock," she whispered. "On the other side."

He stooped to look, and nodded. She was right: The door had been locked from inside.

Isabel took a deep breath. "I've had enough," she whispered. "I'm going to knock."

Jamie looked alarmed. "And?" he whispered.

"I'll ask her why she feels she needs to lock herself in her room."

Jamie considered this. "What if . . ." He broke off.

"Yes?"

He gestured towards the door. "What if there's somebody in there with her?"

Isabel felt that this would make no difference.

"But they may want privacy," Jamie protested, his voice still barely audible.

"This is *our* house," Isabel said. "Ours. She's a guest." She was beginning to sympathise with Grace on this. If Grace resented Dawn's locking of her door because she felt that it revealed a lack of trust, then Isabel resented it because it suggested unfriendliness. If people invited you to stay in their house, then you should at least be friendly towards them. That was basic good manners.

She knocked at the door. Jamie drew in his breath. She looked at him expectantly.

There was no response.

"Dawn?" Isabel called out. "It's Isabel."

She knocked again.

Jamie pointed to the door. He had heard something.

Isabel waited. Then, after a minute or so, she signalled to Jamie that they should make their way back down the stairs. Once down on the lower landing, she closed behind her the door that led to the top flight.

"That was hardly a conspicuous success," Isabel said, her voice returning to its normal level.

"I heard something," said Jamie, fixing Isabel with an earnest look. "I'm really not imagining it. Somebody was in there."

"I had that feeling," Isabel said, adding, "although I didn't hear anything—or I don't think I did."

Jamie frowned. "I'm going to speak to her."

Isabel hesitated. "Are you sure you want to do that?"

He was. "I'm going to tell her that we find her behaviour unfriendly. And I'm going to ask her whether she's made any progress in finding somewhere permanent—or a bit more permanent—to live."

Isabel suggested that it might be easier for her to talk to Dawn—woman to woman—but Jamie was adamant. "No, I'll do it. Dawn is my problem. You've got a whole lot of issues to deal with."

She looked at him with affection. "You worry about me far too much. You mustn't, you know." But she did not want him to stop worrying about her; not really.

"I like to, though," he said. "I just do. That's all that I do."

It was an occasion for complete honesty. "Well, it's very nice to be worried about. It's reassuring, I suppose."

She thought of how lucky she was to have Jamie, and to experience moments such as this; that led her to think of Dawn, who had nobody, she reminded herself, unless, of course, there *had* been somebody in the room with her when they had knocked— in which case her sympathy, if that was what it was, was misplaced. That was the pitfall in feeling sorry for somebody: You might expend your sympathy only to discover that the misfortune that had moved you was not there at all, or that you had been sympathising with the wrong person altogether.

Now she suggested to Jamie that he should be careful not to upset Dawn. "Please be gentle with her," she said.

He promised that he would.

"Remember that we have somewhere to live," Isabel went on. "She doesn't."

"I know that," Jamie reassured her. He smiled and put an arm about her shoulder. "I promise you—I'll be very tactful."

JAMIE WENT OFF to the music room. He was playing that evening in a concert at the Usher Hall and there were several demanding passages that he needed to practise. He liked to play for two hours a day, whatever his commitments were, simply to keep his fingers in working order, as he put it. While he did this, Isabel thought that she would make further inroads into the backlog of her work. The printer's deadline for the next issue of the *Review* was still a good month away, but, as she reminded herself, deadlines had a habit of creeping up on you. Paradise, she imagined, would be a world without deadlines, a state in which nobody ever asked you whether anything was ready and where there was all the time in the world to mull things over. That was not the world she inhabited, but she liked to imagine that it existed somewhere, and one day she would find herself in it.

She sat at her desk, gazing out of the window to the tall yew hedge that separated her front garden from the road beyond it. There was a movement in the foliage, and she saw the shape of a bird within, a blackbird, probably, although a few days ago she had been visited by a thrush and it could always be him. *With thrushes popular . . .* The line came to her unbidden, although if the bird in her hedge was a thrush, then it was understandable that she should think of it. It was Auden, of course, as were most of the lines that haunted her. It came from his poem "Streams," which was one of the first of his poems that she had committed to memory when she was a teenager and had only recently fallen under the poet's spell. Now it came back to her, with its surrounding lines: *Lately in that dale of all Yorkshire's the loveliest,/ Where off its fellside helter-skelter Kisdon Beck/Jumps into Swale with a Boyish shouting,/Sprawled out on grass I dozed for a second/ And found myself following a croquet tournament/In a calm enclosure with thrushes popular . . .* It was the inversion, she thought, that made the line so memorable. It was not *popular with thrushes,* but *with thrushes popular,* which was so much more affecting, so much more beautiful. My yew hedge, she thought, *with unidentified birds popular . . .*

Her phone rang and broke her line of thought. It was Eddie.

She sat back in her chair and smiled. "I know that you're busy," he said, "but I really need to talk to you, Isabel."

She was silent.

"Isabel?"

"Yes, Eddie, I heard what you said."

"I need to talk to you in person—not over the phone. Can you come to the deli? You know that Gordon's gone off."

"Yes, I heard."

"How?"

"Cat told me."

There was silence for a few moments. "She's so selfish. Now she's gone off herself. She just dropped everything and went off to Fife to see that friend of hers—you know the one who runs that restaurant in Ceres. Her. She's gone to see her, she said."

"Oh well, she may need to talk to somebody."

Eddie sounded doubtful. "Oh yes? We all need to talk to people, but we don't drop things just like that—and ask other people to look after our shop for us."

"She's asked you?" asked Isabel.

"Yes. But what about my own job? Hannah has to go to a trade show today. So how can I go and look after Cat's shop?"

Isabel sighed. She was almost expecting this: Nothing, it seemed, was simple.

"And there's another thing," Eddie went on. "I went down to put a notice in her shop saying that we might be open later on, and when I was there two policemen came. They wanted to know where Gordon was."

Isabel asked him whether they knew where Gordon lived.

"They did," replied Eddie. "They'd been round there. But nobody was in."

"Did they say why they called?"

Eddie replied that they had told him nothing.

Isabel closed her eyes. "I'll be round in half an hour."

His relief was palpable. "I wish that Cat was here. She only thinks of herself, you know. She's so selfish."

Isabel was slightly taken aback. It was unlike Eddie to be so forceful. "I know that, Eddie. I think Cat could do with thinking a little more about others."

"And then she expects the rest of us to pick up the pieces."

Isabel sighed. "Yes. That's right too."

Eddie seemed to be getting the bit between his teeth. "And you know something else? I think Gordon's in some sort of trouble."

She waited, and then Eddie continued, "You know that he worked on a yacht in the Caribbean?"

"I did know that," said Isabel.

"Well, somebody went overboard. Did he tell you that?"

"He did say something about it to me."

Isabel tried to remember exactly what Gordon had said. There had been trouble with a chef, she recalled, and somebody went overboard. She swallowed. Had Gordon somehow been implicated in that? He had not struck her as being the sort of person who would do anything violent, but perhaps she was being naive. For all she knew, Gordon was precisely the sort of person to push somebody overboard, and was only now going to be exposed as such.

They ended their telephone call. Isabel remained at her desk for a few minutes, struggling to deal with what Eddie had said. The call had added yet another complication to her life. I am totally entangled, she said to herself. I feel that I cannot possibly extricate myself from the demands that seem to be piling up remorselessly. And then she thought, how many women are in exactly this position: Overwhelmed by the demands placed upon them? The demands of children, of husbands or partners, of the people with whom or for whom they worked; women's shoulders were broad ones, but they always bore so much. She was fortunate, of course: She had what she had; she had help with the house—a rare luxury; she had Jamie's support, which had been unfailing; everything seemed stacked in her favour. And yet, it seemed to her that the pressure upon her was real enough, and weighed heavily.

More than ever before, she was tempted to shrug off her responsibilities and walk away. But how could you walk away when you had a house, a husband, two small boys, a philosophical review to run, and a conscience that simply would not allow it? It was impossible. She looked at her watch. She had promised to see Eddie in half an hour; ten minutes had already passed, so she would have to set a brisk pace if she was to be on time. She stood up and made her way to the door.

CHAPTER FOURTEEN

EDDIE WAS WAITING for her. He had an assistant with him, a young woman whom Isabel had heard of but not met, a student of Byzantine history who worked odd hours to supplement her income. He took off his apron and signalled to her that she should take over.

"Calypso will handle everything," he said.

The young woman smiled at Isabel as she took Eddie's apron. So this is Calypso, thought Isabel, deciding immediately that the name was entirely suitable. The original Calypso, or the one who detained Odysseus for seven years during his long trip home, was reputed to have been exceptionally beautiful—and this Calypso was too, with her silky dark hair and classical profile—features sculpted in straight, descending lines—creating what Isabel would call an ancient beauty; she had a face out of time, she thought.

Calypso noticed Isabel's glance, and smiled at her again. Isabel looked away, almost guiltily, as one may do when an appreciative glance is intercepted and, as may happen, is misinterpreted. Those who attracted such glances, of course, tended to be used to them, and took them in their stride—and as no less than their due. Jamie, she knew, experienced that virtually every day of his life, and was now, she suspected, largely impervious to the turning of heads. Once again Auden whispered in her ear: "The blessed will not care what angle they are regarded from, having nothing to hide . . ." That was from "In Praise of Limestone," a poem that she considered his most sublime achievement. It was true, of course: Most of us have something to hide, if we are honest with ourselves, which, of course, we are not always: some blemish; a side of our profile that makes us look a bit forbidding, perhaps, or possibly sinister—even Count Dracula might have believed one side of his face seemed kinder than the other; a cheek or a forehead on which wrinkles have chosen to concentrate their campaign against youth with particular energy—these are the things we are concerned to conceal. But then there are people like Calypso who, she imagined, would never worry about the lighting under which she would have her photograph taken.

Isabel glanced at Eddie. She wondered what he made of his workmate. She was not sure that Eddie paid particular attention to female beauty, but then she was equally unsure as to whether she really understood this young man. She knew that he had not had an easy start in life, and that something dark and difficult had happened to him, but he had survived that and had grown in confidence. There had been girlfriends, and one of them, Diane, had been serious, although her parents had disapproved of him and the relationship had eventually foundered. He had weathered that, and other, disappointments, but Isabel felt that there was a certain vulnerability there, and she still felt anxious on his behalf. She wanted Eddie to find whatever it was that he wanted in life, but she was not entirely sure that he would.

Eddie invited Isabel to sit down at one of the coffee tables at the back of the deli.

"Would you like a latte?" he asked.

Isabel said that she would, and Eddie signalled to Calypso. She nodded and went over to the coffee machine.

"She makes a mean latte," Eddie said, adding, proudly, "I taught her how to do designs on the milk."

Isabel glanced in Calypso's direction. Her figure, she saw, was well displayed by the stone-coloured leggings she was wearing under a short pinafore dress. These imparted to her body the same sculpted effect that Isabel had noticed in her features. *Calypso's a sculpture* . . . She heard herself saying this to Jamie. He would understand, and say, *Yes, that's exactly what some people are* . . .

"Why are you smiling?" asked Eddie. "Have I said something?"

"No, I was thinking. It was nothing."

Eddie lowered his voice. "What's happening down there at Cat's place?"

Isabel replied that she knew as little as he did—perhaps even less.

"Are the police going to arrest Gordon, do you think?" Eddie asked.

Isabel said that she had no idea. She did not know Gordon very well, she told him, and she thought that there was not much point in speculating as to what the issue was. "I'm sure that Gordon will explain everything when he comes back."

"*If* he comes back," said Eddie. "I think Gordon's disappeared, Isabel. And Cat too, maybe . . ."

Isabel said that she thought that highly unlikely. "Cat goes off in a huff sometimes," she said. "It's just the way she is. Some people are sensitive, I suppose."

Eddie gave her a sideways look. "Very sensitive," he said. And then continued, "But what about their shop?"

"What does Hannah say? Can she spare you?"

Eddie looked anxious. "We're very busy here today and tomorrow. We're expecting deliveries. Hannah's gone to a trade show. Then she has to meet somebody in town and won't be back until after lunch. I could ask her then." He gave Isabel an imploring look. "Do you think you could help out here for a day or two?"

Isabel drew in her breath: This was Pelion being piled upon Ossa. "I've got rather a lot on my plate at the moment," she began. "I don't really know . . ."

Eddie interrupted her. "Just a couple of days. I'm sure Cat will show up. She may even return tomorrow, and then I'll be able to come back."

Isabel frowned. "I have a job, Eddie. You know that. I have my own job and it piles up if I ignore it." She glanced over towards the counter, where Calypso was putting their two cups of latte onto a tray. "What about Calypso? Can't she help Hannah?"

"She's not working tomorrow," said Eddie. "She has her university work, you see. She can't be here all the time."

Isabel thought that surely Byzantine history could wait; after all, Constantinople fell a long time ago. "I see," she said.

Calypso brought them their coffee, handing Isabel her cup first. In the thick, milky foam she had traced a picture of a thistle. It was skilfully executed. Then she passed Eddie his cup; Isabel noticed that she had decorated it with a heart pierced by one of Cupid's arrows. Calypso smiled as she handed it to Eddie. "And this is yours, Eddie," she said. "Specially for you."

Eddie looked up at her and grinned. Then he glanced at Isabel, to see if she had noticed the design on his latte. Isabel met his gaze briefly, and then looked at Calypso, who was still smiling at Eddie. *She's flirting*, she thought. Calypso was flirting with Eddie.

Isabel took a sip of her coffee. She considered what she had just seen. She might be wrong, she thought, but she did not think so. And she was puzzled: What could this extremely attractive, rather sophisticated young Byzantine historian see in Eddie, who had not had much education—not that that was in any way his fault—but who was just so . . . well, so unlikely a match for her.

Calypso returned to the counter.

"She's really nice," Eddie confided in Isabel, his voice lowered to a whisper.

Isabel tried not to show her concern. "Do you get on well with her?" she asked.

"Oh yes," said Eddie. "And I think she likes me."

Isabel hesitated, but then she asked, "Would you like to get to know her better?"

She felt immediately embarrassed by her question. It sounded so coy. *Get to know her better*: Nobody spoke that way any longer.

But Eddie knew what she meant. "Oh yes," he said. "Do you think she wants me to ask her for a date? Is that why she put that heart on my latte? Do you think that's why?"

Isabel spoke with caution. "I don't know, Eddie. It's hard to tell." People were far too ready to throw heart symbols and kisses about. Isabel's hairdresser ended every email, even business ones, with a line of *x*s. Did she really want to blow kisses to her bank manager or accountant? Not that they might not deserve it, thought Isabel; they might even be touched by the gesture, but there were considerations of emotional continence to bear in mind. When we kiss everyone, then our kisses are devalued. And actors, she thought, might bear that in mind when they addressed everyone, even complete strangers, as *darling*, as some did.

"But I think perhaps you should be careful," she continued. "Sometimes people say or do things that they don't really mean. You need to be careful about jumping to conclusions."

"I like her a lot," said Eddie. "She's really cool."

Yes, thought Isabel, Calypso was undoubtedly really cool.

But Eddie, she thought, was not. No, that was unkind, and she reproached herself silently. There was nothing wrong with Eddie—it was just that there was far too great a disparity, it seemed to her, between where Eddie was in life and where she assumed Calypso was. She had that feel about her of the assured young woman from a monied background: the sort whose parent could easily afford to support a master's degree in Byzantine history. Calypso had probably already had a gap year in which she had made an expensive, parent-funded trip to work overseas on a conservation project or on the painting of a school that might already have been redecorated a few years back by a group of privileged young people from far away. There were many such over-painted schools in the gap-year latitudes.

She could imagine what Calypso's life was like. She would be sharing a flat in the New Town somewhere with fellow students, and they were likely to be of the same background. There was nothing wrong with them, but they would have had little experience of Eddie's world. Eddie's Edinburgh was not their Edinburgh: He came from a street where options were fewer—and bleaker. It was all just a bit unlikely, and yet . . . Isabel stopped herself. Why should feeling for another person be affected by social and economic disparities? It was perfectly possible to fall for one whose experience was very different from one's own; that was because the attraction of one for another was, after all, a simple human attraction that did not have to be dependent on shared experience. It was the basis of uncountable romantic stories: a relationship across a divide created by parents or by wider society. It was a story of caste, and the cruelties that accompanied that sort of dividing up of society; a story that we all hoped would end in victory for the lovers, which sometimes happened, but more often did not.

But was Calypso serious about Eddie? Isabel realised that she was getting ahead of herself. All she had seen was a mild flirtatiousness; all she had heard were some wistful remarks from Eddie. And at the back of her mind was Jamie's advice about not concerning herself with matters that were none of her business. People made unwise decisions in their private lives—that was their affair and it was not for her to give them unasked-for advice. But then she thought: Eddie asked me what I thought. *He* involved me.

"So," said Eddie. "Can you?"

Isabel put down her cup. "It doesn't look as if I have much choice."

"I'd be really grateful. And I'll pay you back somehow— promise." He grinned at her, and she noticed that one of his teeth, a top molar, was slightly crooked. But that, she felt, was only human: Isabel had never been entirely sure of the justification for cosmetic dentistry, not being convinced that physical perfection did anything to enhance character—or appearance. Features could be too regular; smiles could be too unflawed. Vanity, she thought, was in the list of the major vices, but perhaps that was an outdated view in the Age of Identity. People saw no reason why they should accept the flesh to which they were heir if the creation of a different physical person was a possibility. And was there anything inherently wrong in that? It would make, she thought, a good topic for a special issue of the journal: *The Ethics of Cosmetic Surgery*, with a leading contribution from Christopher Dove, no less, who was notoriously vain.

Looking now at Eddie, Isabel relented. She did not wish to be grudging. "You don't have to pay me back," she said. "I'm perfectly happy to help out."

Eddie leaned forward. "You'll have the chance to work with Calypso this afternoon," he said. "You'll like that."

She wanted to smile, but restrained herself. "Will I?"

"Yes, of course. Calypso's great, Isabel. She's . . . she's . . ." He frowned as he searched for the right words. "She's seriously smart. She knows everything. Ask her . . . ask her anything. She'll blow your mind."

Isabel raised an eyebrow. "Blow my mind?"

"Big time," said Eddie.

"Well, that's a thought," said Isabel, imagining her brain expanding suddenly into a Roy Lichtenstein flash of red and yellow. Did Eddie see the world that way: a place in which *WOW*, in large, jagged letters, hung above moments of emotional intensity.

Eddie looked at her with the bright eyes of his age. "I'm telling you, Isabel: She's cosmic."

"Cosmic?"

"Yes. Slay."

Isabel had no idea what *slay* meant. She might have asked him, but the context, it occurred to her, shone a light on its meaning. Of course Calypso was slay—one only had to look at her to realise that *slay* was exactly what she was. She suddenly found herself wanting to put her arm around Eddie—this rather unprepossessing young man, with all his uncertainty, his puppy-like manner, and his innocent resort to the shifting argot of youth. She wanted to protect him from the harm that the world seemed to be so determined to cook up for people like him. And some of that harm, in the case of somebody as vulnerable as Eddie, could include being led on by more worldly-wise women who were more or less certainly thinking of no more than a brief affair.

She told Eddie that she would return at lunchtime to release him so that he could go down the road to open Cat's shop for the afternoon. Now she walked back to the house, lost in thought. She felt angry with Cat for absenting herself so abruptly; she felt angry, too, with Gordon for doing much the same thing. There were other possible targets for her antipathy and frustration: Professor Lettuce and Marcus Grant; the squabbling members of the book group; Calypso; Dawn, for her ill manners; the list was a growing one. But then she pulled herself short: Negative feelings towards others were corrosive—it was as simple as that. Forgiveness and reconciliation, tolerance and acceptance were the notes to which one should tune. If she had learned anything from her years of doing philosophy, surely it was that—a simple, homespun truth that you did not have to be a philosopher to realise. She would not allow distaste to corrupt her, and that meant that she would make an effort to *like* Calypso when she worked with her that afternoon: That was her moral duty, for *agape*, as the Greeks called that pure love of others, Isabel had often told herself, is what we should both profess and practise, whatever the temptations might be in the other direction.

And suddenly it occurred to her that here was the solution to the challenges which this chapter of complications had foisted upon her: love—and, in particular, that disinterested and unselfish love of others, *agape*—unconditional love, as it tended to be— that was the answer to everything from the unhappy book group to the machinations of Robert Lettuce and his cousin Marcus Grant; from the enigma of Dawn to the trying unreasonableness of Cat and her disappearing lover, Gordon—*agape* was the solution, and its implementation was down to her, as it is, she suddenly thought, to all of us.

THE DELI WAS BUSY that afternoon, just as Eddie had predicted. Hannah called to say that she would be unable to be back until the following day—would Isabel and Calypso be able to manage? Isabel assured her that they would.

"You're a star, Isabel."

Isabel demurred. "You'd do the same for me."

There was a brief hesitation at the other end of the line before Hannah said, "I hope I would."

"And anyway," Isabel continued, "I have a certain responsibility . . ."

She left the sentence unfinished. Neither of them wanted to be more specific: Isabel had rescued the deli financially after Cat and Leo had gone off to live on the other side of the country, putting Hannah in charge and saving Eddie's job, but she never mentioned this. Good works, she felt, were not to be openly discussed—at least by those who performed them. And those who benefitted, of course, were often also silent, sometimes from resentment. Beneficence sometimes shames us, Isabel had heard one of her philosophy lecturers say, and she had remembered it. It was true: Some would prefer to manage without the kindness of others.

They worked independently, although Calypso occasionally asked for advice on the contents of various salamis and the provenance of the more obscure cheeses. She was squeamish in the use of a knife and refused to use the ham-slicer, shuddering at the sight of the gleaming, spinning blade.

"I'm so useless," she said to Isabel.

"I don't think you are," Isabel replied.

"But I am. All I can do is Byzantine history."

Isabel laughed. She was warming to Calypso, and when, in a quiet moment, they managed to snatch a cup of coffee together, she began to ask her about her life in Edinburgh. As she had imagined, Calypso shared a flat with other students, and it was, as she'd suspected, in the New Town. But those, she reminded herself, were externals.

"And why Byzantine history?" she asked.

"We went to Istanbul when I was fifteen," she said. "I fell in love with it. The great souk. Hagia Sophia. The ships going through the Bosphorus. It was a heady mixture." She paused. "And my name, of course. I know your name shouldn't make a difference, but mine did. I had a Greek grandmother, you see. That's why I'm called Calypso."

Isabel hesitated. "Eddie," she said.

A broad smile spread across Calypso's face. "He's a sweetie, isn't he."

Isabel was cautious. "Yes. He is."

There was a silence. After a few moments, Isabel continued, "I've known him for some time, of course."

Calypso nodded. "He told me. He has nothing but praise for you."

"Perhaps he hasn't noticed my shortcomings." Isabel paused. "It hasn't been easy for him, you know."

Calypso looked concerned. "What hasn't?"

"Life. Everything."

Calypso waited.

"He's very vulnerable," Isabel continued, wondering whether to leave it at that. But she decided to continue, "I must admit I was a bit concerned that . . ." She stopped herself, uncertain as to whether to go any further. But she was committed now, and so she went on, "I was a bit concerned that Eddie might, well, might be falling for you."

Calypso's expression was one of complete surprise. "For me?" she exclaimed. "Eddie falling for me?"

It was obvious now to Isabel that she had misread the situation more or less completely. What had struck her as flirtatious behaviour was probably no more than platonic affection. Eddie was precisely the sort of young man whom women might want to mother. There was nothing more than that in Calypso's gesture with the heart in the coffee.

She wanted to back-pedal. "I may be wrong," she said hurriedly. "And I'm not suggesting you were encouraging him."

"I wasn't," Calypso blurted out.

"It's just that a young man like Eddie might misunderstand," Isabel continued. "In fact, I think that's exactly what he's done."

Calypso looked aghast. "I didn't intend that to happen."

"I'm sure you didn't."

Calypso gave Isabel a searching look. "So, what can I do? Should I speak to him?"

Isabel took a final sip of her coffee. Sooner or later, customers would come into the deli and their coffee break would have to come to an end. She considered what Calypso had said. *Verbalisation precedes resolution* . . . Yes, but verbalisation here would have only one result, she thought: Eddie's confidence would be dented. Any rebuff by Calypso, however gently put, would dent his fragile confidence; Isabel was sure of that. Eddie would be hurt.

Calypso now answered her own question. "I need to disappear."

Isabel waited for her to explain.

"I don't want to hurt him," Calypso continued. "That's the last thing I want. So I have to come up with something. I have to go away."

Isabel opened her mouth to say something, but Calypso had more to say. "I don't need this job," she said. "I've been offered something on the other side of town—a part-time job in Valvona & Crolla. You know that deli off Leith Walk? I can pick up a few shifts a week with them. It would be easier to get to, anyway."

"But what would you tell Eddie?"

"I'd just say I was taking a break. He'd forget about me if we weren't seeing one another regularly. It would die a natural death. Finished."

Isabel was not sure about that. "What if he calls you?"

"Calls don't have to be returned. Not always." She looked away guiltily. "Does that make me sound heartless? I suppose it does. But what can I do? It's just that I think it would be gentler to do it this way."

Isabel was silent. Then she said, "No, you don't sound heartless. Not at all." Calypso was not to blame here, but that did not stop her wondering whether her own intervention, well-intentioned though it was, had simply made matters worse. What if Eddie found out that she had spoken to Calypso about him and had triggered this radical response, would he not blame her for derailing his incipient affair? And how would Hannah react to the news that Calypso would suddenly no longer be available to work in the deli? There were plenty of students in Edinburgh, and some of them might welcome a part-time job in a deli, but a new member of staff would have to be trained and might, as was sometimes the case with students, be an unreliable timekeeper.

They closed the deli shortly before six, a few minutes earlier than usual. Isabel walked back to the house slowly. Earlier on in the day she had felt optimistic that her difficulties were surmountable. Now she looked, and felt, disconsolate as she opened the door and went inside, observed, although she had not even noticed him, by Brother Fox in the fastness of his rhododendron bush.

CHAPTER FIFTEEN

JAMIE WAS STANDING in the hall, ready to greet her.

"The boys have had their bath," he said. "They're upstairs. I told them you might read their story tonight."

"Of course." She put her bag down on the hall table.

"Are you all right?" Jamie asked.

She said that she was; she did not think that one's first words on returning home should be ones of complaint. "It's just that the deli was busy. Non-stop."

He leaned forward to kiss her. "The boys are waiting. I'll have a glass of wine ready for you when you come downstairs."

She returned his kiss. Upstairs, the boys were already in their pyjamas. They smelled of toothpaste and flannelette. They were ready for their story, which was one she had read them time and time again; they could recite it almost word for word, and the ending, of course, was no surprise. But that did not seem to matter: the comfort of the expected, thought Isabel.

After she had said good night she made her way downstairs to the kitchen, where Jamie was waiting for her. He was standing over the cooker, stirring a pot; the table was already laid.

She noticed that there were three places.

"Company?" Jamie occasionally invited members of his chamber orchestra to join them when he was cooking dinner. He did not always let Isabel know in advance—not that she minded. She liked Jamie's musician friends, except for one brass player who had been drunk when he last came to dinner and one percussionist who peppered his language with profanities. "He doesn't mean any of it," said Jamie, who was charitable in these matters, of the percussionist. "It goes with having to make a lot of noise."

Jamie smiled as he answered her question. "Yes," he said. "We do have company."

"Who?"

He pointed towards the ceiling. "Upstairs."

Isabel caught her breath. "Dawn?"

He nodded. "I went to see her. I told you I would."

"And?"

"I invited her to join us for dinner."

Isabel sat down at the table. "You're going to have to tell me," she said.

"Why she was so secretive?"

"Yes. The whole thing. The locking of the door. The failure to answer when we knocked and knew that she was in."

He glanced at his watch. "She'll be down soon."

"You must tell me," Isabel insisted.

"Shame," he said. "She felt really ashamed about what she had done. She thought that you disapproved of her. She said she couldn't face either of us. That . . . and there was something else."

"What?"

He was about to respond when they heard approaching footsteps. "That's her," he said.

Isabel wanted him to whisper an answer to her question, but there was no time. The door to the hall was pushed open to reveal

Dawn, poised to come into the kitchen, but still slightly hesitant, like a visitor not quite sure how she will be received.

It took Isabel a few moments to muster her welcome, but when she did so she rose to her feet and gestured for Dawn to join her at the kitchen table. "I'm so glad you were able to join us," she said. She sounded formal, which had not been her intention, but she could not think of anything else to say. She almost added "at last" but stopped herself. That would have been interpreted in only one way by their guest.

Dawn took her seat, glancing at Isabel as she did so, as if fearful that the invitation might be rescinded.

"Dawn's been busy," Jamie said over his shoulder as he attended to a pot on the cooking range.

"You work night shifts, don't you?" asked Isabel.

Dawn nodded. "Yes. I don't mind too much doing them, though. Some of my colleagues do, of course, especially if they have children."

Isabel smiled at Dawn. There was still an awkward atmosphere, but she was not sure how best to dispel it. Dawn's behaviour had been odd by any standards; might it be best to air the matter? She could say "We were worried about you," or something of that sort, but she thought that this might just make matters worse. It was what Isabel's father used to call "an elephant situation"—where there was an elephant in the room, but nobody could mention the fact.

She cleared her throat. "Have you been comfortable enough up there?" she asked.

The question clearly embarrassed Dawn, who shifted in her seat as she sought to respond. "Yes, of course. It's so . . . so quiet."

"I was worried that the boys might make a noise during the day," said Isabel. "If you were asleep after being on duty . . ."

Dawn interrupted her. "I didn't hear them," she said.

"They can be very rowdy," Jamie interjected. "You know how small boys are. They make a soundtrack for themselves—all sorts of sound effects. Shouted orders, exploding sounds—that sort of thing. Battleground noises."

"None of that reached me," said Dawn. She looked down at her hands, folded together on her lap. Then she looked up, to meet Isabel's eyes. "You must have wondered what was going on."

Isabel had not expected this. For a few moments she did not reply. Then she said, "Not really." It was so palpably untrue, and so she added, "Well, I suppose we did—to an extent." She glanced at Jamie. He had his back to the table, as he attended to a pan on the stove; she could tell, though, that he was listening.

"I owe you an apology," Dawn went on. "I've been a very bad guest."

"But you haven't," said Isabel. "We've hardly seen you."

"That's what makes me a bad guest," Dawn retorted. "You don't ignore your hosts—you just don't." She paused. "But I did."

Isabel raised a hand. "You wanted to keep to yourself. That's understandable. You didn't want to impose on us. There's no need to apologise for that."

"But there's every reason," insisted Dawn. "You took me in and then I stayed up in my room for half the time, pretending that you weren't there. In my book that requires an apology."

Once again, Isabel tried to assure her that no apology was expected—or required. But Dawn was not to be persuaded.

"I admit I was avoiding you," she continued. "I felt so ashamed, you see."

Isabel frowned. "You thought we would . . ."

"Disapprove," Dawn supplied. "Yes, I thought you'd disapprove of me. For going off with Fionn."

Isabel shook her head. "No," she began. "I didn't . . ."

"I feel so ashamed."

"You don't need to," said Isabel. "People split up. These things happen."

"But not in the way it happened. Not with me."

Isabel was not sure what she meant. She looked at Jamie, but he was impassive. He was waiting for Dawn to say more, she thought.

"I drove away with Fionn . . ." Dawn continued.

Isabel shrugged. "Well, as I said, relationships end."

". . . in Andrew's car."

Taken aback, Isabel said nothing.

"And we wrote it off," Dawn continued.

Isabel stared at her. "You crashed?"

Dawn inclined her head, her gaze now fixed to the floor. Her voice betrayed the misery she felt. "Fionn was driving," she continued. "I told him it was my car. It was Andrew's, although we both used it. I told Andrew that I wanted to borrow it to go to work. I lied to him." She paused. "And it gets worse, I'm afraid. I left with Fionn while Andrew was away. He'd gone off to see my mother in hospital in Inverness. He went up by train. He was always very kind to her." She stopped. Her misery was palpable. "I thought you knew about it. I thought that everybody knew."

"I'd heard," volunteered Jamie.

"From somebody in the orchestra?" Dawn asked.

"Yes."

Isabel looked up sharply. If Jamie had known, then why had he not told her? Had he deliberately kept it a secret—and if so, why? He met her gaze, but looked away again quickly. Isabel felt a stab of betrayal. Jamie should have told her, and had not done so because he must have thought that had she known the full story, she might have been unwilling to offer Dawn shelter.

But then Jamie said, "What I meant to say is that I heard that you'd had an accident when you left. I didn't know anything about whose car it was."

Isabel and Jamie looked at one another. This explained his failure to mention it. She looked at him, and said sorry with her eyes. He returned her look. With his eyes he said, I understand why you thought that I had kept something from you, but I didn't—I really didn't. In such a way can couples communicate volumes without the utterance of a word.

Isabel said, "I can see why that didn't look good."

"No, it didn't." Dawn turned away. "I don't know what I was thinking of."

Jamie looked at Isabel again. His expression now was one of concern, as if Dawn's discomfort was causing him physical pain. Isabel hesitated, but then responded. "I can see myself doing exactly the same thing," she said, adding, hurriedly, as she noticed Jamie's frown, "I mean, I don't see myself leaving Jamie . . ." She glanced at him, as his frown became a tentative smile. "I didn't mean that, of course. What I meant is that *if* I left somebody, I could see myself just not thinking about whose car I left in."

"You'd leave by public transport, perhaps," offered Jamie.

Isabel gave him a discouraging look, and he mumbled an apology. "I'm sorry. I wasn't making light of it. What Isabel is saying, I think, is that when it comes to these things, we don't always think straight."

"More or less," said Isabel. "What I'd say, I suppose, is that we've all done things that perhaps we would prefer not to have done—later, that is. We regret impulsive acts. We regret falling for somebody. The scales fall from our eyes and we wonder what we saw in somebody who, only a few days previously, we might have been prepared to follow to the ends of the earth."

Jamie nodded his agreement. "Exactly. So you shouldn't beat yourself up over this, Dawn. And as for the other thing . . ."

Dawn looked anxiously at Isabel.

"I haven't told Isabel yet," said Jamie. "I was going to, but then suddenly it was dinner time."

Isabel waited for the disclosure. She was not sure that she wanted to know anything else about Dawn's desertion of Andrew and ill-starred affair with Fionn. She wanted potato dauphinoise, which she suspected Jamie had cooked for dinner, as that was what he always did. She loved him for that. *I loved him for his potato dauphinoise . . .* That sounded so ridiculous, she thought, but it was true, provided one added the rider that potato dauphinoise was *one* of the reasons why she loved Jamie—there were others.

Dawn, still looking anxiously at Isabel, was about to say something, but Jamie spoke instead. "Dawn was not alone in her room," he said.

Isabel was surprised by the way in which Jamie imparted this information. He might have been gentler, she thought; this sounded almost like an accusation.

"I don't think it's any of our business," Isabel said quickly.

"Timmy was there," Jamie went on. "In fact, he's still there."

Isabel felt acutely embarrassed. She glared at Jamie.

"He's a mouse, you see," Jamie continued.

Isabel's glare became more intense. Had Jamie been drinking while cooking his potato dauphinoise? It was quite unlike him to be so tactless, she thought. They would have to discuss this later.

"An actual mouse," said Jamie, with a grin. "I told Dawn that you wouldn't have minded—that you quite like mice, as far as

I know. Or, at least, that you don't have pronounced views on them."

Isabel turned to Dawn. "I'm sorry," she said. "I'm not sure that I understand what's going on."

Jamie explained. "Dawn has a pet mouse. She wanted to ask us if we minded his coming with her, so to speak."

Dawn interrupted him. "But I was . . . well, I suppose you could say that I was scared. I couldn't face you because of what I imagined you thought of me. And so I smuggled him in. It became difficult. I felt that I was deceiving you after you'd been so kind to me. I felt completely wretched."

Isabel wanted to laugh. She glanced at Jamie, and she saw that he felt the same way. She reached out to touch Dawn. "But what Jamie said is true. Of course I wouldn't have minded. Why should I?"

"The only person round here who wouldn't approve," Jamie said, "is the fox in our garden. We have a fox who lives out there in our garden, you see. He'd probably eat Timmy, I suppose. We'll need to keep them apart."

Isabel felt a flood of relief. She had not imagined that the Dawn issue would resolve in this sudden, almost comical way. But then human drama *is* comic, she thought. Once you got up close to it, it was far less serious than it seemed, and tipped over, in some cases at least, into the absurd or the comic. So many human issues were about very small things, when you came to think of it: like misplaced shame and misplaced guilt. And misunderstandings. And mice.

"I must watch the potatoes," said Jamie suddenly, turning back to the cooker and its simmering pots.

"Potato dauphinoise can curdle," Isabel said to Dawn. "Just like life."

Isabel remembered the keys that had been dropped in the hall. She wanted to ask about them, but then she thought: This is not the time.

THEY LAY IN BED. In the summer months, when Edinburgh was barely dark at midnight, they were careful to close the curtains in their bedroom, but that night Isabel left them open. Their room, then, seemed suffused with something that Isabel called "quarter-light," because it was not quite the "half-light" of which people spoke.

"Are you asleep?" Isabel whispered.

She looked at him. Jamie lay with his arms outstretched, as if in surrender to the night.

"No. I was thinking."

She touched his shoulder gently, her fingers no more than a feather upon his skin. He was always asking her what she was thinking about; she rarely asked him the same question. And yet now it seemed important to her that she should know.

"Robert Burns," he said.

She was playful. "Oh yes? And why Robert Burns?"

"Not tonight, Mrs. Maclehose," he muttered.

She remembered: Mrs. Maclehose was the woman in Edinburgh whom Burns loved, although their love was never consummated. She was the "Clarinda" to whom he dedicated his poems. It was one of the great love stories that never was.

She put a finger to his lips. He kissed it.

"I was thinking of what Burns wrote about that mouse—the one he disturbed with his plough. It's such a wonderful apology to the poor little creature."

"And to the world," Isabel said.

"Do you think the earth will forgive us?" Jamie asked.

Isabel knew what he meant. "If we say sorry quickly enough," she said.

"And will we?"

She could not answer that question. Who could? she thought.

She started to drift off. "Those keys," she muttered. "Those keys we found in the hall."

"I asked her about them," Jamie said. "She said they belonged to a friend. She found them on the hall table after we put them there."

"Why did she have a friend's keys, I wonder," asked Isabel.

"No idea," said Jamie, and then added, "Not everything has to make sense in this life."

"So it seems," said Isabel.

CHAPTER SIXTEEN

WE READ EVERYTHING," Roz Mack told Isabel the following day. "Contemporary. Classics. We're not fussy." She paused.
"Except for some of us—who are *very* fussy."

They were in Roz's living room, waiting for the members of
the book group to arrive. It would be a full attendance, Roz had
said, because the weather was good and the members liked warm
evenings. If the evening sky stayed clear, they would go outside
for tea: Roz prided herself on her south-facing walled garden, and
there was a lawn on which she could spread picnic rugs and cush-
ions. "We sit there like those people in *Le Déjeuner sur l'herbe*,"
she said, "although they seem so static, so posed, and somehow I
don't think they were talking about books."

Isabel laughed. "Monet or Manet?" she asked.

"I get them confused," Roz replied. "Nobody's *déshabillé*, of
course—not in our latitudes."

"Then Manet," said Isabel.

Roz nodded. "A couple of months ago we read Stendhal. It was
The Red and the Black, and last year we tackled *Anna Karenina*.
Every book group should tackle a big Russian novel at some point.
It's a rite of passage, I think. Survive your Russian novel and you'll
be fine."

Except, thought Isabel, you *aren't* fine, which is why I'm here—rather against my better judgement.

At that meeting, they were due to discuss Muriel Spark's *The Prime of Miss Jean Brodie*. "I told you about that," said Roz. "We've read one or two of her novels before this. She's highly entertaining." She glanced at her watch. "They'll start arriving in fifteen minutes. They're usually fairly punctual. I hope you didn't mind coming a bit early."

Isabel said that she did not mind.

"I wondered whether you had had any ideas," Roz said. "I don't want to put you under any pressure, but if you've been able to think of anything, then I'd be interested to know."

Isabel confessed that she had not spent much time considering how she might be able to help. "I've been under a bit of pressure," she said. "Work, and so on." It was the *so on* that had been the trouble, of course, but she did not want to talk to Roz about Cat and Gordon, nor about Eddie and Calypso. Nor Dawn and the issues she had brought with her. And how could one explain Lettuce without sounding uncharitable? So she simply said, "My life has been a bit complicated recently."

Roz looked surprised. "I didn't expect you to say that. I don't know much about your circumstances, of course, but I thought you led . . . well, a rather charmed life. Or do I mean charming? I'm not sure. Anyway, I thought that you had a rather nice job, editing a journal from home, and a comfortable house too, of course, and an agreeable husband—from what I hear."

Isabel pursed her lips. "Are you sure you're talking about me?" But then she realised that she should not make little of what she really did have, and so she said, "All of what you said is true. I'm very fortunate. I have all of that. But then, you see, I seem to get involved in all sorts of issues that prove to be rather demanding. Jamie says . . ."

"Your husband?"

"Yes. My husband says that I should lead a simpler existence, but how exactly do you do that?"

"Nobody's life is all that simple," said Roz. "I think people make a mistake when they look at others, don't see much going on, and then conclude that the life that those others are leading is a simple one. Not so."

Isabel agreed. "In his later years," she said, "my poor father used to worry about shaving in the morning. You'd think that he was planning a major campaign. He'd easily spend an hour getting things ready—the brush, the shaving bowl and all the rest. There was always such a palaver. He didn't have much else to do after he retired. All he had to do was shave."

"Later life is full of mountains that are really molehills in disguise," Roz remarked. "My mother was like that, bless her. She used to worry if the postman was late. We used to have a postman called Jimmy. He came from Skye, and he had that lovely Highland accent. She'd wait for him by the window. He'd stop and ring the bell even if he had nothing for her. He'd usually say, 'Nothing for you today, Rosemary. Maybe tomorrow.' He was so kind. Oh, I know it was a tiny thing, but it made all the difference."

"Kindness," muttered Isabel, almost to herself.

"Yes," echoed Roz. "Kindness. Simple kindness."

"Which lies at the heart of civilisation," Isabel said. "If a society is unkind, then it has no chance of being civilised. It may think it has a civilisation, but it'll be an imperfect one."

They looked at one another. Then Roz said, "I wish I'd known you longer."

Isabel was slightly taken aback. "Well, we've met now."

"Yes, but I wish it had been much before this. I feel that I've missed something. You've been there—living your life not far away from mine, just around the corner, really, and I've been here, and we could have talked about so much."

Isabel was touched. "We'll have the chance to talk in the future. We can have coffee together."

"I'd like that," said Roz. "But I feel I'd be intruding. You've already got your friends, and I suppose I've got mine."

Isabel shrugged. "There's always room for more."

"But I thought you needed to simplify your life. Didn't you say that?"

"Perhaps," said Isabel. "But perhaps we should talk about Muriel Spark—before the others come."

Roz sighed. "They're going to argue," she warned. "They're going to spend their time needling one another over . . . over everything. Just watch it develop. It'll be like an international crisis unfolding in slow motion."

They discussed Muriel Spark, and were still doing so ten minutes later when the doorbell rang. "That's them," said Roz. "They're here."

Virginia and Gemma were at the door. As they entered the living room, Isabel remembered how much Gemma admired Virginia and how she echoed and endorsed her every opinion. Now, as they came into the room, Isabel thought that Gemma's body language confirmed this view of the relationship; Gemma was considerably shorter than Virginia, who was tall and, Isabel thought, had the haughtiness that occasionally went with height, giving an impression of superiority in more than one sense. As Isabel greeted them, she noticed that Gemma was looking expectantly at Virginia—it was as if she was waiting to take her cue from a leader. And there was another thing that Isabel became aware of: It was almost as if Virginia was unaware of Gemma's presence. So might a high official in the Sultan's court, Isabel thought, seem unaware of the lowest of attendants.

Isabel said, by way of a conversation-opener, that she was looking forward to discussing *The Prime of Miss Jean Brodie*. "I love Muriel Spark's work," she said. "She was such an amusing writer."

Gemma glanced at her briefly, before quickly turning back to Virginia, as if to ascertain how this remark had been received by higher authority. Virginia pursed her lips. She had a small, disapproving mouth, Isabel decided: This was not a mouth out of which generous sentiments might be expected to emanate.

"Spark?" said Virginia, not directly to Isabel, but, in full *ex cathedra* manner, to an imaginary audience on the sofa.

"Yes," said Isabel. "Muriel Spark."

"A wonderful writer," said Roz. "I love her work—I always have." She paused. "And there are those who say that *Jean Brodie* is her greatest novel."

"Impossible woman," snapped Virginia.

Isabel was not sure whether she meant Muriel Spark or Jean Brodie. Neither, in her view, was impossible.

Roz seemed good-humoured. "Oh, I don't know," she said mildly. "I rather approve of Jean Brodie."

Virginia's nostrils flared. "Frankly, I don't see what there is to approve of. Unless, of course, one approves of fascism."

This remark was accompanied by a look of such condescension that Isabel felt she had to respond.

"I know what you mean about her political views," she said. "But . . ."

"You'll recall how she admired Mussolini," Virginia interjected.

This was the signal for Gemma to lend support. "Mussolini," she said, shaking her head in disapproval. "He was a fascist, you know."

Isabel suppressed a smile. "So I've heard," she said.

Gemma looked anxiously at Virginia, as if eager to find out whether she had said the right thing.

"What I was going to point out," Isabel continued, "is that there was a lot of political naivety in the nineteen-thirties. People supported causes that they really didn't know enough about. They might take a rosy view of a political party without realising that it really was very intolerant—or downright dangerous." Anthony Blunt, thought Isabel: Anthony Blunt, Donald Maclean, Guy Burgess, Kim Philby . . .

"They knew," said Virginia. "Don't tell me that Jean Brodie didn't know what European fascism was all about."

Isabel pointed out that Jean Brodie was a fictional character. The only views that she might have—the only understanding—would be those attributed by the character's creator. "I don't think we can be sure about what Jean Brodie did or did not believe," she said. "We can get clues from the text, of course, but they might be deliberately ambiguous clues."

Virginia shook her head. "Jean Brodie was a fascist—in every respect. And she was in charge of all those impressionable young girls. Typical."

Typical of what? Isabel found herself wondering. Was she suggesting that it was typical of the authorities to appoint the most unsuitable people to positions of influence over young people?

Virginia did not explain what she meant, but went on to say, "Jean Brodie was a romantic authoritarian—and a fantasist."

"Possibly," said Isabel.

"A fantasist," echoed Gemma, giving Isabel a vaguely reproachful look.

"Probably with an unhealthy interest in teenage girls," Virginia remarked.

Roz frowned at this. Gemma looked away in embarrassment.

"Oh, I don't think so," said Isabel. "She wanted to influence them. That's not the same thing as wanting to seduce them."

Gemma was staring out of the window. Virginia looked up at the ceiling.

Now Roz intervened. "We mustn't have our discussion before the others arrive," she warned. To Isabel, she said, "Sometimes that happens, you know. We start to discuss the book before the others arrive, and then we find that by the time we start, everything has already been said."

"Of course," agreed Virginia, but then went on to observe, "Spark's a bit light—whatever one thinks of Jean Brodie. I find her writing shies away from the issue."

Gemma nodded. "Yes," she said. "It can shy away, I think. You need to engage, don't you, Virginia."

Isabel was irritated by this. She had always resented the way in which some people diminished the achievement of writers who, like Muriel Spark, dared to be witty and humorous. There was Virginia, who, as far as Isabel knew, had never published a word, patronising Muriel Spark, who had entertained and inspired so many. She gritted her teeth. How dare she! And as for Gemma, coming in on the coat-tails of this unjustified bit of intellectual snobbery—her comments were at best risible. She wanted to say something; she wanted to demolish, politely but firmly, this casual dismissal, but just as she was about to fashion a retort, the doorbell rang again.

"I imagine that's everybody else," said Roz.

Isabel bit her tongue. She smiled at Virginia, and at Gemma too. "We must discuss that later," she said.

Virginia waved a careless hand, as if she were putting Isabel's request on some lowly agenda of conversations of too little interest to be worth resuming. Only delayed by a few seconds, Gemma made a similar gesture. Angela, Fredericka and Barbara all arrived at the same time. Isabel recalled that Fredericka was said to dislike Angela; that Angela never read anything; and that Barbara also disliked Angela and was, in turn, dismissive of both Virginia and Gemma, although mostly of Virginia. Virginia, Isabel assumed, would have little time for Angela in view of her failure to read even the thin intellectual fare that made up the group's chosen books.

They sat down. Isabel noticed that Virginia and Angela both made for the same chair, but Virginia reached it marginally before Angela and sat down with a deft twist of the hips before the other woman could lay claim to it. Once seated, Virginia looked at Angela with the smug relief that Isabel had last seen on the face of the winner of musical chairs at the last children's party she had held for Charlie. Most guests at that function had been small boys from Charlie's class at school, and the game had ended with a scrummage and damage to a small Victorian bedroom chair that Jamie had unwisely introduced into the game. But while one might expect such attitudes among the six- and seven-year-olds, one did not expect it in a book group in one of Edinburgh's staider suburbs.

Angela moved to a place on a sofa, sitting down next to Gemma, who smiled at her in welcome. Isabel was not sure how those two got on, although she was coming to realise that the default position in this book group was, as Roz had implied, barely concealed hostility. As she thought of this, Isabel wondered if there was any point in Roz's proceeding in the face of the deep-seated antagonisms and difference of opinion that had been so obvious to her, even from her brief experience of the group. Surely it would be better, she thought, to call it a day with these difficult individuals and to establish a new and harmonious group made up of people who appeared not to be at one another's throats. Yet Roz persisted, and Isabel found herself admiring that. Resolving conflict was always a worthwhile goal, even if there were times when it involved considerable effort. *Blessed are the peacemakers . . .* Yes, she thought, although their efforts, unfortunately, did not always bear fruit. And this, she suspected, would be one such situation: The members of this book group, she felt, were fundamentally incompatible, and that, she decided, is what she would tell Roz when she broke to her the news that she would not be coming to another meeting after this one. "I would have liked to have helped," she would say, "but there are limits to what anybody can do."

Isabel found a seat next to Fredericka. She watched as Roz took her own seat and started proceedings.

"This is the second meeting that our new member, Isabel, is enjoying," Roz began. "I'm sure that you'll all join me in saying how glad we are to see her."

The members looked at her and, with the exception of Virginia, smiled. Isabel found herself gazing at Virginia, who sucked in her cheeks and turned away. There will be no dealing with you, Isabel said to herself. You're . . . She searched for a word. *Impossible*, came to her. That was what some people were: It was as simple as that—they were impossible.

There were a few items of routine business, including fixing a date for the next meeting. Then Roz announced, "The book."

There was an immediate silence. Isabel glanced at Roz; she saw tension in the way her hands were clasped; she saw anxiety in the way she looked about the room at the members disported before her. She saw how Roz's gaze fell upon Virginia, and locked upon her, as a heat-seeking missile will lock in on its target. She saw the gaze returned, cold and unwavering, and she saw immediately the old, familiar challenge. Roz was where Virginia wanted to be: It was as simple as that. There can be only one leader of any group, and Roz was that person—by founder's title, no doubt, but that was enough. It was *her* book group, and Virginia would like it to be *her* book group.

Isabel thought: This is the ancient story of any playground.

Roz dragged her eyes away from her challenger. "First question, I suppose," she continued. "How many have read *Jean Brodie* before? I mean, before we took it on."

There was some hesitation before hands went up. Nobody put her hand up immediately, and Isabel drew a conclusion from that. This conclusion survived what happened next, which was that every hand went up, Gemma's being the last—raised only after a quick glance towards Virginia. Isabel decided that nobody had read *The Prime of Miss Jean Brodie* before, even though it was one of the best-known Scottish novels of the twentieth century. Yet nobody wanted to admit to not having read it.

Isabel suppressed a smile. This was the *Anna Karenina* rule— the rule that said that everybody claimed to have read *Anna Karenina*, even if they had not. Not to have read *Anna Karenina* was not something to which people seemed willing to admit, just as they were not prepared to admit that they had never read Walter Scott, or *Moby Dick*, perhaps. Every culture had its shibboleths with which people were expected to be familiar. But the bar to be surmounted was not high: In Scotland, as long as one knew, even vaguely, who Walter Scott was, that would be enough to allow access to most circles, just as, in the United States, an awareness of the existence of a tree in *A Separate Peace* might be sufficient in undemanding circumstances. And here, unexpectedly, the *Anna Karenina* rule had just manifested itself among the members of this squabbling, irredeemable book group. Isabel allowed a smile to break across her face.

Fredericka noticed. She half turned to Isabel, and gave her

an unfriendly look. Isabel noticed this, and realised that she had unwittingly made an enemy. Fredericka was perceptive—Isabel imagined that she might be the most intelligent of the members—and she had sensed, correctly, that Isabel knew that she, Fredericka, was not telling the truth when she raised her hand. Fredericka's look had been one tinged with resentment, and that was exactly how people felt when their untruths were detected. They felt cross because somebody had seen through them.

Virginia broke the silence that followed the introductory plebiscite. "I rather like going back to a book I've read some time ago," she said.

Gemma nodded her agreement with this observation.

"Although, of course," Virginia continued, "a book has to have a certain density before one can do that."

Gemma nodded her head. Of course that was right: Density was required.

Virginia was getting into her stride. "For example, *Anna Karenina . . .*"

It took all of Isabel's self-control not to gasp. *Anna Karenina!* This was synchronicity of the most providential kind. Once again, Fredericka noticed, and turned a disapproving eye on Isabel. It was the sort of look one might get if one consumed popcorn at the opera.

Virginia had more to say about Tolstoy. "I can go back to *Anna Karenina* time and time again. But Muriel Spark . . . I don't think so, somehow. Not that I'm saying that *The Prime of Miss Jean Brodie* is a flawed novel. I'm not suggesting that."

"No," muttered Gemma. "Not that."

Fredericka overcame her disapproval sufficiently to lean towards Isabel and whisper, "She's the Greek chorus, you know. Her over there. Little Miss Mouse. She agrees with everything—

and I mean everything—that Virginia says." She paused. "Even when it's patent rubbish, which it is—most of the time."

Roz gave Fredericka a discouraging look, although Isabel did not think that the whisper had been loud enough to be heard. For her part, she felt that she could not respond. She was busy mentally composing a Venn diagram that demonstrated the channels and flow of the forces at work in the room. And it was at this moment that the solution occurred to her. It was so obvious. Of course. Of course.

But would he agree?

He might; in fact, she thought he probably would. He liked adventure—he always had.

CHAPTER SEVENTEEN

THERE WAS CORRESPONDENCE to deal with the following morning. Isabel sorted her incoming mail, both physical and electronic, into two categories: good and bad. The starkness of this division could be problematic at times—in that there were letters that contained elements of both—but in general it worked, particularly since she made it a rule to deal with the bad first before allowing herself the pleasure of the good. Bad letters were, of course, bills—which she always paid promptly—letters from officialdom in any form, and complaints from readers of the *Review* and, in some cases, from dissatisfied authors of papers. Any letter from Robert Lettuce or Christopher Dove was automatically consigned to the bad pile, a process that gave her a secret pleasure, but also led to feelings of guilt. On several occasions she had extracted a communication from Lettuce from the bad pile and placed it in the good, experiencing some of the satisfaction that comes from doing the right thing even though one would dearly love not to do so. Yet you had to be careful with such feelings, Isabel thought: Smugness lay just below the surface of satisfaction, ready to lure one into its embrace. It was very pleasant being smug, there being no need to concern oneself over improvement when one is perfect as one is.

Now, at her desk, Isabel surveyed the two contrasting piles. The bad pile had been dealt with the previous day and was blessedly empty; the good pile, though, had two letters awaiting a response. She picked up the first of these. She had read it quickly when it arrived, and set it aside for a considered response. It came from an old friend of hers, the theologian Iain Torrance. He wrote from time to time with suggestions for topics for the *Review* and she usually embraced his suggestions enthusiastically. Iain did not shout his opinions, but he was, she thought, almost always right. His advice, she felt, could be encapsulated in a simple suggestion—of the sort that people adopted as their personal motto: *Stop and think.* There was too little stopping, she thought, and too little thinking, too, in a world that promoted the instant response, the knee-jerk reaction. Such responses afforded little room for nuance.

She read through his latest letter. "How about a special issue on partisanship?" Iain wrote. "There is immense pressure on people today to take sides immediately and completely. People appear not to want the opinion of critical friends—they want uncritical partisanship. I find it depressing." Isabel did too, and wrote a quick note to Iain. "A brilliant idea," she said. And then she asked him to be the guest editor, and if possible, to ask his critical friends to submit papers. That, she added, was not an entirely serious suggestion, but she thought he would appreciate it.

She turned to the next letter, which was from another friend, Edward Mendelson, sending her a copy of an article he had found on Auden's view of Thomas Cranmer's liturgical prose. "He admired it," he wrote. "It was to him the apogee of the English language." Isabel agreed, and started to write a note of thanks to Edward. Somehow, halfway through, it turned into a note of gratitude to Cranmer himself, for what he had done for language.

"He gave us so much," she wrote. "Those gorgeous phrases—the parataxis, the asyndeton, the assonance." She put aside her pen, and thought for a few moments of the mistreatment handed out to Thomas Cranmer—the excoriation, the long months of imprisonment, and finally the burning at the stake for heresy. That was not entirely Rome's fault, Queen Mary herself having issued the final order; history, she reminded herself, was such a tangle of guilt.

Isabel looked at her watch. It was that odd hour between noon and one, when a decision needed to be taken as to whether to break early, or to continue to work through what would otherwise be a lunch hour. She sat back in her chair and thought about this, enjoying the feeling of having complete freedom to choose between alternatives. Isabel spent little time on the never-ending arguments between believers in determinism and those who espoused the cause of free will, but, sitting back in her chair, with the midday sun falling through her study window in dust-speckled shafts, she had a sudden sense of exhilarating freedom. I am free to choose, she said to herself, and the choice will reflect something that will have occurred within me, right here, and that was not decided long years ago when I was subjected to this or that influence.

Grace knocked on the door. Isabel looked up. "A person from Porlock," she said.

Grace frowned. "From where?"

Isabel laughed. "Sorry, Grace, I was thinking of something, you see. No great thoughts, I'm afraid, but still . . . And the person from Porlock, of course . . . well, Coleridge was sitting in his study writing down the poem that had come to him in a dream— 'Kubla Khan'—and somebody knocked on the door and stopped him completing it. It was a person from Porlock, you see."

Grace looked confused. "Oh," she said. "And where's Porlock?"

"I'm not quite sure," said Isabel. "Somewhere in Somerset, I think. But it stands forever as a symbol of interruption."

"I've never heard of it," said Grace. "Nor of that person, whoever he was."

"History doesn't record that," said Isabel.

"Anyway," Grace said. "I've put him in the kitchen. I told him you were working but I'd find out if you could see him."

"Him being?" asked Isabel. She had not been expecting anybody, and she was not sure that she wanted to see a visitor.

"Professor Lettuce," said Grace, with the air of one who knows that the news she is bearing will not be welcome. "That big, greedy slug. There's some cake on the kitchen table—I'll be able to tell if he's taken a nibble." She paused. "Should I tell him you're washing your hair and can't see him?"

They both smiled at the reference. *I have to wash my hair* was the excuse that young men were given by young women who did not want to go out with them.

"No," said Isabel. "I don't think I should lie about my hair."

Grace was used to Isabel's moral reasoning around situations that she herself considered perfectly straightforward. "There are times when it's unkind to tell people the truth," she said. "I don't see what's wrong with protecting them from something they won't want to hear."

Isabel shook her head. "No, it's not that simple, Grace. Sorry."

"So you want to see Lettuce?"

She explained that she did not necessarily *want* to see him—not in the strong sense—but that she *had* to see him. "So, I suppose you could say that I want to see him because I know I have to see him," she said. "Do you see that?"

"No," said Grace. "What I want to know is whether you would like me to bring him in here from the kitchen. That's all I need to know."

"In that case," said Isabel, "wheel him in."

Grace frowned. "Wheel him?"

"Not literally. Lettuce can walk."

Grace gave an involuntary shudder. "Awful man," she said.

Isabel felt that she had to say at least something in defence of Lettuce. He was under her roof; she owed him a duty of moral consideration. "Some people are not as dreadful as we may think they are—not when you get up close to them."

Grace gave another shudder. "I wouldn't let Lettuce get close to me. No, definitely not. About two yards would be as close as he'd get to me, personally."

"Poor man," said Isabel. "He wants to be appreciated, you know, just like everybody else."

"I'm not going to appreciate him," said Grace. "Nor that smarmy friend of his—what's he called? Bird?"

"Christopher Dove,"

"Yes, him. He's even worse than his boss, I think."

"Possibly," said Isabel. "Although, once again, perhaps we have a duty to give him a chance."

"Not me," said Grace, firmly. "Now, shall I go and tell him you'll see him?"

"Thank you," said Isabel.

As Grace left the room, she turned and said, "Call me if you need me—I'll be just outside."

Isabel assured her that Lettuce was not dangerous. "Ridiculous, yes, but not dangerous."

"You never know," said Grace, adding, darkly, "You know what men are like. They're capable of anything."

Isabel smiled. "As are women, Grace."

Grace looked doubtful. "Well, I won't be far away."

Once Grace had shut the door behind her, Isabel allowed herself a smile. The idea that Lettuce could attack her, or even make a pass at her, was absurd. Sitting down at her desk, she straightened the piles of paper before her: She did not want Lettuce to see her with an untidy desk.

Grace showed him in, and then left, drawing the door closed behind her, but leaving it very slightly ajar.

"Your housekeeper?" Lettuce asked as he lowered himself onto the chair that Isabel offered him.

"Yes," said Isabel. "You've met her before, I think."

Lettuce looked uncertain. "I'm not certain," he said. "Perhaps."

Isabel thought that this was typical of Lettuce: He would only notice people whom he deemed to be important—a mere housekeeper would be beneath his notice, she suspected.

"You're very fortunate to have somebody to help you in the house," said Lettuce. "I just have my wife."

Isabel looked at him in astonishment. Did Lettuce consider his wife to be no more than a domestic helper?

"I'm not sure how your wife would feel about that," she said.

"Oh, she loves housework," said Lettuce airily. "She's never happier than when she's sweeping something up, or vacuuming, of course. She loves vacuuming."

"Are you sure she loves it?" Isabel asked.

Lettuce looked surprised. "Well, she's never complained," he said.

Isabel looked up at the ceiling. There was no limit, she thought, to this man's insensitivity. Surely even the most unaware of men must have realised by now that the days of treating women as unpaid domestic skivvies were over.

She decided to be gentle with Lettuce. "Well, I'm sure you help her, Robert."

Lettuce chuckled. "I'm afraid I'm not much good at that sort of thing. I do the philosophy, you see, and she does the housework. It's a division of labour."

Isabel stared at him. She had a sudden intense yearning for an old-fashioned hat pin, those long and bejewelled devices that used to be inserted in women's hats but that were now largely confined to vintage clothing shops. It would give the very highest level of satisfaction, she thought, to stick such a pin into a non-vital part of Lettuce—not to hurt him, of course, but simply to bring it home to him that this was not a world in which he could continue to express such views. Or rather—because Isabel was tolerant and believed in freedom of expression—such views could be expressed, but only at the risk of the sort of swift refutation that hat pins might provide.

But if she stuck a pin into Lettuce, the consequences could be grave. He might deflate—one never knew—and, if he did, he might simply shoot off, as a punctured balloon would do, pro-pelled through the air by escaping pressure. Or he could turn out to be full of green vegetable liquid, which would ooze out of the pinhole in a slowly spreading lactescence.

She stopped herself. This was not what she had intended; she had abjured pettiness and recrimination in her dealings with Lettuce; she would, instead, invoke the healing power of *agape*. That had been her firm intention, and she should not fall at the very first fence.

"I'm sure that you're useful about the house," she said, trying hard to sound upbeat.

"I flatter myself in that department," Lettuce said. "I enjoy cooking, for instance—not very often, but once or twice a month I make a bouillabaisse. We both enjoy a bowl of bouillabaisse."

Isabel inclined her head. She could not help but picture Let-tuce seated at a table, a white napkin tucked into his collar, tack-ling a bowl of bouillabaisse to an accompaniment of loud slurping sounds. *Once or twice a month* . . . Cooking would always be fun if one had to do it only once or twice a month.

Lettuce had presumably decided to call in connection with the proposed conference on the virtues and the vices. She was ready to discuss that, of course, but not on the terms that he envisaged: What she had in mind was something very different.

She took a deep breath. This was the moment of dramatic denouement. This was the salad bowl in which Lettuce would meet his end.

"I'm glad you came to see me," Isabel said. "Because I have rather thrilling news for you. The conference of virtues and vices . . ."

She was interrupted by Lettuce's raising of a small finger. "I thought we might put vices first," he said. "Vices and virtues. It sounds better, and, perhaps, reflects the way things are in the world today."

Isabel felt a momentary irritation. "I don't see how that can be . . ."

Again, he interrupted her. "The vices, I would have thought, are more prominent than the virtues at present. There's more bad behaviour around, I feel, than there is good."

Isabel was not inclined to argue. "Well, it's a small point."

Lettuce smiled sweetly. He has a cupid-bow mouth, Isabel thought. She had never noticed that before, but he did. One saw that from time to time in fleshy faces like Lettuce's: The mouth was tight and precise, rather like Betty Boop's. Dear Betty Boop, thought Isabel, inconsequentially. *Boop boop de doop* . . .

"Small points are often big points in disguise," said Lettuce, and smiled again.

"Be that as it may," said Isabel, collecting herself and trying to abandon thoughts of Betty Boop. Professor Boop, she thought. That would be a fine name for a professor of philosophy at one of those liberal arts colleges in the Midwest, perhaps in the college town in which her mother's cousin had lived—and had been married to a man who wrote books on butterflies. How innocent the world was then; how pristine. Professor Boop would have driven a large blue car that had seen better days, and his students, who would love him dearly, would say, *There goes Professor Boop in his Oldsmobile.*

"Be that as it may," she continued, "I have some rather good news. As you may know, the *Review of Applied Ethics* is reasonably well funded. And we have, as it happens, a small fund that we can use to bring together people who deliver papers on certain subjects. We then publish them either as special issues, or in the course of our normal publication schedule."

Lettuce watched her. The small mouth was closed, but opened slightly as he took a breath. Lettuce, she observed, was breathing through his mouth. What was wrong with his nose? It was probably just a bad habit—what in horses is called a *vice*. The extraordinary linguistic coincidence struck her forcibly, and she smiled.

"Yes?" said Lettuce. His tone was suspicious.

"Well, it occurred to me that we could save a great deal of money by holding the conference on virtues and vices . . ."

"Vices and virtues," interjected Lettuce.

"*La même chose,*" said Isabel evenly. "The *Review* could host, and fund, the conference ourselves in the community centre round the corner. They have a good-sized hall, which we can hire for next to nothing, and excellent catering arrangements. And they have a team of volunteers that is always looking for things to do. These are well-qualified people—retired professors and so on. They would be well capable of handling the administrative side of things—and all *pro bono*. They wouldn't charge a penny."

Lettuce stared at her. His mouth opened, and then closed again. Remember to breathe, thought Isabel.

"I imagine that the Matheson Trust will be delighted to save all that money," Isabel continued. "They'll be able to fund something else with it—something that otherwise wouldn't get support. Everybody ends up better off."

Lettuce's eyes narrowed. "But the application is at an advanced stage. The money's approved, I believe."

"Never too late to make a saving," said Isabel breezily. "I shall point that out to a member of the trust when I see her next week. That's not Marcus Grant, of course—he's just one of them. No, the person I'm thinking of is called Andrea Matheson—she's a cousin of George Matheson. Do you know her?"

Lettuce shook his head.

"She's a charming woman," Isabel said. "She's very public-spirited. A good bridge player. A lovely person."

She might well be, for all I know, thought Isabel. She had never met Andrea Matheson, of whose existence she had only recently become aware after making a few well-directed enquiries. But Lettuce did not know that she did not know Andrea. And she had not lied to him; she had not claimed an acquaintanceship she did not have. She had merely said that she was a charming woman, which she probably was. And she had not said that she had already arranged a meeting with Andrea: All she had said was, "when I see her next week"—and one could say that quite truthfully, even if one only had an *intention* to see her. As for bridge—that was a mere detail, but an important one. Lettuce would think that she played bridge with Andrea Matheson. Let him think that; once again, she had told no lies.

It was working. Isabel saw the movement of Lettuce's thoughts written plain on his features. She saw the calculation. She saw him thinking of his cousin's plight. If the other trustees heard that the *Review*'s generous money-saving offer was being rejected, then enquiries would be made as to why this was so. That would mean that the scheme that cousin Marcus had cooked up would be exposed.

Lettuce now spoke. "That's very generous of you," he said.

Isabel waved a hand airily. "Think nothing of it," she said. "Although I do hope that you won't mind not getting all those fees. I know how those things don't matter to you, though. The important thing is scholarship, after all. I know that that's what you have at heart."

He was looking at the floor. Poor Lettuce, thought Isabel.

And now thoughts of *agape* returned.

"You know, Robert," Isabel said, "I've always admired your work. I don't know if I've ever spelled it out, but I do. You've made such a major contribution to philosophy—you really have."

Lettuce was not prepared for this. He looked up sharply. "That's very . . ." He stumbled over the words. "That's very generous of you. Very." And then he added, "Very."

"And I wanted to ask you something," Isabel went on. "I was wondering how you would feel about the *Review* devoting a whole issue next year to the discussion and appreciation of your work. Would you mind too much if we did that?"

Lettuce's mouth opened. He sucked in air—he might need half the air in the room, thought Isabel—such was his emotion.

It's so easy, Isabel thought. The work of *agape* is so easy, if we only allow it the room it needs.

"I'm so honoured," said Lettuce, his voice barely audible. It was as if he felt that speaking any louder than he did might break the spell that had fallen upon him—that spell of blessedness and good fortune.

Isabel took a further step. "In fact, it might be better if we were all to devote our energies to that, rather than to a conference on virtues and vices."

He did not try to change the order to vices and virtues. All that was behind him.

"Thank you so much," he said. "Thank you, Isabel. And, if you'll allow me, I'd also like to say how much I admire all the work you've done. You've done so much good with your *Review* and, indeed, with everything."

She saw him out of the door a few minutes later. As he walked down the garden path, he turned and waved to her, as if bestowing a benediction, which, in a way, he was.

CHAPTER EIGHTEEN

It was two weeks later. It was evening: one of those long, drawn-out summer evenings, when the light still lay across Scotland like a gentle, translucent veil of gold. Jamie sat on one side of the kitchen table, and Isabel on the other. Charlie and Magnus were upstairs asleep; they had both been at a trampoline party—there were constant birthday parties at that age, making the social calendars of those six- and seven-year-olds as crowded as those of an unreformed socialite—and they were tired out. Bouncing depletes the reserves of energy even of small boys, who otherwise seem capable of going on indefinitely. Their heads were now on their pillows and were filled with the things of small boys' dreams: rockets and dogs and railway engines, innocent things that they would, Isabel hoped, not abandon too quickly as they went through life. Even an adult life has room for old steam engines and bits of string, for bows and arrows, and construction sets.

Jamie was doing the cooking. He had offered to do so since it was a Saturday, and by tradition he cooked on that evening—and on others, of course. She was expecting potato dauphinoise, which she could have, she said, at any time, but he had chosen to do something quite different. He had taken off the shelf his copy of one of Mary Contini's cookbooks, *A Year at an Italian Table*. He and Isabel knew the Continis, and he had even dared to cook for Mary and Philip a few months earlier. They had complimented him on his dishes, and had assured him that they really meant it.

That evening he was trying a Neapolitan seafood risotto, using a shellfish stock that he had prepared a few days earlier. Both he and Isabel liked risotto in all its forms, but this one was slightly more ambitious than the usual mushroom version Jamie made.

Isabel watched him from her side of the table. Before her was a glass of white Italian, a Vermentino that Valvona & Crolla had recently imported. "Philip says this is particularly good for those moments when everything is going well," Isabel said. "Do you agree?"

"That the wine suits such moments?" asked Jamie. "Or that everything is going well right now?"

"Both," said Isabel. "But start with the wine."

Jamie turned from the cooker to take a sip from his glass. "Yes," he said. "Perfect. Or should I say *perfetto*?"

"Either will do," said Isabel. "Or both. Italian *perfetto* might be even more forceful than its English equivalent. They use their hands to underline the perfection. Language is not only a matter of words, don't you think?"

He smiled. It was fun being married to Isabel and to follow her conversation wherever it led—and it led to some pretty unexpected places.

"I wish I was Italian," he said, taking another sip of the Vermentino.

She looked at him. "Isn't it enough to be Scottish?"

He hesitated, but only briefly. "Yes, of course it is. I love Scotland." He paused. "I love it more than I can say."

There was a moment of silence between them. Sometimes that happened when they talked about Scotland.

"I love Scotland because it breaks the heart," he said quietly. "As MacDiarmid said. Remember?"

Isabel knew the poem—how could she forget it? MacDiarmid had said that he did not want the rose of all the world—that the little white rose of Scotland would suffice. That rose, he said, broke the heart.

She nodded. But Jamie had said that he would also like to be Italian. Why was that?

"Because of everything," he replied. "Because of Florence and Siena. Because of the films of Pier Paolo Pasolini. Because of Verdi. Because of Botticelli and Caravaggio. Because of . . . of *risotto ai frutti di mare* and Vermentino from the hills of Tuscany. Because of all that." He paused. "What would you be, Isabel, if you weren't Scottish, that is."

She reminded him that she was half American. "There was my sainted American mother, remember."

"Of course. Could you do without the Scottish bit? Is that what you'd prefer?"

She said that she would not. She was happy with both heritages. But she would not decline to throw her hat in with her mother's people if she were ever pushed to do so. "America is a good country," she said. "It sometimes gets it wrong—who doesn't? But who does everyone turn to when things get really bad? Doesn't that tell you something?"

Jamie said that he thought it did.

"America's a great idea," she said. "Think of the music and the fun and the marching bands."

Jamie laughed.

"And the things that have nothing to do with marching bands and popcorn: the great universities and the Library of Congress and T. S. Eliot."

"He jumped ship, though, didn't he?"

"Perhaps. But then Auden went in the opposite direction."

Jamie nodded. "The fickleness of poets."

"Anyway," said Isabel. "You asked what I might like to be— if I weren't what I am. Well, you won't laugh, I hope, if I tell you that I would love to be Swedish. I really would. I've wanted to be Swedish for ages, but . . ."

"But you never seem to get there?"

She shook her head. "No, I haven't. I've watched all those Bergman films. I've had platefuls of *smørrebrød*. I've tried to get depressed. I've done my best, I really have."

Jamie laughed. "You can't become Swedish, you know. It's one of those closed identities—of which there are quite a few. But it's even harder to be Finnish. You have to learn Finnish if you have that in mind, and that's impossible, I gather. Even for Finns. A lot of them say they haven't really mastered the language although it's their native tongue."

"And I have a Swedish car," Isabel continued. "I feel quite Swedish when I'm driving."

A pot behind Jamie started to boil over. This was the arborio rice, and he needed to attend to it. Over his shoulder he said, "May I ask you something, Isabel? How did you arrive at your solution for the book group?"

"Sudden, blinding insight," said Isabel. "Not that I want to sound self-congratulatory, but it came to me. You know how solutions sometimes jump up in front of you? It was like that. I suddenly knew."

Jamie turned back to face her, and smiled broadly. "It worked, didn't it?"

"So Roz said. She called me this morning, by the way. I meant to mention it to you. She said that several members had been in touch with her about yesterday's meeting. They were all extremely pleased."

"Once the idea came to you, were you convinced it would work?" asked Jamie.

Isabel thought for a moment. She had felt some misgivings, but nothing serious. "It was a bit of a punt," she said. "But I think the basic supposition made sense."

"The basic supposition being?"

"That single sex groups may work—sometimes—but that when they don't work, the reason is the simple fact that they're single sex."

He waited for her to continue.

"You see, I could tell," she said, "that those women were just going to carry on needling one another. The chemistry was all wrong, for whatever reason. Some of them were competitive, some were arrogant, some were neither here nor there. I saw all that and realised that what they needed was a man in the book group. If there was a man, they'd lose interest in their private quarrels. They wouldn't want to show themselves up in the presence of a man."

Jamie burst out laughing. "This is sounding very old-fashioned," he said. "Even a bit reactionary."

Isabel shook her head. "No," she said. "Ordinary psychology—folk psychology, if you like—doesn't have to be reactionary. It tends to be based on long observation of how human beings tick. And one of the things you can see if you only open your eyes is that men and women can behave badly when they're in single sex groups. This applies as much to men as it does to women—perhaps even more so in the case of men. Men can behave in a very foolish and immature way when it's just them in the room, so to speak."

Jamie agreed. "Yes, they can." He thought of something. "Did I ever tell you about what happened at school when it first stopped being a boys-only school? Did I tell you about that?"

Isabel shook her head.

"The school used to be only for boys when I first went to it," said Jamie. "Then, when I was in my penultimate year there— I was sixteen-ish—they started to admit girls. I remember the first day they joined us. We had three girls come into our class of nineteen boys. And I remember that one of the boys was using a wooden ruler to flick pellets of paper at this poor guy called Winston Churchill Macgregor—yes, that's what his folks had named him, can you believe it? He just called himself Win, but somebody had seen his school record, which had his full name on it. He was a bit uncoordinated, and he was hopeless at ball games. He played chess quite well, but sixteen-year-old boys are not all impressed with that sort of thing. The only thing that impresses them, I think, is themselves. Anyway, I remember that on the day that the girls joined us, some of the boys were picking on poor Win Macgregor and they handed one of the girls a ruler and offered to show her how to flick pellets at him. She looked at them with utter scorn and said, 'But why?' They looked sheepish and just gave up. And everything was different from then on."

"Poor Winston Churchill Macgregor," said Isabel. "Did things get better for him?"

Jamie brightened. "Yes, they did. He married an Italian model and went to live in Milan. His father-in-law had a fashion house there. Nobody could believe it."

"A happy ending."

"Very happy. But it makes the point, doesn't it. Girls were a civilising influence."

Isabel agreed. "I think they are. But there is the counterpart, remember: There are cases where groups of women will be improved by the addition of men. Not always, of course, but sometimes. And I think this has been one of them."

Jamie looked thoughtful. "I was a bit worried when you asked me to join the book group. But it went really well last night. They were all very polite to one another. I'd say that they were on their best behaviour."

"No disparaging remarks?"

"No."

"No trying to put other members down?"

"Not that I saw," said Jamie.

"Well, there you are: success. And that's very much what Roz said when she telephoned this morning. She's very grateful." Isabel paused. "And you don't mind continuing to be a member?"

"Not at all," said Jamie. "I've been wanting to read more—I think we talked about that, didn't we? When you were talking about living on an island. You said I'd have more time to read."

Isabel remembered. Perhaps they would discuss that again one day.

"I think more men should join book groups," said Jamie. "They don't know what they're missing."

"Many men don't know what they're missing in general," observed Isabel.

Jamie looked at her, uncertain how to take that remark. But Isabel just smiled. She did not intend to explain, possibly because she was not quite sure what she had meant, although she thought it was probably true.

HE SERVED THE RISOTTO, which lived up to its enticing smell. He poured a further glass of Vermentino. He filled two water glasses with San Pellegrino mineral water. He put a piece of ciabatta bread on Isabel's side plate, and then sprinkled it with olive oil from a small clear glass jug.

"So you saw Cat this morning?" Jamie asked.

"Yes. I went down to her shop."

Jamie asked her whether Cat had told her about Gordon.

"She didn't say much about him," she said. "But I think that's the last we'll hear of him. She said that there had been some problem in Antigua. She said that Gordon was implicated in something that happened on board, but she was not sure what it was. She said that she was not going to stick with somebody who could keep things from her. It's over, she said."

"Oh dear. Poor Cat. She doesn't seem to pick the right men, does she?"

"Some people are like that," said Isabel. "And some men too."

"We're all flawed," agreed Jamie. "Each in our particular way. We look for happiness, but we stumble on the path. We all stumble."

She remembered Dawn. "Is Dawn all right?"

Dawn had moved out. She had found a flat and was sharing with another nurse and a radiographer. The radiographer was a long-distance runner and had involved Dawn in the sport. "They have miles and miles to go," said Jamie.

Isabel thought about that. We all had miles and miles to go, in our individual ways.

They finished the risotto. There was cheese to follow—plain Parmesan, but aged for almost five years, which made it special.

"Five years is quite a long time in the life of a cheese," said Isabel.

ABOUT THE AUTHOR

Alexander McCall Smith is the author of the No. 1 Ladies' Detective Agency novels and of a number of other series and stand-alone books. His works have been translated into more than forty languages and have been best sellers throughout the world. He lives in Scotland.

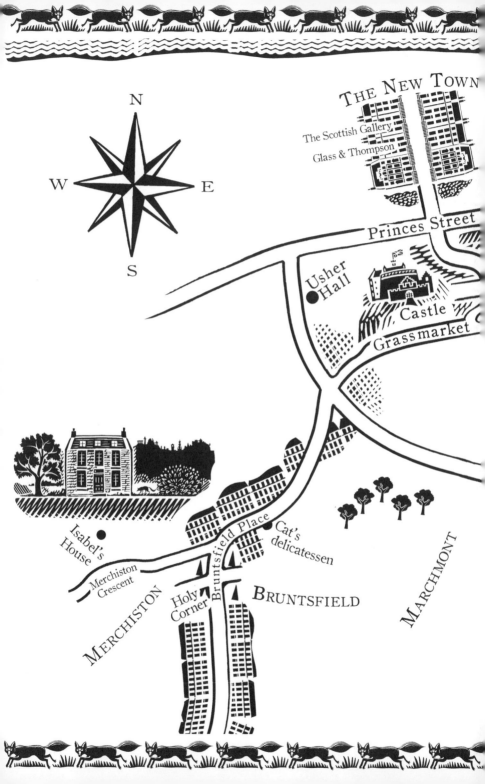